Guardians of Zion: The Guardians Crest
Copyright © 2018 by Michael Chrobak

Seneschal Publishing; Oakley, California
www.seneschalpublishing.com
Twitter: @SeneschalBooks

Book Cover Artist:
Kristyn / Drop Dead Designs
http://www.dropdeaddesigns.com

ISBN paperback: 978-0-9981350-6-9
ISBN eBook: 978-0-9981350-7-6

First Paperback Edition
Printed in the United States of America

Other Books by Michael Chrobak

Brother Thomas and the Guardians of Zion Series

Book One: Foundations of Faith
Book Two: The Paladin of Panama
Book Three: The Guardians Crest

Other Titles

Where Angels Dwell

For all those brave enough
to share their dreams

INTRO

Welcome to *The Guardians Crest*, the third book of the *Brother Thomas and the Guardians of Zion* series. As I've previously shared, this series came about as a way to explore the concepts of The Fruits of the Holy Spirit through the use of fantasy. In the first book, *Foundations of Faith*, I expressed my understanding of the concept of *Faith*; and in the second book, *The Paladin of Panama*, I took a look at *Chastity*. This time, I will be exploring *Kindness*, but from a different vantage than in the past.

The spiritual presence of *Kindness* manifests itself as an understanding, sympathy and concern for those in need. The opposite of this, in my opinion, is a form of loathing, or hate. There are no beings more perfect to describe this, than the demons of Hell. These are beings who hate everything, and think only of themselves.

Therefore, this book will begin back at the start of the story, back when Thomas was on his confirmation retreat. Only, this time, the story will focus on the antagonist point of view. Why? Because being unkind is such an easy thing to do. In fact, being unkind can be as easy as adopting an apathetic position regarding any part of God's creation. We don't have to take part in hateful acts to be unkind, we only have to allow them to exist.

Every time we walk by someone being picked on or taken advantage of, we are choosing to be unkind. Every time we don't stand up for those less fortunate, we are choosing to be unkind. Every time we see something happening that makes us uncomfortable, and rather than take action, we simply say 'Not my problem', we are choosing to be unkind.

I will admit, so far, this was the toughest book to write. I started writing in the fall of 2017, got about halfway done, and then threw it all out. I just didn't like what I had created so far, so I started again. And again. And again. In fact. I wrote enough words to have written two complete novels, but not a single word of that work made it into what I finally chose to release. The reason why this happened is simple; I was focused on what I wanted to say, not where the story needed to go.

For me, it was a great example of how easily we can be swayed away from what we are meant to do, and instead become focused on what we want to do. When this happens, when we turn from what God has intended for our lives, and put our intention on what we want to do, we put ourselves at risk of falling from grace. We become self-absorbed, withdrawn from the world around us, we stop trusting others, think that no one understands us, or begin to feel isolated or depressed.

This is the story that needed to be told. Sure, it would have been easier to just introduce another one of the Guardians, have them fight against and defeat the powers of evil, and continue on into the fourth book. But life isn't always that simple, and choosing to adhere to the Fruits of the Holy Spirit is definitely not an easy thing to do, either. There will always be conflict.

Therefore, for this story to be honest in both its message and its intent, I felt it was time to tell the story from the other side, to give the demons—who have been hard at work trying to stop Thomas and his friends—a chance to have their story told. In my mind, understanding how the forces of evil work within our hearts and minds is a critical factor in understanding how to use the spiritual powers we have against these forces.

When I started writing from this understanding, suddenly the words began to flow again. There was less resistance, and the story not only made sense, but it definitely felt right, too. Now, rather than just adding one more book to the series, I honestly feel I have created something that will help the reader understand what kindness is, and how important it is to the spiritual journey we are all on.

Being kind to one another isn't just something we *should* be doing, it's something me *must* be doing, and doing every opportunity we get. Yes, that's hard to do, but the more we practice being kind, the easier it becomes, and the stronger our defenses are against Satan and his dark army. And, to be honest, *Kindness* is the strongest weapon we will ever have in the battle of good over evil.

Are you ready to join in that battle? Then read on, brave adventurer! It's time for you to discover *The Guardians Crest!*

PART ONE

Be kind, for everyone you meet is engaged in a battle.
— St. Philo of Alexandria

CHAPTER ONE
ON THE OTHER SIDE

What makes a person choose to do evil? Does it come from a single moment of challenge? Can it be from just one event? Is that when we choose darkness? Is there a darkness already hiding in the corners of our hearts, waiting for just the right moment to come forth? Or, is it the other way around? Maybe we don't choose the darkness. Maybe the darkness chooses us?

Furcas spat on the ground, then watched the acidic fluid sizzle and foam as it reacted violently with the rich, fertile soil, leaving behind nothing but a deathly gray stain. The ground he stood upon was good soil, and for that, he hated it all the more. He stroked the back of his weathered hand across dry, cracked lips, wiping the lingering spittle away, then hacked and spat once more. Of all the assignments he could have drawn, the one he now attended had to be the worst.

For hours now he had stood in this spot, his eyes fixed on the back wall of a large wooden building as the morning sun broke through the fog. Inside the building he was watching, a retreat was underway; a weekend of religious and social activities designed to prepare young people for the Sacrament of Confirmation. Just being this close to such an event made his stomach churn and his blade-hand ache to draw forth the cold, hard steel hanging at his side. He'd been denied the use of force, however, by a demon whose rule he could not disobey; at least, not for now.

A few paces behind him, his midnight-black demon-born horse, Gauerdi, pawed at the ground, as if trying to erase his own shadow. The horse, too, was impatient and bored.

"Aye, Gauerdi. Aye. This task is not worthy of a Knight of Abaddon. Nor his mare. Still, here we are, and here we will stay 'til this fool of a mission is over."

Gauerdi responded with a blow and a nicker. Then the pure-black horse turned his head and wandered away, grazing on the dew-soaked grass. Furcas watched for a moment, envying the animal in his ignorant bliss, and then turned his attention back to the building, and his task of watching and waiting.

His eyes locked on the dull-gray walls, no more than a stone's throw away. Though in truth, it wasn't the building he was watching, but what was gathered inside. Humans; and mostly young, teenage ones, too. There was nearly a hundred of them, seated in chairs arranged in rows of ten seats each. Using his demonic powers, Furcas could discern not only the potential and kinetic energy within each human within the room, but the strength and fervor of their spirit as well. The brighter the light he perceived, the purer would be their spirit; and the purer the spirit, the stronger would be their faith.

Within the bodies of the one-hundred or so young people gathered, only eight hearts burned with a passion bright enough to notice. Another dozen or so flickered, but most were as cold and dark as stone. Furcas didn't care about the brightly burning hearts. They were not part of his mission. Their lives were going to be inconsequential. It was one thing to have a strong faith; it was entirely another thing to use it.

No, the hearts he had been sent to watch were the ones that barely glowed. He knew that, kindled at the right time, even the smallest spark could ignite the dormant faith that waited within. That was something the Devil's Cavalier hated to see; cold, barren hearts set ablaze; yet that was exactly what he was to watch for. A heart on fire—especially a heart as young as those of the teens gathered for this retreat weekend—would be capable of fantastic deeds.

Not all of the barely-glowing hearts were worth watching, for only a few cold hearts ever did come to life. No, out of every human inside the building he watched, there was only one that had the power to change the course of humanity for generations to come; only one that could threaten his master's plans. That one heart belonged to a fifteen-year-old boy; and his name was Thomas.

Furcas could easily pick Thomas out from the crowd. The young teen's spiritual energy barely registered; so cold was the light of his faith, and so thick and heavy were his doubts. But that's what made Thomas so dangerous, and it was what made this mission so critical, boring as it was. Furcas' instructions had been simple; watch Thomas every waking moment, and set wards around his cabin when the boy slept.

Furcas had been on over-watch assignments at retreats such as this one hundreds of times before. He knew nothing important would happen this early. Nothing of any significance ever happened until late on Saturday night. Right now it was only Saturday morning. The weekend was just getting started.

And so, after spending another half-hour watching the building, with no sign that anything significant was about to occur, Furcas rested, placing his worn and tired body against the trunk of a tree, convinced he could just as easily watch the building while reclined, as he could while standing. There was no reason to be uncomfortable, after all. He would most likely be on watch for quite some time.

A group of butterflies caught his eye as they flitted and danced, and he couldn't help but hope that one of them would come close enough for him to catch and crush in his hand. But the butterflies must have read Furcas' mind, and they fluttered away, adding a layer of frustration to the boredom and impatience already plaguing Furcas' thoughts. If only he had something to do, other than scratch at itches that weren't really there, or chew nervously on his chapped lips.

Breathing in deeply, Furcas sighed. It was a miserable, depressing sound, but it helped him relax, and for that he was grateful. He stretched out his legs, trying to find a position that would allow his tired, old bones to rest while he waited. Nothing too comfortable, of course. Comfort was not something demons desired. Just a position that would allow him to save his energy as he attended to his task. His instincts reminded him once more that nothing would happen this early in the weekend. Not yet.

Trusting his instincts, he relaxed even deeper, allowing his body to relax and sag against the cold, hard tree, while the fog continued to lift, revealing a perfect blue sky above, dotted here and there with clusters of clouds. Furcas watched them float by, hating them for what they represented. As he watched his eyes began to flutter—each blink lasting longer than the last—and his breathing began to slow. Then, after one rather lengthy blink, his eyelids failed to rise back again, and Furcas began to snore.

※

While Furcas slumbered, the unimaginable happened. Four small sparks leaped from the brightest heart in the room, a heart belonging to a priest named Dominic. The nearly invisible embers arced through the air, and landed squarely upon the boy, Thomas. The first one landed on Thomas' chest, burrowing deep into his heart. Suddenly, the boy began to pay attention to Father Dominic's words, the same words which had barely captured his attention until now.

The second spark landed on Thomas' head, finding a home within his mind, and his thoughts began to stir. Parables and scriptures Thomas had heard hundreds of times before began to make sense in a way that they never had. And as those stories opened their secrets to him, Thomas' curiosity became like tinder, surrendering to the flames of his now ignited faith. The stronger his curiosity grew, the deeper the connection Thomas made to his faith, and the more brightly the flame in his heart began to glow.

The third spark struck Thomas' feet, filling the young man with a desire to live a purposeful life. This desire added to the tinder, and the flames quickly doubled in size. Thomas began not only to consider what his life meant, but what it was that he stood for, and what his purpose might be. Though these thoughts challenged and frightened him, the faith burning inside his heart strengthened his resolve. He knew his life may not have been of much significance before, but based on the feelings growing inside, he began to understand how easily that could change.

The final spark bore with it a call to Christian action. As it drew near, the spark divided into two, each part finding and disappearing into the palms of Thomas' hands. Now: aware, awake, driven, and committed; Thomas couldn't have been more prepared to be who he had been born to be. The flame within his heart burned with a passion and fervor that rivaled even the greatest of saints. A golden halo, invisible to everyone within the room, appeared over Thomas' head, and a euphoric peace permeated his soul.

※

Had Furcas been awake, he would have seen the sparks jump from Father Dominic to Thomas, and watched as the once-dead fire in Thomas' heart burst to life. He would most likely have cringed at the golden halo over Thomas' head. But he didn't see any of this. However, Gauerdi did. The horse, which had been created from the molten fires of Hell itself, was trained for spiritual battle, and had been granted the ability to sense even small fluctuations in spiritual energy.

The jet-black demon-steed raised his head and whickered. His ears pricked back as he turned his attention towards his master. He knew the danger of what those four sparks represented, and he neighed a loud warning. When that warning went unheeded, Gauerdi clopped over to where Furcas reclined against the tree and nuzzled his master's face.

"What is it, boy?" Furcas groaned softly, not yet opening his eyes. "Are you as bored as I am?"

Gauerdi nuzzled more urgently, then gave a hard snort. This time, Furcas understood. His eyes flashed open and he sat up straight, nearly knocking his head against Gauerdi's jaw. Even before the cobwebs of sleep had cleared his mind, he knew something was amiss.

"Eh? What's this?" he gasped, seeing the newly kindled flames burning bright, and knowing without asking that the heart belonged to Thomas.

"What happened? Who woke the boy's faith?"

Gauerdi whinnied loudly, tossing his head.

"The priest, you say?" Furcas asked.

Furcas stepped to the edge of the tree line, the closest he dared approach. Leaning forward, he squinted his eyes, picking out the steady glow of Father Dominic's faith. The priest's heart was burning more brightly as well, revealing something Furcas had not previously seen. The man was supposed to be just a common, ordinary friar, not someone with the power to ignite a cold, barren spirit such as the one Thomas had. Furcas was witnessing a miracle, and it made him ill.

At that moment, Father Dominic's heart opened a fifth time, fluttering just long enough to release one more spark. In that brief moment, Furcas realized he had been duped. Father Dominic was no ordinary monk! Instead, Furcas was looking upon someone who had been blessed by the most hated and most powerful enemy of the underworld: Saint Dominic himself!

There was nothing Furcas could do about it now. It was too late to stop Thomas' burgeoning faith, and it was too late to call for support. He would have to rely on the only weapon in his arsenal that had a chance of reversing what had just taken place: Doubt. If Furcas could make Thomas doubt this newly forming faith—or better yet, doubt his worthiness to have such a strong faith—he may yet quench the fire that Saint Dominic's agent had just lit.

Whispering to Gauerdi, Furcas began to rise "Let's see if we can stop this, shall we?"

Gauerdi tossed his head and nickered as he leaned his shoulders and chest against his master's back in support. Furcas let his weight rest against the muscular beast as he raised his weathered hands before him. Curling his bony fingers like claws, Furcas began to chant in the most ancient language he knew.

> *Inta maṉitaṉai oḷiyiliruntu piṇaikkiṟāṉ*
> *(Bind this human from the light)*
> *Avaruṭaiya itayattaiy maṉataiy payamuṟuttuṅkaḷ*
> *(Fill his heart and mind with fright)*
> *Avaratu āvi ātmā paṟakka viṭuṅkaḷ*
> *(Pray his spirit soul take flight)*

Over and over he chanted, while around his hands wispy clouds began to form. As the vapors coalesced, twin streams began to flow towards the building, and those gathered within. Furcas' chants continued growing louder, the words now carrying a passionate, desperate plea. He closed his eyes, allowing the poem to become a dark and powerful spell. A few feet before striking the building, the two vaporous streams separated, each one flowing around the building from opposite sides.

Now that he was dealing with someone who held the blessings of a Saint, Furcas knew there was no way he would be able to enter the room. Though, he already knew that he didn't have to. He just had to stop Thomas from accepting the changes that Father Dominic had already begun within him.

His mouth continued reciting the spell as his mind reached out psychically, trying to connect with Thomas' mind. Feeling their minds connect, Furcas began to fill the boy with as much doubt as he could. This wasn't the first time he had done something like this; sway the thoughts or actions of a human through enchantment. In fact, enchanting humans was one of his favored skills. He had enchanted thousands of humans before today.

Furcas knew that once a human began to doubt their worthiness to have a deeply rooted faith, the pillars on which the Christian faith was built would crumble. This time, however, something was different. This time, the target of his enchantments had help. Father Dominic was using his own faith as a shield. If he had any chance of winning the battle, Furcas had to separate the two. As long as Thomas was close to Father Dominic, Furcas would not have the strength to win on his own.

"Damn you, Dominic," Furcas hissed as he prepared for an intense battle of wills. "This young soul will be mine. You have not the power to deny me, priest!"

Furcas leaned forward, pressing his weight into his spell. As he did, his chants lost some of their strength, becoming desperate, and the rivers of fog began to thin. Never had he faced such a disciplined resolve. The only thing he could do now, was to be patient and wait for the most opportune time to strike. Furcas and Father Dominic were locked in a stalemate of wills. If either of the two dropped their hold on Thomas, even for a moment, the other would win. Furcas pressed hard, forcing the priest to reply in kind.

Suddenly, he felt Father Dominic waver, and Furcas knew he had gained the upper hand.

"So, the blessings of Saint Dominic are weaker than the legends portray!" he sneered, pressing his slight advantage even more.

As he watched, the inferno inside Thomas' heart began to falter and fade. At any moment now, Furcas would break through, and the battle would be won. He just needed to draw Thomas away from Father Dominic, as far as he could. And then, in the very next moment, he got his chance.

Inside the building where Thomas and Dominic were, the humans began to stir. The priest's talk was over, and the group had been excused for a break. Thomas, who was obviously feeling the effects of the spiritual battle being waged for his soul, headed for the door that would lead him outside. Furcas could see the young man was dizzy and weak. This was the chance he needed, but it wouldn't last long.

Letting his hand drop, he clicked his tongue in a practiced command, and Gauerdi responded, walking in front of Furcas and allowing his master to mount. Furcas grabbed the reins and placed one foot in the stirrup, and then swung his other leg over the saddle. With a sharp tug and a kick of his heels, he drove his mount forward, heading towards the front of the building where Thomas would emerge. He only had to get close enough to touch Thomas, if even just his clothes, or his hair. If he did, he would own Thomas' soul. But he also knew that Father Dominic wouldn't give up, and Furcas prepared for a fight. As long as the boy's thoughts were still on the words he had heard Father Dominic speak, Furcas couldn't win. He had to distract Thomas somehow. But how?

A plan formed in his mind, one that he had high hopes would work. Winding the twin streams of energy that still poured from his hands, Furcas twisted them like a rope. Then, with a powerful flick of his wrist, he cast the rope around Thomas' feet just as the boy stepped through the doorway leading outside, causing Thomas to stumble and fall. The teens who witnessed Thomas fall broke into a chorus of laughter, the effect of which was exactly what Furcas had hoped for. A heavy veil of embarrassment fell over Thomas' mind, blocking out Father Dominic's invisible support. As Thomas stood, the embarrassment began to harden his heart. Furcas pressed on these new feelings, forcing Thomas to wallow in his humiliation. And then, rather than just taking a moment to calm himself in the fresh air, Thomas began to run away.

Seizing the opportunity, Furcas whispered hoarsely, "Run, Thomas! That's right. Run! Keep running. To the end of the trail. Out into the field. Just keep going. Don't look back, don't stop. Just run!"

As the words registered in his mind, Thomas froze. Furcas could see the hairs on the back of the boy's neck stand on end, an obvious sign that the boy could sense his presence. Suddenly, and without warning, the bond linking Thomas to Father Dominic shattered, and Thomas began to run faster now.

To Furcas' surprise, Thomas was fast. Inhumanly fast. Even though the connection between the boy and the priest had been severed, it seemed Thomas still had help. Suddenly it was Furcas who began to doubt, realizing he had underestimated the importance of this young man.

"*Perhaps,*" Furcas considered silently, "*Thomas is not just a boy at all. Perhaps he's blessed! Or even worse, perhaps he is a Guardian!*"

The Guardians of Zion were humans who had been born with the power of angels. Humans like Saint Dominic, Mother Theresa, or even Jesus' mother, Mary. If Thomas was a Guardian, then it signaled the onset of dangerous times to come.

"There hasn't been a Guardian born in nearly one-thousand years!" Furcas whispered to himself, realizing that it would do no good to simply snuff the boy's faith; it would only return again, and when it did it would be even stronger still.

As he pressed Gauerdi in pursuit of Thomas, Furcas thought back to the moment he had been given his mission, and the final words his master, the Demon Prince Astaroth, had said.

"This is a mission of the greatest importance, Furcas. You must turn the boy. You must keep the light from reaching him. But, if he cannot be turned, then the boy must die."

Cursing once more, Furcas drove his heels, hard, forcing Gauerdi to respond. The horse's hooves churned clouds of dust as they thundered along. Though, the faster the horse raced, the faster Thomas ran, until both pursuer and pursued were moving at lightning speed. Furcas could tell he was gaining on his prey, he just wasn't gaining fast enough.

Rounding a corner of a building at the far end of the grounds, Furcas tried again to twist Thomas' thoughts. He whispered words he hoped would make the young man believe that he would be seen, that he would be questioned for running away, and that he would have to explain why he had run. As he pressed these thoughts, he saw Thomas' resolve crack. The ploy was working.

Thomas began to slow. And then, the unspeakable happened. Rather than turn his thoughts away from his faith, as Furcas had hoped, Thomas prayed aloud.

"God, don't let anyone see me."

Curious what it was that had strengthened Thomas' resolve, Furcas took his eyes off the boy and looked ahead, seeing for the first time where it was they were headed: The chapel. If Thomas made it inside, Furcas knew the chase would be over. Although Gauerdi was already at his limit, with saliva and blood foaming at his mouth, Furcas slapped his open palm on the beasts' haunches, drawing an accusatory blow, but earning another increase in speed.

The distance to the chapel shrunk rapidly. Furcas knew it was going to be close. Too close. Though he believed he could reach Thomas before Thomas reached the chapel, he pulled Gauerdi's reins to the right, placing his steed on a path to cut between Thomas and the open chapel door. If he couldn't catch the boy, he would at least block Thomas from reaching safety. Then, to shorten the distance further, the knight stood in the saddle and reached forward, trying desperately to touch even just the fabric of Thomas' shirt.

With his fingers just inches away, Furcas flinched as Thomas prayed once more.

"God, please help me!"

With a sound like thunder, a mighty wind struck, knocking Gauerdi against the wall of the chapel, causing his front legs to trip. The horse stumbled and fell, throwing his master into the air. The same wind that had upended the horse also lifted Thomas off the ground and thrust him through the chapel's open front door, well out of Furcas' reach.

The heavy wooden door slammed shut.

Thomas was safe.

Furcas had failed.

Sprawled across the damp ground, dazed in pain, Furcas knew who was responsible for the wind. There was only one being with the strength to stop Gauerdi when the horse was at full speed. Blinking his eyes, Furcas turned his head to the left. There, less than twenty yards away, stood an immaculately crafted angel with long, flowing golden-blonde hair, striking silver-blue eyes, and dressed in radiant armor of crystal and gold. In one hand the angel held a titanium sword, and in the other, a matching shield. Behind the angel, a pair of snow-white wings were tucked.

"Go away, Light-Bringer!" Furcas cursed with a venomous snarl.

"Save your strength, Shadow-Spawn!" the Archangel Michael replied. "You've lost this time. Take your devilish tricks and go home."

"What do you care of this one boy? You never interfered with any of the others I turned! What is this one human to you?"

Michael unfurled his wings, creating a powerful and commanding sight.

"You know as well as I the course this boy will travel. He is Chosen. You feel it the same as I."

Furcas spat at the ground, looking to see if this time it would produce the result he wanted. When it sizzled and failed, just like his last attempt, he ground his teeth and quietly mumbled an ancient curse. Michael's eyes became sharp at the words, and the angel leaned towards Furcas with a powerful glare.

"If the boy is so special, Angel, then why even let me get close? Why not drive me away from the start?"

Michael grinned, then leaned back and laughed, causing his hair to cascade over his shoulders and drift with the breeze. "Do you honestly believe you were doing the Devil's work, imp?"

It took only a moment for Furcas to realize what Michael meant, and at that moment, he realized the true depth of his defeat. Thomas' faith was fragile, that much was true, but only because it had yet been tested. Nothing yet had happened for Thomas to choose between faith and fear. The moment that Thomas had prayed had been that first choice. Torn between the embers of faith that Father Dominic had kindled, and the fear and doubt that Furcas had cast, Thomas had chosen faith. And in so doing, the boy hadn't simply prayed; he had set his feet firmly on the path of righteousness, discovering a strength he didn't realize he had. Thomas had found not only his faith, but his purpose as well. Furcas had provided exactly what the boy needed to make that choice. Furcas had been used.

"Curse your meddling ways!" Furcas bellowed, gnashing his teeth and curling his hands into fists.

Michael smiled, then did the one thing demons hated most; he quoted scripture. "He will guard the feet of His saints, but the wicked shall be silent in darkness."

Furcas slowly got to his knees, feigning that his injuries were worse than they were. His mission may have ended in disaster, but there was still a chance to retain his position within Satan's kingdom, if nothing else. To do so, he would have to hand the Prince of Darkness a prize greater than that of a faithless teen. He would have to bring him the Archangel Michael's wings.

Tensing his muscles, Furcas prepared to pounce. Slowly his hand moved towards the great sword hanging at his side as he watched the Archangel warily. He was no match for Heaven's greatest warrior, but perhaps he could take the angel by surprise. Furcas had battled angels before and had yet to suffer defeat. This false sense of confidence urged him on. Plus, he had nothing to lose. Failure to complete his mission would result in his banishment from Hell at least. He didn't want to think about what else it might entail. Furcas had no choice left, and nowhere else to go.

Bending his knees, his hand firmly around the hilt of his sword, Furcas attacked, driving towards Michael as he drew his blade soundlessly from the sheath. Furcas had obtained the advantage of surprise, still, the Archangel's response was quick. Furcas watched as Michael's wings wrapped over the front of the angel's body, then locked in place, becoming as hard as steel. Unable to stop his swing, Furcas felt the blade vibrate harshly as it clanged harmlessly off the wings.

Furcas was defeated, yet still he attacked, each of his swings growing wilder and more barbaric than the last. Michael simply stood his ground, allowing Furcas to waste his energy in useless attacks. Finally, after what felt like hours, his sword fell. Furcas, covered in sweat and breathing heavily, crumbled to the ground in defeat.

"Do your worst, Light Bearer," Furcas sighed.

"Though I would like nothing more than to do just that," the Angel replied, "I have my orders. Your time has not yet ended."

"You cursed being!" Furcas spat. "You know what fate will await me if I return to the shadows! I would much rather die!"

"Not by my hand, you won't. Not today, at least," Michael stated in a matter-of-fact tone. "You have no choice, demon. Unless…"

Furcas knew what Michael meant by 'unless.' There was a third option; a choice the Demon Knight never believed he would consider.

The Abyss.

A realm of existence which was neither Heaven nor Hell, nor did it belong to any part of creation. The Abyss was an endless, empty void. It was the place where *The Unjudged* lived; where those who had never chosen a side in the battle of good over evil waited for the moment they would stand before the powers of Darkness and Light. Though Michael could not cast Furcas to the Abyss without a direct command from God, if Furcas asked to be sent, it would be possible.

"I need a moment to choose, Angel. Grant me that?" Furcas asked, garnering a single nod in reply.

Furcas began to consider his options, knowing there were three choices he could make. The first would be to return to Hell, defeated, and with no prize to guarantee his existence in the Kingdom of Shadows. If he were banished from Hell, he would spend the rest of eternity wandering the physical world, locked in the dominion of Man. His powers would be reduced to only those agreed that humans could have: the seven virtues, the seven vices, and the Fruits and Gifts of the Holy Spirit. He would no longer have Demon Sight, he would have to give up his armor and horse, and his power to enchant and persuade would be all but gone.

His second option would be for his existence to end; but the only beings powerful enough for that were like the one standing before him now. If the Defender of Heaven had no desire to break the tentative truce the two realms currently held, then none of the other angels would, either. It was impossible for Furcas to end his own existence, which meant this was not a viable choice.

The third, and perhaps the easiest option, would be to permit the Archangel Michael to send him to the Abyss. There, he would wait for Judgement Day, never knowing anything other than emptiness in the barren void. Furcas thought long and hard on this final choice, dreading the thought of being cast to the Abyss more and more with each passing moment. He could not see himself uselessly riding out the tide of time.

No, the Abyss would not do, either. Though it would be the easiest choice to make, there would be no possible way to change the course of his future, nor could he ever return to the Shadow Realm. With the first two options being unacceptable in his mind, Furcas knew what he needed to do, regardless of how much he didn't want to do it. He would have to return to Hell, face Astaroth, and await the decision of his fate. Strengthening his resolve, he turned his eyes to Michael.

"So, you have chosen, then?" Michael inquired.

"I have," Furcas replied.

"Then let the die be cast. Though I would rather see you, and all like you, permanently removed from Creation, I understand God's purpose in maintaining your existence. I doubt I would be as benevolent if the choice were mine to make. Be glad that it is not."

"Has anyone ever told you that you use far too many words, Light-Bearer?" Furcas nagged.

Archangel Michael smiled, nodding in respect.

"Farewell, imp. We will meet again soon."

With that, Michael stretched his wings fully to each side, placed both hands on the hilt of his sword, and raised the sword up high, the point of the blade facing the ground. Furcas closed his eyes, knowing what was to come. Then, with a mighty cry, Michael drove the sword downward, the tip biting deep into the soft, loamy soil. A flash of white exploded from the blade, and the world around them vanished like mist.

A moment later, Furcas opened his eyes, seeing he had been delivered to the Gates of Hell. His companion, Gauerdi, was at his side. The blood-red crystal portal sensed his presence, and opened with a hiss. Furcas lead Gauerdi through the mighty portal. The gates slid shut with an ominous clang.

CHAPTER TWO
THE FOUR WINDS

"Failed?" Satan bellowed, the word striking Astaroth like a powerful blow, causing him to take a cautious step back.

The Prince of Darkness began a slow, determined march around his dark-green, moldavite crystal throne, his obsidian boots hammering sparks from the dais' bone-white stone. The entire underworld trembled in reply. From time to time the Demon King's deep red eyes burned magma-white, while twin bolts of flame blasted Astaroth for having brought such bad news. Though the news was not his fault, Astaroth endured the lashings.

The winged demon stumbled each time the flames struck, but did nothing to resist, knowing how much more he would suffer if he tried to dodge or parry the blows. Between each blow, the demon searched for the courage and the words to reply; his hollow, empty, black eyes darting from side to side as if seeking someone— anyone—to pass this task to. There was none.

Astaroth was the Aide de Camp; the one who stood at Satan's right hand. It was his job—and his alone—to bring news such as this, regardless of the response that news might bring.

"The human boy had help, My Lord," Astaroth explained to Satan, straining to maintain a confident expression while his body was bent in submission and respect. "He was helped by one of our...brothers."

Satan's hand slashed in a wide arc before him as he heard the final word, sending a surge of dark energy that shattered everything in its path.

"Which one?" he bellowed.

"The Archangel Michael," Astaroth stated, his body flinching as the words crossed his lips.

Satan froze, his eyes flashing white-hot once more. Astaroth could hear him grinding his teeth.

"Michael," he spat, the word filled with rage.

Astaroth said nothing, hoping the grin he would have loved to have shown was not actually displayed. He knew the rumors; that it had been Michael who had cast Satan from Paradise, banishing the Demon King to dwell in the underworld until Judgement Day. He could see the rage boiling in Satan's eyes, could feel the tension in Satan's jaw, and as his master's fingers curled tightly, so too did Astaroth's curl; though not with anger, but with fear. His master was ready to explode; and the only thing left unbroken in the room, was Astaroth himself. Then, just as Satan's rage reached its' peak, it faded, swallowed back into the furnace of the Dark Lord's bowels where it would stew and boil until another day.

"Bah! Furcas was weak," the Demon Lord hissed, his face buried in a deep scowl. "He should have known Michael was there." Satan sighed, his eyes burning holes in the floor as his thoughts wandered. "He has grown old, Astaroth. His time is done. Banish him."

"At once, My Lord," Astaroth replied as he bowed and backed out of the room.

Upon reaching the antechamber, Astaroth saw Furcas leaning against a wall, picking his teeth with a dagger as if his very existence wasn't at risk. Next to the knight was his familiar midnight-black steed.

"I told you to leave the horse behind!" Astaroth growled at the indifference Furcas displayed.

The knight only shrugged, seemingly ambivalent to Astaroth's concerns.

"So?" Furcas inquired emotionlessly. "What did Satan choose? Are we to be banished, then?"

Astaroth glared at the lower-ranking demon, his normally solid black eyes burning red hot.

"Yes," Astaroth sighed, "the Prince of Darkness chose banishment. You are to leave at once."

Furcas nodded, then reached out a hand to grasp Gauerdi's reins.

"Come, old friend. 'Tis time to go."

Gauerdi whickered, shaking his head.

"No, Furcas. Not Gauerdi. Only you."

Furcas froze, then turned towards Astaroth.

"Gauerdi goes with me," he said, feigning the confidence to stand up to Astaroth's temper.

Astaroth narrowed his eyes and stood tall.

"You have little ground to stand on here. Let me remind you, Satan was generous in his decree. For whatever reason, he did not use the word 'permanent'. However, if you continue to press, I do hold the power to amend your sentence. If you ever want to see the Dark Towers again, be careful what words come next from your accursed lips."

Furcas returned the stare with an empty, unreadable look, only the tiniest of frowns on his weathered and worn face.

"Come now, Astaroth, who will watch over Gauerdi while I'm gone? You?" Furcas inquired plainly. "You know how childish Gauerdi gets in my absence. Do you truly want us apart?"

Astaroth sighed, knowing the demon spoke the truth. Separating the two would mean some other demon would have to care for the mount, and there were few demons, if any at all, who cared about anything other than themselves. He might as well let Gauerdi go with Furcas, if only to keep the horse from getting in the way.

"Fine. I'll grant you a choice. Your weapons and powers? Or the horse?" Astaroth proffered, knowing the huge advantage Furcas would have if he maintained his powers in the human realm. Yet, to his surprise, Furcas simply shrugged, and then removed his sword belt and set it to the side.

"Not here, you fool!" Astaroth growled. "Am I now to be your *servant*? Tend to your own blade!"

Furcas simply grinned as he reattached the belt around his waist. Astaroth knew the banished demon was enjoying this one last moment to be a thorn in his side, but he was not in the mood to allow it to continue.

"You have one earth hour," Astaroth said, turning his back on Furcas and picking up an hourglass. "Store your items, dress in human fashions, and be outside the gates before this sand runs out."

He flipped the hourglass over and placed it on a shelf cut into the wall. He then pushed past Furcas and returned to Satan's throne room. Behind him he could hear Furcas whispering to Gauerdi, followed by a noise that sounded as if the two were sharing a laugh. Astaroth ground his teeth in anger, yet simply walked on.

"Furcas will be gone in one earth-hour, My Lord," he informed the Prince of Darkness.

"Good," Satan responded, not even turning to face his aide. "Now, I've been thinking about this situation while you were gone. I believe we only have one choice,"

Satan muttered, as if speaking to himself. "If this boy, Thomas, is under God's protection, then we'll have to strike from a different direction. What do you know about his family?"

※

"Jules?" a timid voice whispered outside the white, six-panel bedroom door. "Are you awake?"

The door cracked open, the hinges voicing their displeasure with a soft squeak. A thin shaft of dim yellow light spilled into Julianna's room from the hallway, rousing the shadows that had gathered overnight. A petite, well-kempt hand slid through the narrow opening, groping along the pale-lavender wall until it found the switch and flicked it upward, bathing the room in a brighter, white light.

At once the shadows hid; some moving to the narrow spaces behind the dresser or desk, while others ducked into the closet or under the bed, all the places Julianna once believed monsters lived. If only she knew how right those thoughts had been, for even now, in the darkest of these spaces, a strange energy stirred. Ever since she was young, she had sensed there was something in the room with her, watching her, especially when she thought she was alone, though she had never been able to find anything there.

"Are you awake?" her mother asked again as the door creaked open further.

Julianna emitted a soft, sorrowful moan as her arms stretched out from under her jumbled pink comforter. She pushed the quilt aside, exposing her shoulders and head.

"I'm up, Mom," she replied as the door continued to open until there was enough room for her mother to slip inside.

"Just a warning," her mother, Angela, whispered, "your father's still asleep. Let's not wake the bear."

A forced smile stretched across Angela's tired face, and though the words had been uttered as if in jest, Julianna was not amused. She could see the way her mother's cheeks sagged; the way her eyes seemed to cry out; and the disheveled way she wrapped her threadbare robe about her small frame. No matter what her mother's smile implied, the words held no humor. The warning was clear. Her father was not to be disturbed.

Julianna wasn't afraid of her father, not physically anyway. He had never struck her, or anyone else that she knew of. He was just an angry man, and sometimes that anger rolled out like waves surging against the fragile walls that protected her self-esteem, eroding them until there was barely any left. Plus, today was one of those days when she would much rather not deal with her father's crazy ways.

Today was a special day. Today, Heather Murphy, who had been Julianna's best friend since daycare, would become a teenager. Tonight was Heather's party. It was going to be a dance party, too. The first 'no-parents-allowed,' live-DJ dance party that Julianna had been invited to, and she couldn't wait. She had been looking forward to this birthday more than she had ever looked forward to any of her own. Only a few kids ever turned thirteen in sixth grade, especially this early in the school year, and Julianna was glad that Heather would be the first. She liked having a best friend who was a full year older than she was, and yet still in the same grade.

Glancing towards the door, Julianna realized her mother was still there, as if waiting for something. She couldn't think what that something might be.

"I said I'm awake. I'll get up when you close the door, okay?" Julianna stated a bit roughly, immediately wanting to pull back the tone of her words, if not the words themselves.

With no more than a slight frown, Angela slid back out of the room, pulling the door closed behind her. Julianna took a deep breath, then sighed. Her heart ached for her mom; for the terrible way her father treated her; for the strict rules he enforced; for the strength of character her mom pretended to have, and yet lacked. And her heart ached for her own life, knowing how easy it would be to wind up becoming like her mom.

Somehow her older brother, Thomas, got by without the restrictions and frustrations that Julianna had to deal with; like being the last girl in sixth grade allowed to wear makeup and jewelry, or do other things that kids her age normally did. Julianna's ears were still not pierced, and her makeup kit included only two items; cherry-flavored lip gloss and pastel eyeshadow, both of which she could only wear for special occasions, and only with her father's consent.

Though her father hadn't stated that Heather's party counted as a special occasion, Julianna hadn't asked. According to her, it was going to be. It was the first act of defiance she had ever found the courage to take. But that was how special this night was going to be for her. Now, all she needed was to get out of the house before he was awake. If she did, then he couldn't search through her overnight bag; the one she suddenly realized she still hadn't packed.

Pitching her sheets to the side of the bed against the wall, Julianna slipped her legs over the other side and sat up. She reached down to retrieve the cell phone she had dropped four hours ago when she had finally fallen asleep, checking to see if either of her three best friends had messaged her.

Stacey, Heather, Jasmine, and Julianna had been inseparable for the past few years. There was rarely a moment when the four weren't all together, as if they were joined at the hip. So infamous was their friendship that their fourth-grade teacher, Mr. Donovan, had nicknamed them *The Four Winds*. A huge Greek mythology fan, Mr. Donovan had once explained to the girls what their nickname meant.

Stacey Johansson was *Boreas*, the Greek God of the North Wind, and the one responsible for the winter storms. With her steel-blue eyes and platinum-blonde hair, Stacey certainly looked the part. Though, at first impression she appeared gentle and kind with a Disney-princess personality, Julianna knew that Stacey had a much darker side. Anyone who had crossed Stacey the wrong way could attest to the cold-hearted way she sought revenge.

Mr. Donovan had given the nickname, *Notos*, God of the South Wind, to Heather. With her thick, golden tresses and ever-sparkling pear-green eyes, Heather had always been one of the most popular girls in school. Julianna knew exactly how Heather had earned her nickname, and how she kept it, too. Her oldest friend was a bit of a manipulator, a trick she had learned from her parents during their lengthy and bitter divorce. Julianna knew, if there was something Heather wanted, she would always find a way to get it. No matter what.

The third girl of the foursome was Julianna's least favorite friend, Jasmine Tantiangco. Had it been up to Julianna, Jasmine would never have been added to their group, but unfortunately, that wasn't her choice. Heather was the one who made those decisions. For some reason, Heather took a liking to Jasmine, even though Julianna couldn't understand why.

Jasmine was just a few inches over four-feet tall, with pale fawn skin and jet-black, almond-shaped eyes. She had worn her hair—which was just as dark as her eyes—in the same shaggy pixie cut since the first grade. Because of her competitive nature, Mr. Donovan had awarded Jasmine the name of *Zephyros*, the God of the West Wind. *Zephyros* was a jealous and competitive God. He was also the God of spring, new life, and rebirth; an energetic and playful God, and yet, a God that still held the power to destroy. Julianna knew that Jasmine was all that and more.

This left *Eurus*, the God of the East Wind, for Julianna. According to Mr. Donovan, the Greeks only had three seasons, which meant *Eurus* had been the least important of the four; a situation Julianna felt she aligned with only too well. Although she believed there was something special about herself, the rigid discipline her father imposed had never allowed her to find out exactly what that was.

There were times when Julianna felt she was beautiful, and she was always having people tell her how striking her forest-green eyes were when surrounded by her long, curvy, dark-chestnut locks. It was just that, with the restrictions her father placed on makeup and attire, Julianna always felt far too plain. On those days when her father did give his consent for her to dress up, Julianna would transform, both inside and out. The timid, shy, insecure, and quiet young girl disappeared, and a confident, secure, bold young woman took her place. It was these days when she truly felt herself. Though, the world beyond her immediate family had never seen her like that. Tonight, however, they would.

Though Julianna had already made the decision to go against her father's wishes, she still had to maintain the courage to put her plan into place. It was in these moments she wished she had Stacey's tenacity, Heather's gift of persuasion, or Jasmine's confident strength. But she didn't have those. All she had was a feeling that burned inside, pushing her to do things her way, to disobey her father's wishes, regardless of what that might cost.

As Julianna continued searching for the courage she required, the dark energy hiding in the shadows flashed briefly, then twice more, as invisible waves of emotional energy floated across the room, aimed for Julianna's heart. The subtle push was all that was required. Suddenly feeling daring, Julianna stood and moved to her dresser. She knew there was little chance her father would visit Heather's party. Therefore, in her mind, what he didn't know wouldn't hurt him. She would have more than enough time to return to the puritan appearance he demanded before he picked her up on Sunday morning for church.

She knew Heather and Stacey both had appointments to have their hair done this morning. It was the first stop on the list of errands Heather's mom would be chauffeuring the girls to and from. Julianna had secretly been stashing her allowance away for months. While her friends were having their hair done, Julianna was going to ask one of the ladies who worked at the salon do her makeup, and probably her nails, too. She had saved just enough. As long as she washed off the makeup and removed the paint from her nails, there was a chance that her father would never know. With a roguish smile, Julianna's decision was made.

Inside her top dresser drawer, behind a pile of unmatched socks and unfolded underwear, a hidden secret lay. She shifted the multi-colored clothing to one side, uncovering a small, worn, jewelry box. She held the box in her hands, breathing deeply as she gazed upon the mother-of-pearl inlay that decorated the rich walnut top. Though she had looked upon the artwork a thousand times, the beauty of it never grew old.

Carefully, she placed the box on her dresser and opened the lid. Inside the nearly empty, velvet-lined tray, only four items lay: a simple pair of diamond stud earrings, a bracelet made of the finest braided gold, a matching necklace with a red jasper pendant, and a folded piece of paper with the word *Julianna* written on the front with a shaky handwriting. Julianna would recognize that handwriting anywhere.

The box, and the items inside, had been a gift from her grandmother. Julianna had received it only a week before her grandmother has passed away. It was all she had left to remember the woman who had been her most favored relative. When she had spent time with her paternal grandmother, Julianna felt as if no one else existed in the world. And, in her grandmother's mind, no one did. For that reason, Julianna loved the gift more than almost anything else she owned.

She unfolded the note, being careful that the paper didn't rip along the folds, and then she silently read the script inside.

Julianna,

I wish I could live forever. We've barely just become friends. But cancer is a mean and heartless thing. It doesn't care about wishes. So, I must go. But know that, just as I did when I was alive, I will be thinking of you and praying for you always. You will never be far from my heart, no matter where your life might take you, no matter what you might become. I love you now as much as I ever have, and I always will. Keep these jewels close to your heart. They will one day hold a value beyond anything you can imagine.

You will always be my most precious Jewel, my Kósmima, my star.

Grandma Berenike

The words became difficult to read as her eyes filled with tears. She tried to swallow back the sorrow she felt when she read the words, but her throat was dry and tight. Placing the letter to the side, Julianna grabbed a few tissues, one of which she dabbed at her eyes, and the others she lay flat on the dresser's top. She then placed the jewelry in the tissues and carefully bundled them up. She placed her small treasure inside a sock, then placed that in her Monster High overnight bag, the same one she'd had since she was five. Julianna then filled the rest of the bag, first grabbing a plain, knee-length blue dress—one that she hated to wear—and a pair of taupe flats.

The dress was not the one that she wanted to wear. The dress she wanted to wear was hanging on a rack in a small boutique shop in the mall. Julianna had tried in on, just for fun, the last time she and her friends had gone to the mall. It had fit perfectly, and she had promised herself that she would wear it someday. She wished that today would be that day, but she had no idea where she would get the money to buy it. Stuffing the plain blue dress in her bag, she sighed, then grabbed another boring, ordinary outfit to wear to church on Sunday.

Finally, she grabbed the jewelry box once more. Running her finger along the lining, she found the cut she had made in the velvet, and pulled the lining away from the box. Underneath was the money she had saved. Julianna pulled the money out, quickly counted it, and then set it on top of her dresser. Glancing at her phone, she realized she only had a few minutes left before Heather's mom would be there to pick her up.

To complete her subterfuge, she removed the sweatpants and oversized t-shirt she had slept in and replaced them with the baggiest pair of jeans she owned, an oversized grey hoody, and her favorite Chucks: lemon yellow with purple laces looped in a ladder pattern. Before she placed her feet in the shoes, she slid the small stack of bills under the bottom liner of the left shoe, saying a quick prayer that, should her father wake up before she left, he wouldn't think to search inside her shoes. Julianna turned to look in her mirror, and what appeared to look like a ten-year-old skater-punk looked back. Not exactly the look she going for, but definitely one that her father would approve of.

Finished packing, she slung the bag over her shoulder, grabbed her Hannah Montana sleeping bag—also a relic from her early childhood—and headed down the hall. On her way to the front door, her phone buzzed. Glancing at the screen, she stopped dead in her tracks as she read the text.

It was yet another challenge from Jasmine. A challenge that was beyond anything Julianna ever imagined that Jasmine would do. A challenge that was not only very personal, but was Julianna's worst nightmare.

I bet I can kiss Devon before you do tonight.

CHAPTER THREE
GAME ON

Jasmine Tantiangco had always been a thorn in Julianna's side. As early as first-grade, Jasmine had chosen Julianna to be the target of every challenge she could think up, and Jasmine thought up quite a few. At first the challenges had been simple things like: how much they could eat, how long they could stand on their heads, how fast they could swim, or run, or bike, or even pee. Everything and anything could turn into a challenge for Jasmine, and to Jasmine, none of it was a game. Julianna knew her friend wanted nothing more than to win, and that she would do whatever it took to ensure she did.

Julianna had tried to ignore the challenges, but that only made things worse, and Jasmine wouldn't stop berating her for being afraid to lose, even though everyone at the school knew she most likely would anyway. So, Julianna had learned to accept Jasmine's challenges right away, and then compete only hard enough so it seemed like she was trying, all the time knowing she rarely, if ever, had a chance.

But this time Jasmine had taken things too far. After all, the four friends had made a pact three years ago, at the start of third grade. They had agreed they would never fight over a boy. Once one of them called dibs on a boy, the others knew to stay away. To start their new pact, they had each picked one of their classmates, the one they hoped would one day be their boyfriend. Julianna had chosen Devon. He was supposed to be 'hands off.'

In third grade, Devon McDonald had been one of the least attractive kids in their class; something that Jasmine had made fun of Julianna about for months. Still, Julianna had picked him, and over the years, she stayed with her choice. She didn't see Devon the way everyone else did. They saw him as a red-headed, freckled-faced goofball whose nose was a bit large, and whose ears stuck out too far. But Julianna thought he was funny, and smart, and that he had the most perfect sky-blue eyes.

Over the three years since then, Devon had changed. He was no longer the unattractive, uncoordinated goofball he had been in the third grade. Now, his lanky frame had developed into an athletic physique, and his hair—which had become more auburn than red—had grown out, hiding his awkwardly shaped ears. Most of his freckles had faded, and those that remained made his sky-blue eyes gleam even that much more. Julianna had chosen her 'someday-boyfriend' well, and by the looks of things from the text she had just read, she had chosen better than Jasmine was willing to admit.

"Not now. Not tonight," Julianna groaned silently as she read and re-read the text.

For weeks she had been dreaming of how Devon would ask her to dance, how they would hold hands, how he would lead her away from the dance to a place where the full moon shone just for the two of them. There, he would cup her face in the palms of his hands and, in a most perfect and gentle way, he would give Julianna her first kiss. Now Jasmine was going to ruin all of that.

Julianna didn't even know if Jasmine liked Devon, or if she had simply chosen this challenge for the same reason she had chosen all the others; that Jasmine wanted to win. It was very possible that Jasmine cared nothing about Devon, nor did she care about Julianna's girlish, romantic dreams. She only cared about being the victor in yet another race to be first. The kiss she intended to win from Devon would mean nothing to her. It would be a wasted, empty moment. Nothing at all like the moment Julianna had dreamed for herself.

As she read the text once more, her lips silently mouthing each word, she felt her throat get tight and her eyes grow moist. This was just one more situation where she was sure to feel inconsequential and meaningless. Becoming Devon's girlfriend was supposed to change all that. Jasmine didn't need a boyfriend like Devon, but Julianna did. Having a boyfriend like Devon meant Julianna would eat lunch with the popular kids. It would mean she would be the envy of every girl at school as she walked the hallways wrapped in Devon's varsity jacket. It didn't matter to her that he didn't even have a varsity jacket…yet. Details like that never shattered her dreams. Now, Jasmine's text just had.

A string of words cursing Jasmine flooded into Julianna's mind, all of which were of a nature that she would have been grounded for life if her father had heard her say even one. Still, she muttered the words with as much passion and volume as she was willing to risk. Her heart pounded in her ears and her entire body grew tense. She had never felt this angry before, or this determined to fight back. Little did she know that it was the strange energy drifting in the shadows of her room that was twisting and tweaking her emotions, dampening her fear and increasing her resolve. Still, Julianna had far too much experience competing against Jasmine, and far too many examples where she *had* tried, and yet had still lost. She began to feel desperate.

As her desperation continued to grow, Julianna's grip tightened on her phone; her fingers turning white as she squeezed so tight the phone nearly burst. In the back of her mind, she began to imagine doing the same thing to Jasmine, if only she found the courage. All of a sudden the feeling that someone was in her room intensified, and Julianna began to feel nervous. Then, a voice sounded in the depths of her mind, making her gasp.

"What are you going to do?" the voice asked.

Julianna had heard this voice before. It was the same voice that was always telling her she wasn't pretty, or smart, or that her ears were too small or her eyes were too big. It constantly reminded her that her legs weren't shaped right, or that the small mole on her cheek made her look like she had a disease. She was used to hearing this voice, and had lived with its insults and negativity for years. But it had never before asked her a question.

"What do you mean?" Julianna silently replied.

"Are you just going to give up?" the voice asked.

The words stunned Julianna, and she unconsciously took a step back. Giving up and letting Jasmine win was what she had always done. After having been beaten by her undersized friend over and again, it had become natural to think Jasmine would always win. Now, she began to think differently. She began to trust that her inner voice wouldn't have asked the question unless there was a chance *she* could win. For whatever reason, this time the voice wasn't saying mean things to her. This time, it was urging her to see herself in a different way.

With that thought in mind, Julianna's eyes took on a fearsome glow, as every memory of the world she had grown up in came crashing together, spurring her to respond. For years she thought she was letting Jasmine win because it was the easy way out. She had never felt that it would make much of a difference if she had won. Now, she realized Jasmine was nothing more than a bully; just like her father was to her mom.

Though her mom had moments of strength, and would at times even argue with Julianna's father, Julianna realized her mother was just going through the motions. Her mother wasn't brave, or stubborn, or resolved, and neither was she. The one thing Julianna feared the most was becoming just like her mom. But that had already come true. Just as her mother had never truly stood up to her dad, not when it mattered, Julianna had never stood up to Jasmine. She had let Jasmine push her around, let herself feel worthless, and not only let herself be seen as weak, but feel like she was, too. Suddenly, beating Jasmine was the most important thing in her world.

"No more," she thought. *"Tonight, things change."*

"So? What are you going to do?" the voice repeated.

Julianna knew what she was going to do, and it all started by finding a way to get that dress; the one she had tried on and promised herself she would wear someday. Today would be that day.

Julianna didn't respond to her inner voice, but she did respond to Jasmine's text. With just two simple words, Julianna drew a line in the sand.

Game on

※

"What news, Astaroth? Where do we stand?" Satan asked impatiently as the demon approached.

"Things are coming together better than we hoped, My Lord," Astaroth answered, still halfway across the room. "The female child has been easy to persuade. A most opportune situation is beginning to unfold, one which we can use to further weaken the bonds that hold this family together. At your word, Lord Satan, I will tear their family apart."

"And how will your plans affect Thomas?" the Demon King inquired.

Astaroth grinned. He knew that the question was only a trap. Satan already knew the answer to the question, and had only asked it to ensure that Astaroth knew the answer as well.

"Our predictions are he will turn inward, bury his emotions, and become too afraid to ask for help. Much like his father, he will isolate himself from the world as he becomes more and more desperate. If everything goes as planned, I expect Thomas will give up."

Satan, who until now had appeared to be absentmindedly picking at a loose crystal on the edge of his throne, turned his full attention to his aide, his gaze burning deep into Astaroth's mind, seeking any sign of weakness or deceit. Finding none, he turned away.

"You have my approval," he said with a wave of his hand. "I give you my authority to make whatever decisions need to be made, and to command whatever resources are required. Now, go!"

Astaroth exited as he always did; bowing his head low as he backed out of the room and returned to his den. There, a quintet of lesser demons awaited his commands.

"You, Sitri," he said, pointing at a demon that resembled a leopard with eagle's wings. "The one called Jasmine will be yours to command."

Sitri nodded, then waved his hands, creating a cloud of vapor into which he vanished from view.

"Zepar," Astaroth said, moving his attention to the next demon in the group, one who resembled a knight dressed in blood-red armor with a helm that completely covered its face. "Your target will be Heather."

This demon, too, disappeared in the same fashion as Sitri had. Astaroth pointed to the third demon.

"Ose, fly quickly to the mother. Stay alert! Strike the moment the others do, not a moment sooner! And Raum," Astaroth said, turning to a large, crow-like demon as Ose began to fade, "you will take the father."

When Raum had vanished, Astaroth addressed the final demon.

"Finally, Barbas. Your target is Julianna. Please note, I will not tolerate failure, not like Furcas failed with her brother," Astaroth spoke these last words with contempt, his face twisted and filled with disgust.

The demon vanished, leaving Astaroth alone, allowing him to prepare for the task of interceding in Julianna's life, a task he now felt would be much easier than first assumed. With his demon-sight, he would not only be able to watch the events unfold, but could continue to place pressure as needed, bending the young girl to his whim. As he thought of all he could accomplish in the next few hours, his eyes began to burn, and an evil smile stretched slowly across his face.

※

Angela Berenike, Julianna's mother, sat at a computer, going over the family's finances and paying a few bills. Next to her was a cup of tea and a half-eaten slice of whole-wheat toast. Her senses were on alert, listening for any sound that her husband was awake. She heard the shuffling sound of someone coming down the hallway, and prepared herself in case it was him.

"Mom? Where are you? We need to talk!" she heard her daughter's voice call out.

Angela frowned. Julianna had obviously forgotten her earlier warning about 'waking the bear.'

"In the office, dear," Angela replied, her voice barely audible. "And please, keep your voice down!"

As she waited, she could hear Julianna's footsteps striking hard on the laminate floor, a sign that her daughter was in one of her moods.

"Mom, I need money," Julianna blurted out the moment she entered the room.

"How much?" Angela inquired.

"I don't know," Julianna said, shrugging her shoulders and pursing her lips.

Angela Berenike paused a moment, giving her daughter a knowing and experienced look. She could tell Julianna already knew exactly how much money she needed, and she gave her a look that let her daughter know just as much.

"Maybe a hundred bucks?" Julianna admitted bashfully. "I need a new dress."

"What's wrong with your blue dress? I think you look pretty in that one," she stated, knowing full well what Julianna's reaction would be.

"Mom…seriously? I look like a nun, or like I'm Amish or something. No one my age wears anything like that. You know who does? Little old ladies, like the school librarian. Did you know she has the same blue dress?" Julianna replied.

Angela's lips pulled to the left as she gave her daughter a half-frown, and a knowing look appeared in her dull, tired eyes.

"First, tell me why," she stated, setting her brows.

Julianna huffed, then sighed, but Angela noticed that she didn't look away, not like she used to do when she was younger.

"This is one of those times when you're not going to back down, isn't it?" Julianna quietly asked.

Angela simply smiled, letting the sparkle in her eyes inform her daughter that she knew the answer to her question already.

"Okay," Julianna began. "It's Jasmine, mom. She's at it again."

Angela felt her fingers tighten on the arms of the chair. *Jasmine!* The girl had been a pain from the moment she had first come into Julianna's life. Though her daughter hadn't told her about all of Jasmine's challenges right away, after time, Angela had figured it out, and when she confronted Julianna about the situation, her daughter had confessed.

"What is it this time?" she inquired.

"Do I have to tell?" Julianna begged.

Angela knew the look her daughter was giving her. She knew that the challenge Jasmine had just put forth would either be something that would publicly embarrass her daughter, or it was about a boy.

"Is this about Devon?" she casually asked, watching as Julianna's eyes grew wide.

"How do you know about Devon?" Julianna said, the words coming out slow from the shock.

"Can we just say that I have my ways, and leave it at that?" Angela suggested.

The fact was, Angela didn't want her daughter to know how it was she had found out about Devon. If she did know, it would definitely destroy the trust it had taken years for the two to develop. The sad truth was, Julianna's father forced her to search their daughter's room when Julianna wasn't home. He would stand in the doorway and watch while she searched, too. Then, when she finally found something of interest, such as her daughter's diary, he made her read it through it. Though, at least he never demanded she read it out loud.

Angela knew it was a violation of her daughter's privacy, and she had prayed for years that he would stop asking her to do it. Now, the embarrassment of her daughter finding out, whether she had been forced to or not, weighed heavily on Angela's heart. She looked again at Julianna, praying that her daughter would be so upset at Jasmine, that she would let this moment slide. When Julianna said nothing, Angela sighed.

"I'll make you a deal. You tell me why, and if it's a good reason, I'll seriously consider letting you get a new dress," she said, hoping the lure would be enough.

Julianna gave her a sideways glance, then nodded.

"Yeah, it's about Devon," she said, showing her mom the text.

Angela felt her eyes grow wide as she read the words, and her heart went out to her daughter.

"And your response, this 'game on' part, is that what the dress is for?" she asked.

Julianna nodded, then wiped away a tear.

"Mom, no one outside of our family has ever seen me dressed up. Maybe if I had a new dress, a really fancy one, it would be enough to beat Jasmine this time. Maybe Devon wouldn't even know Jasmine was in the room."

Angela sighed, her mind flooding with an image of her daughter in the plain, blue dress she had just suggested Julianna should wear.

"You know she's right. The dress is not one designed for a young girl her age. She needs something more," the demon, Ose, whispered in her mind.

"But I don't think that I should. Her father would never approve!" Angela answered, believing she was simply answering her own thoughts.

"Why does he need to know?" the demon suggested as it picked away at the wall of fear and doubt surrounding Angela's heart, igniting a small spark, a desire to be treated as an equal and with respect.

"What kind of dress do you want?" Angela asked, surprising both her daughter and herself as the words came to life.

"I…I don't know…" Julianna stuttered, her face still draped in shock. "Wait, are you saying yes?"

Angela thought about it, wondering if she was in fact doing exactly that, saying yes; and if so, what the potential repercussions of her response might be.

"Assuming I do, there would have to be a few restrictions in place."

"Like what?" Julianna asked, her newfound excitement draining rapidly away.

"Like, nothing too revealing, and it has to have full shoulders. It can't be sleeveless, or have a low neckline. And it can't be too short, nothing above the knee," Angela replied, suddenly feeling emotional as her throat begin to tighten. "I don't care how old you think you are, in my mind you're still my little girl."

The image of her daughter shifted as tears filled her eyes, and she quickly wiped them away.

"Mom, I'm twelve, not six," Julianna replied with a quiet confidence. "I'll be a teenager this summer. I'm not a little girl anymore."

"You're right, Jules," Angela said after a moment's pause. "You're not a little girl anymore. I mean, look at you. You're becoming a woman right before my eyes. A beautiful, strong woman."

"Then I can get a new dress?" Julianna asked with an expectant gleam in her eyes.

Angela paused. Half of her was still screaming to say no, afraid of what Julianna's father would do if he ever found out. But those screams faded quickly as the demon working inside her heart continued to dampen her fears. Finally, those fears vanished altogether as Angela found a resolve she had never known before. Rising slowly from the chair, she took hold of her daughter's hand.

"Come with me. Let's see how much I've got stashed away."

The two walked to the kitchen where Angela proceeded to remove several cans from a shelf in the pantry, setting each one aside. Finally, she found the one she was looking for and held it tightly in her hand, breathing deeply.

"Ah…here it is," she said.

With a twist of her wrist, she cracked the can open, revealing a secret no one but she knew. Rather than lima beans like the label showed, inside was a tight roll of bills. Though it was mostly fives and tens, there were a few larger bills as well.

"I've been saving this for an emergency," she said as her eyes locked with her daughter's.

She rifled through the bills until she found five twenty-dollar-bills, then held them tightly in one hand.

"This should be enough," she said as she twisted the rest of the cash back into a bundle.

"What about my hair and nails?" her daughter asked as she reached for the bills. "Heather's getting hers done this morning. Maybe they can fit me in too?"

Angela's grip tightened on the bills as her daughter tried to pull them away. She began once more to wonder if she was doing the right thing, but the die had already been cast. She knew if she got in trouble for letting her daughter wear a new dress, one that had not been approved by her husband, it wouldn't matter if she had also let Julianna have her hair and nails done.

Smiling as she accepted the possible fate of her decision, Angela let go of the first stack of bills, then reached back inside the fake can of beans and pulled out one-hundred dollars more. Before she gave them to her daughter, she resealed the can and placed it towards the back of the pantry once more, surrounding it with cans that really did hold inside what their outer labels said. Finally, she turned to her daughter.

"Nails? Manicure, buff and polish only. No French tips, acrylics or gels. Hair? Cut and styled, not too short, and no coloring, highlights, weaves, or whatever else is popular right now. Agreed?" she asked, once more holding the money out towards her daughter.

Julianna's eyes shone with excitement and hope as she reached for the bills, but Angela pulled them back.

"Agreed?" she asked again, this time more sternly.

"Okay! Agreed," Julianna relented as she waited for her mom to pass the money to her once more.

"And make sure you wash it all off before church. And tie your hair in a bun or something until it grows back out," she said as she released the money. Then, feeling more relaxed about what she had just done, Angela added, "If there's enough left over, get yourself a pair of shoes, and ask Mrs. Murphy to help you pick out a new slip."

Julianna smiled, and her eyes were sparkly and bright. In her mind, Angela could already see her daughter in the new dress, her hair perfectly styled, her makeup done just right. Suddenly, as both women began to shed tears, Julianna threw her arms around her mother's neck and hugged her tight.

"Thank you, Mom," Julianna said, the words sputtering out, and Angela knew her daughter was truly grateful for the gift she had just received.

As mother and daughter embraced, two invisible demons floated out of the kitchen and through the house until they found a dark, quiet corner to hide in. There, they set about sending a signal to Astaroth that they had something to report.

CHAPTER FOUR
PRELUDE TO A KISS

Astaroth stirred the coals in the bottom of a heavy, bronze brazier, watching as the thick top-layer of soot was displaced, revealing softly glowing embers underneath. As the coals were exposed, they began to change color; from cherry, to pumpkin, to gold. Above and around him on the cold rock surface of the ceiling and walls, dark shadows danced. Fairy flames twinkled upward with the rising heat. Even the air was fluid, giving the illusions of movement to objects on the other side of the room.

Reaching down, Astaroth clutched a small scoop, the bowl of which was bedecked with holes, much like a sieve. He thrust the blade of the shovel deep into the embers, then lifted and shook the scoop; ash and cinders fell through the holes, and the larger chunks broke apart. He continued to shake until all that remained was a brightly burning ember the size of a child's fist. Gently tipping the scoop, he allowed the ember to slide out, catching it in a small, stone cup. He placed the scoop back on the floor, then carried the stone cup to a semi-circular table covered with a jumble of items: alembics, mortars, retorts, and aludels; all tools of the alchemist's trade.

Sorting through bottles of various colors, he chose three, two of which were blue, while the third was dark jade. With one hand he pulled the crystal stoppers from each flask while his other hand retrieved a mortar. Astaroth sprinkled small amounts of the crystalline substances from each of the vials into the mortar, then ground them into a fine powder with a stone pestle. When he was satisfied, he added the mixture into the stone cup which he gently swirled allowing the multi-colored powder to cover the ember, causing it to smoke, pop, and hiss. As the reaction reached its peak, Astaroth took one step back, leaning slightly away from the table. A moment later, the mixture in the cup flared and a dense cloud of pearlescent vapors formed into an oval-shaped disc.

The disc glimmered softly, and then began to spin, rotating faster and faster until Astaroth could no longer distinguish the top of the oval from the bottom. And then, an image began to appear. As the image solidified, Astaroth saw the head and shoulders of a leopard.

"What news, Ose?" Astaroth inquired at the first sign of movement in the phantasmal shape.

"Everything goes as planned, Lord Astaroth," Ose replied, his image flickering slightly, the words not quite in synch with the movement of his mouth. "The female child is on her way and Barbas is following. I have convinced the child's mother to allow the child certain liberties that will certainly anger the child's father."

"Ah, the father. Certainly a key part of our plan. Any word from Raum on how his efforts have fared?"

"Raum arrived to find the adult male asleep. He is currently filling the man's dreams with memories of his past, specifically the darker memories the human had attempted long ago to forget. Raum and I will continue to twist the emotions of the two adult humans throughout the day, as you have commanded. When the time comes for them to fall, they will be well prepared."

Astaroth considered the news carefully, searching for any possible holes in his plan. From what he could tell, the plan was moving along with near perfect precision;

though perhaps a bit too fast. He needed to make sure everything came together at the same time, or the changes he was preparing for Julianna could fail.

"Not until I say," Astaroth growled, his dog-like face grimacing. "Not until all of the pieces are ready. For now, just watch and wait."

"As you command, Lord Astaroth," Ose said, bowing with respect as both his image and the glimmering disc faded away.

※

The rest of the morning and afternoon was filled with chaos as Mrs. Murphy, Heather's mom, rushed the girls from one stop to the next, trying to fit in far too many activities in the rapidly diminishing hours before the party was scheduled to start. During this time, three demons were at work, and they did their jobs well. Every time Mrs. Murphy paid even the slightest attention to Julianna, Zepar, the demon assigned to Heather, filled his target's mind with jealousy and contempt, and constantly reminded Heather that this special day was supposed to belong to *her*, not Julianna.

Sitri, the demon assigned to Jasmine, had an even easier task. It was this demon's job to ensure that every change in Julianna's appearance was seen as a direct threat to Jasmine's challenge of who would win Devon's first kiss. Even without the demon twisting her thoughts, Jasmine would have been concerned, for Julianna was blossoming before everyone's eyes. The previously ordinary, plain, diffident girl that Julianna had been since pre-school was becoming more radiant and confident with every stop the group made.

The biggest change had been with her hair and makeup, the transformation being completely unexpected. Underneath the puritan façade, Jasmine realized, Julianna was gorgeous. With her hair and makeup done just right, her childish features became beautifully mature. And when Jasmine saw the dress and matching heels that Julianna picked out, for the first time ever Jasmine was afraid she had issued a challenge that she might not win.

Though she was a fierce competitor, Jasmine had never believed herself to be beautiful or attractive. Her small stature made her feel like she was still a child at times. Julianna, however, was tall, and though a bit gangly, was learning to carry herself with style and grace. Jasmine knew there was no way that Devon would fail to notice Julianna now.

The third demon was Barbas, the one that Astaroth had assigned to Julianna. With subtle tweaks and gentle influencing words, Barbas continually pressed on Julianna's vanity, allowing the young woman to see herself through a new self-assurance as her heart began to swell overconfidently with pride.

Finally, everything had been prepared, and the birthday dance party was about to begin. The inside of Eagle's Hall, the location where the party would be, had been thoroughly transformed. No longer was it a drab, wood-paneled building where seniors met to play Bingo or Wednesdays. Instead, it now looked like the ballroom of a medieval castle. Every inch of the ceiling and walls had been covered in murals painted to resemble dark gray stone walls, and instead of the typical fluorescent-tube lighting, there now hung crystal chandeliers bedecked with flickering LED candle-shaped lamps.

On one side of the building, four food stations had been set, ready to provide as much pizza, tacos, hamburgers and nachos as the kids could consume. On the opposite wall stood two dessert stations, and a mocktail bar that served brightly-colored drinks bearing even more colorful names. On the stage, a live band waited for their turn to perform, while a DJ pumped club tunes from a dozen Marshall stacked amps.

Spilled across the dancefloor, nearly fifty sixth-grade girls and boys milled about in clusters of three, or four, or five. The girls were dressed in sparkles and glitter, with dresses and high-low skirts that billowed when they moved. On their feet they wore brightly colored heels that made their ankles wobble as they walked. Their eyes were wide, flickering with excitement, anticipation, and awe, and the gloss on their lips sparkled as bright as the gleam in their eyes in the flashing lights. The boys looked handsome in their dress shirts and trousers that their mothers ironed for them or had paid to have pressed. Their eyes, too, were wide, though not from excitement. To the last one, they were scared. Not one had ever asked a girl to dance before, and they wondered who would have the courage to be first.

In a small, dusty room behind the stage, the Four Winds made their final preparations, pulling and tugging their dresses into place while admiring themselves in one of the many available mirrors, and constantly tweaking or tossing their hair. This was the last chance for photos before the party began, and a professional photographer captured each moment with five different cameras that she had strapped across her shoulders and back. Her assistant shuffled nervously from one spot to the next, holding a screen to diffuse the flashing lights. In the midst of it all, Heather's father couldn't stop staring with pride at his daughter all grown up, while he layered all four girls with compliments and praise.

For the moment, the girls had forgotten all about the tension that had developed through the day, though it wouldn't be long before those feelings returned. The exhaustion from the hours of shopping and errands, coupled with far too little rest the night before, was evident in their excited, yet tired eyes.

Then, at exactly one minute before eight, the lights dimmed, and a single spotlight began to sweep in random circles over the crowd. The music became charged with anticipation, and all eyes turned towards the stage. A second spotlight appeared on the left side of the stage where Jasmine, Stacey and Julianna now stood. The light followed them as the three girls walked to the middle of the stage and paused, each one giving a quick curtsey to the audience as the DJ introduced them by name. When all three had been introduced, they turned in unison to face the right side of the stage, where the randomly meandering spotlight suddenly locked onto a prearranged spot. All eyes turned to see what was coming next, and everyone froze.

The music reached a crescendo, and Heather stepped into view. The crowd burst into applause as the DJ formally announced the birthday girl. Framed in bright white light, Heather looked radiant, and her smile couldn't have been any wider. This night was all for her and she knew it.

With the grand introductions over, the four girls placed their arms around each other as they made their way to the stairs on the side of the stage. The DJ stepped away from his turntable, and the band took over, starting off with one of the most current popular songs. A chorus of screams drowned out the music as excited, caffeinated and sugar-rushed pre-teen girls began to hop and bounce and twist, each in their own unique way. The boys started moving towards the outer walls, though some stayed, either because they were brave, or because they had been unable to escape the grasp of one of the girls and were now trying their best to not look as foolish as they felt, dancing in front of their friends.

Heather and her three best friends left the stage, the spotlights following as they made their way to the center of the room where they, too, began to dance. Gone were the thoughts of the challenge Jasmine had issued. Gone were the feelings of jealousy and spite. The Four Winds were all blowing the same direction once more.

As they continued to dance, one or the other would suddenly spin away from the group, rushing off to grab one of the other guests and bring them to the center where their newly captured friend would stay for a dance or two before flowing back into the throng as new faces were dragged in to take their place. The mood was elevated, excited and bursting with emotions, and it stayed like that for the entire length of the band's first set. Then, as the band took a quick break, it became quiet for a moment, granting the youth their first opportunity to breathe, or speak, or release the smiles that had been plastered across their faces for nearly an hour-and-a-half.

Heather marched as confidently as she could in the four-inch heels she wore, heading straight to the table of honor that had been set up just for her and her three closest friends. Julianna, Jasmine and Stacey obediently followed, and then took their assigned seats as a waiter approached and handed each of the girls a paper menu listing all of the food and drink options available. With their orders placed and the waiter departed, the girls began to gossip about some of the other guests.

"Can you believe she wore that dress?" Stacey said, pointing to their first unknowing victim.

"Oh, I know!" Heather replied. "And those shoes! It looked like she's wearing her grandma's clothes!"

"Not as bad as Tamara's dress!" Julianna exclaimed. "Did you see how far up that slit went?"

"Oh, she definitely thinks she has it going on," Stacey said, roasting the oblivious victim of their fashion critique. "At least all the guys look really cute!"

"Oh, yeah!" Heather nodded in agreement. "You better keep your hands off Tony. Tonight, he's all mine!"

"Ha ha! You can have him," Stacey said as she shook her head. "My eyes are on David. Rawr, rawr!"

"Wait, David Lawrence? Or David Kingman?"

"Oh my God! Did you really think I meant David Kingman! Gross! The guy ate boogers in third grade!"

"Oh my God! I forgot about that! It's kinda too bad, though. He's cute."

"Hey, he's all yours if you want him."

"What about Matt? He's looking really hot. I don't think I've ever seen him with his hair slicked back like that. He has really pretty eyes, don't you think?"

"Yeah, he does! He should stop wearing glasses and keep his hair that way."

The waiter returned with their drinks. On the tray stood two hurricane glasses filled with a bright watermelon-colored slush with huge strawberries slipped over the rim and tall peaks of whipped cream; a pilsner style glass filled with a neon green liquid and dark blue boba pearls; and a champagne flute filled with sparkling apple cider and frozen kiwi chunks. The girls, oblivious to the movements of the waiter, continued chatting as if he wasn't even there.

"Did you guys see Keith?" Jasmine chimed in. "I never thought I'd say this, but he's cute!"

"So, does that mean you're not going after Devon then?" Heather asked.

"Oh, no…" Jasmine said, lowering her voice as her eyes flickered with a wicked glare. "It's still on."

CHAPTER FIVE
DANCING WITH THE DEVIL

Astaroth twisted his hand, spinning the handle of a fire poker, the tip of which rested on the floor. The poker spun to the left, then, as he reversed the motion, it spun back to the right. Small, light-gray circles were left behind on the dark-gray stone tile floor. The Crown Prince of Demons was bored. It had been hours since he had employed his five most-trusted lesser demons, and he had had nothing to do since then, but wait. Before him, rather than just one spinning communication disc, he now had five, each one showing him the image of a different demon. Currently, all five were at rest, not fully dormant, but close enough, saving their energy for the events yet to come. Behind each, he could clearly see the image of the target that he had assigned them to, and by so doing, he knew that the time had come.

"Arise, my demons. The time has come," he growled only slightly louder than a whisper, and then sat back with anticipation to watch the events unfold.

Sitri was the first to respond, nodding his leopard-shaped head and unfurling his eagle-like wings as he spiraled invisibly into the air above the table where the Four Winds sat in silence. Then, decreasing rapidly in size, he dove straight for the smallest of the four, heading straight for Jasmine's heart. As soon as the demon was in place, he began to flood the young girl's mind with images of a future he knew his target would want nothing more than to avoid; a future where Julianna won the latest challenge, and Jasmine failed.

With experience born from millennia of twisting the fate of human hearts, the demon twisted Jasmine's emotions; changing them to feelings of embarrassment, defeat, insecurity and loss. All of which were feelings he knew Jasmine was familiar with. They were the same emotions that drove her competitive nature. The demon knew that the competitive young woman feared losing more than anything else, and the extra urgency he placed upon her only stoked the flames of the fires she had fought to avoid most of her life.

Suddenly, Jasmine stood, turned, and raced across the dance floor.

※

The moment that Jasmine had stood up and raced across the room, Barbas knew that the time had come for him to begin his work. In his demonic form, which was half-lion and half man, it was hard to see the grin he wore as he tossed his jet-black lion's mane and uttered a low growl. Then, turning his chocolate-brown eyes towards Julianna, he simply placed an invisible paw over her head, knowing as long as he held it there, she would be unable to move. While he kept the young girl captive, Barbas whispered in Julianna's ear, filling her mind with knowledge of the plan Jasmine was in the process of acting out. Every move Jasmine was planning, Julianna now knew, and yet she was paralyzed, unable to respond.

Barbas could feel the desperation rising from the pit of the young girl's soul as she watched the events unfold. He grinned an evil, wicked grin.

※

Julianna wanted nothing more than to chase after Jasmine, to stop her from doing what it was she was planning to do, but she couldn't. For some inexplicable reason, she felt too stunned to move. All she could do was watch, and despair.

※

As Sitri and Barbas enacted their part of Astaroth's plan, a few miles away, in a typical ranch-style home on a quiet residential street, Ose and Raum awoke. Raum twisted his large crow-shaped head, looking first with one eye, and then with the next, at the adult humans who sat nearby. He was urgent to begin his part of the plan, for it had been some time since he had used his powers to destroy. Beside him, the demon Ose, who was also in a leopard-like form, lay curled in a ball, purring like a common housecat. Raum unfurled his raven-black wings and shook noisily, rousing the demon-cat. Ose raised his head, his eyes fully alert and his ears pricked up.

"It is time, Ose," Raum said, his giant obsidian eyes beginning to glow.

"Yes. I know," Ose replied, giving Raum a sideways glance, as if to remind the demon which one of them was currently a cat, and which was a bird.

"Do you want to make the first move? Or shall I?" Raum inquired, not responding to Ose's unspoken threat.

"Please," Ose replied, waving his leopard-like paw forward, casually, as if he couldn't be more bored.

Raum grinned, then pointed his beak towards the scene before them, and nodded his head.

※

At that moment, the Berenike's television flickered, and then went black. Angela gasped as she heard her husband's frustrated growl. She watched, transfixed, as he held the remote before him, pressing buttons in a seemingly random way. Silently, she began to pray that his fingers would somehow strike the buttons in the correct order, and the screen would leap back to life. Yet, for a full thirty seconds he continued, his frustration growing with each new attempt. With another growl, he tossed the remote in her direction, showing no concern for the force of the toss. The remote bounced off of her chest and landed on the floor at her feet.

"Can you figure out what's wrong with the damn TV, please?" her husband grumbled, his eyes suddenly looking hard and fierce.

Angela swallowed, trying unsuccessfully to force back the feelings of dread. She knew there was nothing she could do that her husband hadn't already tried. She also knew that the inclusion of the word 'please' was in no way indicative that he was attempting to soften his mood. He was simply holding back his anger, which, though currently aimed at the non-working television, could just as easily be directed towards her. She had been in too many situations like this before, and she prepared herself for the verbal assault that she feared would soon pass over his lips.

Back from his quick venture into the depths of Jasmine's heart, Sitri was now reclined along one of the supporting rafters, high enough from the floor to be hidden in the shadows of the barn-like roof, yet close enough to impact the situation taking place below him on the dance floor. Between his forepaws he held what looked like a marionette's paddle, its invisible strings draping down to the side of the dance floor where Jasmine now stood.

Jasmine had a strange sensation that her body was somehow acting of its own accord as she approached Devon. She took a moment to cherish the look in his eyes, then reached her hand towards him as she heard her voice say, *'Dance with me'*. Devon smiled as he took her hand, and Jasmine led him through the crowd just as the DJ began to play the first slow song of the night.

As most of the crowd began to disperse, being too shy to slow dance this early in the night, Jasmine and Devon had the floor to themselves. She turned to face him, and holding his arms at the wrist, placed his hands in position just above her waist. Then, she extended her arms to place her hands around his neck, which, due to the difference in their height, meant they were forced to stand fairly close. Jasmine could only imagine what might be going through Julianna's mind as she looked on from the sideline, and she tried to steal a glance or two in her direction each time the pair spun that way.

If there was one thing that Zepar knew, it was how to make people fall in love. It was one of his favorite powers, after all. And since his part in the plan had yet to begin, he found himself with a bit of free time on his hands. He decided the best way to spend it, was to play around with a few young, innocent, easily persuaded hearts. As he watched Jasmine and Devon swaying slowly in the near darkness, he wished the dance was taking place outdoors. There wasn't much he could do within the confines of the building they were in. Still, since the roof of the building had been designed with several skylights, it gave Zepar an idea. Though the moon had not yet risen far enough to be seen through any of them, he knew exactly what to do.

Julianna's heart dropped the moment she heard the softer music begin to play, and she watched in still-frozen horror as Jasmine and Devon took their place, their arms wrapped around each other. This was supposed to have been her dance, her moment of triumph. It was supposed to be her out there winning over Devon's heart. She wanted to scream, but still her body would not move. And then, as if it had been planned to happen, the clouds overhead broke apart, and a single beam of moonlight broke through one of the skylights above, bathing Jasmine and Devon in a heavenly light. As if on cue, every young woman in the room audibly sighed. The sound washed over Julianna like a tidal wave.

※

Twitching his tail playfully, Ose watched as Angela Berenike fumbled with the TV remote. The more she fumbled, the more the demon pushed her fear. He knew if he pushed her far enough, the fear could become terror. Humans always acted in strange, unpredictable ways when they were terrified. He started imagining what strange behavior his target might begin.

※

"I don't know what's wrong," Angela said, her eyes pleading with her husband. "Maybe you can watch the game on your phone?"

She watched as the look in her husband's face darkened, and she began to feel more afraid of him than she had ever felt before. As he stood up from his chair and walked towards her, her mind raced, trying to think of anything she could do to assuage his mood. Though he had been in moods like this more often than she cared to recount, this time it seemed far worse. She considered asking what was wrong, but she had made that mistake before and wanted nothing more than to avoid an argument that she could never win.

He reached the spot where she sat and held out his hand. Believing he wanted her to give him back the remote, she extended it out towards him, hoping he would simply take it. Instead, he slapped it out of her hand, then leaned forward and picked up her cell phone from off the table beside her. She went pale as he stood over her and unlocked her phone.

⁕

"Oh my! Julianna is just about ready to burst!" Barbas sneered. "Shall I release her yet?"

Sitri shook his large, spotted head.

"Not quite yet. Now that Zepar has set the mood, let's wait just a moment and see how this plays out."

⁕

Jasmine had never felt the way she had when the moonlight first broke through. It was like she was floating on air. Even with all the time she had spent twirling and flipping and tumbling during her floor routines, or her dismounts, or her vaults, she had never had this same feeling of utter weightlessness. It consumed every part of her, leaving her nothing to do but stare into Devon's beautiful blue eyes. As she did, she could tell that he was feeling the same way. She hadn't planned on things happening the way they were. This was just supposed to be a competition, a way of proving once more to Julianna that she was better than her. She had just planned on dancing with Devon, then asking him to give her a quick kiss, nothing romantic or extended. Just enough for everyone to see, just enough so Julianna would know that she had lost the challenge.

But now, something else was taking place, something Jasmine knew she couldn't control. Though she had imagined a moment like this happening someday, she had always thought she would have been able to decide with whom it would happen, and when. But now that it *was* happening, she could only let things flow. As she stared up at Devon, for the first time seeing how handsome he actually was, she raised up on her tiptoes, and closed her eyes. A moment later, she felt an explosion of emotions as their lips touched, and Jasmine Tantiangco knew, she had fallen in love.

※

"Do you recall earlier today, what the adult female said to her child? Just before the younger woman left for the mall?" Raum inquired of the demon standing nearby.

"I do," Ose responded, then grinned wickedly. "How fortunate for us that the female child complied!"

Raum extended his right wing before him, tilted back his head, and softly chanted the words of a spell.

※

Roger Berenike saw terror flood into his wife's eyes as he reached for her phone and instantly knew there was something she was hoping he wouldn't see. He immediately began to search through the device, hoping to find exactly what that something was. First, he checked the phone log, but nothing there seemed amiss. A few phone calls had been made throughout the day, but he recognized the phone numbers for those. Next, he checked the text messages. Again, he didn't see anything strange. Not at first, anyway.

Then, he his intuition told him to check the text messages sent between his wife and their daughter from earlier that day. When he opened the conversation, he found it to be almost empty. There were only two texts. The first text was sent from his wife to their daughter telling her to have fun at Heather's party. That one didn't seem amiss. He knew Julianna was going to be at Heather's birthday party tonight. They had discussed it earlier in the week. And there was nothing out of the ordinary in the way his daughter replied, though he did feel that her response was a bit over-excited for what he believed was supposed to be just pizza and movies with Heather and a few other friends. Why his daughter had said she would tell her mom all about it tomorrow when she came back home made him wonder if perhaps he had been duped. Perhaps the party was not as simple as a movie night with friends. Perhaps they were going to meet up with some boys as well.

He glared at his wife as his anger surged. Still, there was no evidence that his wife had withheld information from him. It was just a feeling he had in his gut; a feeling that pushed him to continue to search. Turning his attention to the pictures folder, his eyes suddenly went wide. In a sub-folder titled 'Dance', were photos of his daughter he could only assume had been taken earlier that day. Julianna with a new hairstyle. Julianna with painted nails. Julianna in a fancy dress. All items he would have never approved. He turned his eyes back to his wife, his heart racing and his anger threatening to explode. When he looked at her, he could see she was frozen in fear.

※

With a low growl, Barbas lifted his paw, releasing Julianna from the spell he had placed upon her. He then leaned back as he eagerly watched to see what came next. Beside him, he could hear Sitri chuckle with delight.

※

Julianna felt her stomach tighten as she watched Jasmine walk back to their table. Her hands, now free to move again, were filled with pins and needles, like she had slept on them wrong. Her thoughts were dark and dangerous, and her eyes were cold and hard, while a vicious sneer stretched across her face. She could feel Heather's and Stacey's eyes upon her, though neither of those two spoke. Step by step her nemesis approached the table, a gleam of triumph in her eyes.

"And that," Jasmine gloated, "is how it's done."

Julianna felt her shoulders hunch and her hands ball into fists. She swallowed hard, trying to keep from breaking into tears. Jasmine just stood there, grinning at her. Then, as if a fuse had burned down to the primer, Julianna felt herself explode. Her right hand shot out, grabbing the closest thing it could; which happened to be one of the colorful drinks: a Strawberry Kiss. Her hand locked tightly around the icy-cold glass as she thrust forward, launching the contents at Jasmine's head. The world became surreal and time seemed to slow as she watched the watermelon-colored liquid splash over Jasmine from her face to her hips, completely drenching Jasmine's brand new dress.

CHAPTER SIX
STRAWBERRY KISSES AND TACO BAR WARS

As if one person in two separate forms, Heather and Stacey gasped. Jasmine, too shocked to do anything, simply froze. Her eyes were shut tight as the sugary slush slid down her face, erasing the joyful, love-struck look that had been there just a moment before. For the longest time no one moved, or blinked, or even breathed. The only sound was a soft plip-plip-plip as small watermelon-colored drops fell to the floor. When Jasmine finally did open her eyes, they were burning red.

"What the hell was that for?" Jasmine screeched, her eyes locked on Julianna. "You ruined my dress!"

Julianna simply sneered.

Gathered together once more, Barbas, Sitri and Zepar watched from their hiding place in the deep shadows, the grins they wore were the only outward sign that they were proud of the chaos they had created so far.

"Zepar, I believe this is where you come in," said Sitri in a low, rumbling tone.

"That it is," Zepar nodded, then turned to where Heather sat and began softly chanting a spell.

Sitri knew the spell Zepar was casting. It was one designed to turn Heather against Julianna, not just for this day, but for the rest of their lives. From the moment the spell took hold, and unless Zepar released the curse, Heather would slowly go from being Julianna's best friend, to being her worst nightmare.

※

"What the hell, Jules?" Heather demanded, turning towards Julianna with fury in her heart.

"Yeah, Jules," Stacey echoed. "What the hell?"

"You had better not ruin my party!" Heather commanded, throwing the words like daggers.

With her eyes locked on Julianna, Heather waited for a reply. As she did, she noticed movement from the corner of her eye and glanced in that direction to see Jasmine turn and stomp away. Heather turned her attention back to Julianna.

"Are you going to say something?" she asked, crossing her arms in a stance that mimicked the way she had seen her mother stand when she was mad.

Julianna just stood there, her eyes flicking from Heather to Jasmine and back again.

Heather could tell Julianna wanted to go after Jasmine. A part of her didn't blame Julianna, either. She knew that Jasmine had just broken the pact that the four had made. But still, this was *her* party. All of the attention was supposed to be on *her*, not Jasmine or Julianna. Without even looking, Heather knew that a crowd had gathered, and more than a few phones were already out, recording the event.

"None of this better wind up on Snapchat or Twitter," Heather threatened as a small blob that looked a bit like mud sailed through the air, striking Julianna on the side of the head.

※

"Oh, Sitri," Barbas purred. "That was a brilliant shot! Give her a few more!"

Sitri grinned back, and then nodded his head.

※

Julianna felt the blob strike her, though she had no idea what it was. It felt like being hit with a snowball. A moment later, she felt another blob strike with a soft *thump*, this one on her lower back. She spun around quickly, the movement causing the first blob to slide from the side of her head and hit the floor with a *plop.* Her eyes searched through the dim lighting until she found the source of the attack. About twenty feet away, next to the taco bar, stood Jasmine. In her hand was a metal serving spoon, covered with refried beans.

Before Julianna could even think, Jasmine scooped out another spoonful of beans, and then flicked the spoon forward. The mound of beans rose in a perfect arc as it soared across the room. Then, having reached the peak of its arc, it began to fall. Julianna tried to spin out of the way, but her movements seemed sluggish, and before she could move, it struck her right on the chest.

※

"My turn," Barbas announced as two invisible bolts shot out like lightning from the tips of his fingers, heading straight into Julianna's heart.

※

Julianna didn't see the bolts that flashed across the room, but she felt them when they struck. They hit with the force of a wrecking ball, shattering the last of the fragile hold she had on her caged-up emotions. At that moment, as the last vestiges of her restraint fell apart, she had only one thought.

Revenge.

Without realizing it, her hands balled into fists, her lips curled into a snarl, and her body prepared to attack. With a scream that released every ounce of frustration she had ever felt, she launched herself at Jasmine. The room began to blur as her eyes shed tears filled with hate, spurred on by the years of pent-up anger she had unconsciously stored. Though most of the emotions had been set aside for some future day if she ever found the courage to stand up to her father, tonight she didn't care who the target of her anger was. The emotions weren't picky. They just bubbled up and out, coaxed by the machinations of one of the most powerful demons to ever have crossed through the Gates of Hell.

Julianna watched as the cocky smile Jasmine was wearing quickly disappeared, replaced by a look of surprise and shock, as if after having beaten Julianna at so many challenges in the past, she couldn't conceive that Julianna would have the courage to strike back. Dropping the metal spoon, Jasmine spun on her heels and sprinted away. Julianna followed shortly behind, trailed by a few dozen newly-appointed videographers. Behind that group came Stacey and Heather, who were shouting angrily at everyone to get out of their way.

※

"So, Jasmine isn't as tough as she made out to be," Barbas whispered to his fellow demons.

"We aren't done yet. Let's get these two alone, away from the crowd. Then we will see what comes," Sitri answered, guiding Jasmine towards the hallway that would lead her back behind the stage.

※

When Barbas had whispered those words, he had allowed Julianna to hear them inside her mind, as if they were her own. Had she not been in a fit of rage, she most likely would come to the same conclusion; that Jasmine wasn't as tough as Julianna had let herself believe. But she barely had enough room for her thoughts of revenge.

As her rage boiled over, she realized that the target of her anger was getting away. Jasmine was fast; much faster than Julianna had expected, though Julianna was still wearing her wobbly heels. She slid to a stop, nearly falling over, and kicked off the heels, not caring where they landed, then sprinted forward again in her bare feet. Without the insecure footwear, Julianna regained the advantage. Her strides were now nearly twice the length of Jasmine's, and her legs turned over at a surprising rate.

The two girls raced through Eagle Hall, darting around tables, dashing past groups of party guests, circling the entire inside of the building twice, with Jasmine waving her arms frantically at anyone in her way, and with Julianna always just a few steps behind. Then, with a sudden burst of speed, Jasmine flew back across the dance floor and raced up the stairs of the stage, then headed towards a door that led to a hallway behind the stage. Julianna was now barely five strides behind. Behind them the throng of pre-teen videographers clogged the way, making it impossible for Heather and Stacey to get through. Then, as Julianna passed through the same door Jasmine had just entered, a strong gust of wind flashed across the stage and slammed the door shut so hard that it jammed.

Jasmine and Julianna were alone.

Though the demonically-sealed doorway proved an obstinate barrier for the humans trying to get through, the demons entered easily. Sitri flashed down the hallway, staying in the shadows, as he raced towards the far end where Jasmine was headed. Barbas stayed closer to the doorway where Julianna had come to a stop and waited for her eyes to adjust to the darkness.

"Anytime you're ready, Barbas," Sitri growled, moving his arms in small circles.

With each completed circle a crimson hoop appeared, each one wrapping around Jasmine's arms and legs, bringing the smaller girl to a stop and leaving her helpless to move.

Suddenly frozen in fear, Jasmine started to beg for mercy. "Jules, stop!" she cried, her almond eyes wide with terror and wet with tears. "It was just a joke! I'm not going to steal Devon. You can have him! Just stop!"

Barbas leaned forward and gently touched Julianna's wrists. As he did, the darkness of the hallway was ruptured by an eerie violet-blue light that seemed to be emanating from Julianna's hands.

A part of Julianna heard her friend's pleas and wanted to stop, but that part of her was no longer in control. A different, more violent and darker part of her had taken over, and she had no intention to stop.

"You kissed Devon! You knew he was mine! We made a pact! All of us! You, me, Heather, Stacey! We made a pact!" Julianna growled, her hands tightening into fists until her knuckles grew white and the violet-blue light flashed into twin balls of flame.

"It was supposed to be a just challenge, like all the others! I didn't mean to fall for him!" Jasmine explained.

Her plea fell on deaf ears as her admission caused Julianna to feel nothing but rage building on rage. Part of her fury came from emotions she had originally stored for her controlling, demanding father. Part of it had once been meant for her subservient and weak-willed mother. Some of it had even once been held for her brother, Thomas, for having escaped all of the restrictions of their father's rigid rules; just because Thomas had been born a boy. All of these emotions mixed with the feelings she had built up from the years of losing challenge after challenge to her so-called friend; the same friend who now knelt before her, begging for mercy.

But any mercy that Julianna might have had was now buried so deep inside, she wouldn't have known where to look to find it.

"It's too late, Jasmine," she seethed. "I've had enough of losing to you! I'm never going to lose again!"

"Strike her down!" Barbas' voice whispered inside Julianna's mind, causing the young woman to flinch.

"What? How?" Julianna said aloud, looking around for the source of the voice.

Jasmine's face twisted with confusion as she watched Julianna speaking to ghosts.

"Your power. Turn it against her. Channel all your anger into your hands. Feel them burn!" Barbas continued.

"What power?" she demanded.

"Trust me. Center your anger. Focus your rage. Pour it out through your hands like the liquid fire it has become."

Julianna clenched her fists even tighter, her nails cutting deep into her palms. Her breathing became slow and heavy, and spittle sprayed through her clenched jaws. Her mind fed her images from her past; memories of being told she couldn't do or have the things her friends did. Everything she had ever wanted in life had been denied to her, and now Jasmine had taken away Devon's first kiss. Even if it had just been one of Jasmine's challenges, it had still happened.

"Don't hold back, just let it flow! Don't try to control it. Let it out!" the inner voice demanded.

Still believing the voice to be nothing more than her own thoughts, Julianna complied, letting her emotions build until she burst into tears.

"I hate you!" she screamed at Jasmine, then thrust her fists forward, watching as they spewed forth electric, violet-blue flames.

The dim hallway became as bright as day as the twin balls of flame sped toward Jasmine, whose body was so locked in terror, she was unable to move.

"I hate you! I hate you! I hate you!" Julianna repeated over and over, taking small, purposeful steps towards her terrified ex-friend. With each step another blast of fire shot through the air, knocking Jasmine further and further down the hallway. Then, as Jasmine tried to crawl away, Julianna let loose with every painful memory she had ever had.

Raising her hands above her head, she screamed, "I wish you would DIE!"

At the same time she brought her hands back down, and a solid wave of energy, powered by pure hate, slashed through the air, making a crackling sound, like lightning. Jasmine was lifted off her feet and thrown the remaining length of the hallway, where she crashed hard against the concrete wall. Her body slumped to the ground, then lay still.

Seeing what she had done, Julianna screamed once more, as another blast of energy shot out. With Jasmine lying unconscious on the ground, this one crashed into an electrical panel hanging on the side wall. The gray-painted, metal box exploded in a shower of sparks as every fuse in the box blew at once.

Eagle Hall went dark.

So, too, did Julianna's heart.

CHAPTER SEVEN
THE CAVE

Julianna found herself in a dark, expansive cavern, the walls of which were invisible in the depths of the dimly lit chamber. The ceiling was decorated with stalactites reaching downward, and the floor with stalagmites reaching up. In some places they touched, creating columns, and in one area several columns had joined together, forming a wall. A low, heavy fog clung to the ground, as if the ground was covered with a flowing, bioluminescent moss. Misty fingers clawed up from the fog, twisting gently in the constant breeze. The only other sounds were the gentle pitter-pat of her heart, and the plops and plinks as water droplets struck the floor.

Drawing in a deep breath, Julianna felt the cool, moist air tickle as it entered her lungs. The same breath returned to the cave as a small, tentative cloud. It was cold in the cavern. Cold, and dark, and lonely; though, Julianna could tell, she was not alone.

"Hello?" she called out, hearing the echo of her words replay in the depths. "Is someone there?"

Though she was in a strange and mysterious place, she felt no fear, just a burning curiosity as she wondered where this place was and how she had arrived here. Spinning in an unhurried, deliberate circle, she took in the sights and sounds of the room. There was something there. She could feel it.

"Hello?" she called again, her words now sounding a bit frightened and urgent.

"Hello, Daughter of Eve," a deeply confident and masculine voice sounded from the gloom. "I've been waiting for you."

Julianna felt a chill walk down her spine.

"Waiting? For me?" she inquired. "Why?"

"Ah, good! A child of few words. So different from most of your kind, especially those of your age. Nothing but endless chatter."

Julianna heard her invisible companion chortle and snivel as if laughing at his own comment.

"Well? What do you want?" she asked, becoming a bit indignant.

A deep, throaty chuckle was her only reply. Whatever this invisible creature was, it was enjoying frustrating her to no end.

"It might help if I knew where you were," she said, looking over her shoulder as she turned around.

A heavy sigh washed through the cave.

"As you wish. Though, you might want to prepare yourself," the voice stated, emotionlessly. "I'm over here; just to your left."

Julianna spun slowly to her left, at first seeing nothing. And then several of the vaporous tendrils rising from the fog began to coil together, becoming a long rope that reached towards the cavern's crown. There, they formed a dense cloud, which coalesced as the cloud fell back towards the ground. As the cloud dispersed, it revealed a creature of fantastic design.

The main torso and arms of the creature were like those of a man, while its two muscular legs looked like they should be on a lion. They were powerful and large, with huge padded paws for feet. The skin of the creature's main body was ghostly gray, and was stretched taut against its narrow, bony frame, giving it the illusion of frailty. On its back were a pair of dark-gray, leathery wings—like those of a dragon—with sharp spikes at the tips. In one hand it held a serpent, and in the other, a spear. Its head was not like any creature Julianna knew, real or fantasy. Its eyes were colored in reverse; the parts that should be white were black, and the parts that should bear color, were a pure silver-white.

Above its eyes, Julianna saw what she assumed were its ears, though they resembled those of a vampire bat, standing upright and alert, and twitching in response to every sound. Behind the ears rose a pair of twisted horns that ended in sharpened points. Its mouth and chin protruded forward, reminding Julianna of a muzzle of a dog. There was no hair on its body or head, though a covering of dark scales dressed the creature from chest to thigh, and similar scales covered the back of its hands and tops of its feet.

The breeze—which drew constantly through the cavern—brought to her nose a horrible smell, causing her face to twist with disgust. It smelled of rotting garbage, fear, and death.

"What...what are you?" she asked hesitantly.

"I believe the proper greeting is, '*Who* are you?'. But you're frightened and confused, so I'll overlook the faux pas," the creature said. "I, am Astaroth, your...Guardian Angel."

The last two words came out filled with contempt, and a vicious snarl pulled back his lips, revealing two rows of razor-sharp fangs. A black, forked tongue darted between the dagger-like teeth as his snarl turned to a mocking sneer. Julianna simply stared at him, disbelieving his words.

"You don't look like an angel," she said cautiously, taking two steps back.

"And you don't look like a killer," Astaroth replied haughtily.

Julianna looked up at Astaroth, her eyes glistening in the soft yellow glow of the endless fog. Her face was locked with confusion as her mind raced to understand why Astaroth would have called her a killer. She took two steps back, but when Astaroth did not move towards her, she allowed herself to relax.

Though she wanted to inquire about his comment, she wasn't sure she wanted to hear his reply, and instead she asked, "What is this place?"

"The land of dreams," Astaroth said quietly, then, narrowing his eyes and lowering his voice, he added, "and nightmares, too."

"So, you're saying I'm dreaming? That this is all just a dream?"

"In a way, yes. That you are dreaming is mostly correct. Though this is far more than a simple dream. You and I are real in every sense of the word, that I assure you. Please, pinch yourself if you don't trust my words."

Julianna did exactly that, and then flinched.

"You see? Now, would you have been able to dream that pain?" Astaroth inquired.

"I...I don't know. I don't have many dreams, not that I can remember. Definitely none that were as clear as this." She paused as she considered what next to say, then settled on another question. "Why am I here?"

The silver parts of Astaroth's eyes flickered red as he narrowed his gaze. Then, with a wave of his hands, he sent a tiny ribbon of electric light towards Julianna. It struck her on the sides of her head, just at the temples.

"Let me help you remember," he said.

Julianna felt a shock, like the kind her brother used to tease her with after rubbing his socks on the carpet. With the jolt came memories: the party, the dance, the kiss, the fight. As they flooded back in, her stomach was felt the same anger and fury she had felt before. Once more she recalled how she chased Jasmine, and how Jasmine had begged for mercy. She recalled how the violet-blue fire lashed out from her hands, smashing into and sending Jasmine crashing into the wall. And she saw Jasmine's body as it slumped lifelessly to the floor.

"Oh my God!" Julianna gasped. "Did I...?"

"Kill her?" Astaroth finished for her. "You certainly wanted to, didn't you?"

Julianna felt her eyes begin to tear.

"No...I didn't. I mean, I guess I did, in a way. I was angry, sure, but I didn't want to *kill* her!"

"It was your voice that said you wished she would die, was it not? Tell me, as your...angel...how am I supposed to know if you truly want what you pray for, or if you're just thinking out loud?"

Julianna bent her head, knowing the creature spoke the truth.

"Answer me!" Astaroth suddenly commanded, his words filled with anger. "Was it you that shouted that you wished her to die?"

"Yes! Yes! It was me," she admitted, beginning to wail. "I said it. I said those words."

"Said them, yes. Anyone can say words. But did you mean them?"

Tears rolled down her face as Julianna looked for the answer inside her heart. She didn't have to look far.

"Maybe? I don't remember. I was upset, okay?"

"Did you mean what you said? Yes, or no?"

She didn't want to answer, and instead bit down on her tongue, hoping Astaroth would change the conversation, or go away. Her hope was denied.

"I will ask once more, Daughter of Eve, did you mean what you said?"

As her tears began to flow uncontrollably, Julianna could only nod her head.

"I'm sorry," he sneered, "was that a yes?"

Julianna nodded a little more firmly, still unwilling to say the words out loud.

"Perhaps there is something wrong with my ears. Your head is bobbing up and down, but I don't hear any sound. Just that revolting, sniveling, whimper. Though it pains me to be so forgiving, I'll grant you one last chance. And please, for your own sake, kindly use words this time," he stated, slowly and succinctly, emphasizing each word. "Did you, or did you not, mean what you said?"

Julianna gulped back tears, trying to regain control. Why she had to state the answer out loud, she didn't understand. In her mind, she had already nodded her head. That should have been enough. Still, she began to feel frightened of what this creature might do to her if she failed to reply, and so, she grabbed every bit of strength she had and bellowed out her response.

"Yes! Okay? Is that what you wanted to hear?" she shouted, gasping in air before continuing on, the final words barely loud enough to be heard, and sounding thick with remorse. "Yes. I wanted her dead."

A sound reached her ears. Was Astaroth laughing?

"Now, that wasn't so hard," Astaroth finally said as a wisp of fog rose from the ground and began to coalesce, twisting into a shape that sent shivers up

Julianna's spine. The creature that formed from the fog reminded her of a small, skinny, bald monkey, but with a head like a snake. Its skin was the color of ash. The creature was carrying an object that it handed to Astaroth. When the object was handed over, Astaroth spoke to the creature in a language that Julianna didn't understand.

"Master pani mudinduvittadu enru solla. Andap pen ipodu nammudiathu," which meant, *'Tell the Master that the task is done. The girl is ours now.'*

The creature nodded, then disappeared. Astaroth carried the item over to Julianna. As he drew near, she saw that it was some form of fabric. He held up the edge of the fabric, letting the item unfold. It looked like a cloak or a robe of some kind. Astaroth motioned for Julianna to turn around.

"Come, you look cold. Let me wrap this cloak around you. It will keep you warm," he said, though a sudden flicker of warning in Julianna's gut told her the cloak was something much more.

Julianna obliged, feeling the weight of the garment as he draped it across her shoulders and drew the hood over her head. Though she felt the fabric where it touched her, it seemed to have no weight. It also felt as if it became a part of her in some way, like it was bonded to her.

"This cloak will help you focus your powers, and it will hide them, too. At least, it will hide them until you are called to use them again. Used in the wrong way, your powers can do irreparable damage. As you've already seen, they can even kill," Astaroth instructed.

"What powers?" she inquired.

Astaroth grinned.

"Ah, yes, your powers. You've felt them burning inside for some time now, haven't you?"

Julianna considered the creature's question. It was true. She had felt something strange lately, but had simply added it to the myriad of other strange things her body was going through. As far as she knew, the strange sensations had just been part of becoming a woman.

"I guess so," she said, a bit embarrassed to be speaking about these things with a stranger.

"And, haven't you felt like perhaps you don't belong in this world? That you are different in some way? Haven't your thoughts become a bit…darker lately?" he continued inquiring.

Again, the beast was right. She had felt like her thoughts had changed, and she had felt like she didn't belong, or like this wasn't supposed to be her life. For the past few months, she had even been thinking about running away and living on her own, somewhere far away from the tension and stress of her life at home. How did Astaroth know this? Was he really her Guardian Angel like he had said he was? Was this his way of protecting her from becoming something or someone she was never meant to be?

The cloak around her tightened, and suddenly, Julianna was afraid. As her fear began to rise, so too did a sense of remorse. She hated what she had done to Jasmine. She never wanted to do something like that to anyone ever again, though a part of her knew that she would.

"Did I?" Julianna groaned. "Did I kill Jasmine?"

"Don't flatter yourself!" Astaroth spat. "Your powers aren't *that* strong. They've barely begun to hatch! The only way you hurt her at all was that you had help."

"Because of help? What did he mean?" she thought, then realized what else Astaroth's statement meant, and a brief flicker of hope flashed in her eyes.

"So she's not dead? She's okay? Are you sure?" Julianna asked optimistically.

Astaroth made a sound like metal scraping on metal. It took a minute for Julianna to realize he was grinding his teeth.

"I did not say that, either! Oh, the joy you humans experience when you're putting words in other's mouths!" Astaroth replied.

Julianna stared at the beastly creature for a moment, choosing her next words carefully.

"What happened to Jasmine? How bad did she get hurt? Please, I need to know!"

Astaroth flashed her a wicked smile.

"Let's just say she won't be dreaming of Olympic gold any longer. You may not have killed the girl, but you most certainly killed her dreams!" he said as he grinned at his own joke.

Julianna tilted her head to one side, still wondering exactly what injuries Jasmine may have attained. Then, touching the edge of her new cloak and feeling a strange sense of familiarity, she asked, "What I did to Jasmine, was that my power?"

Her expression gave away her thoughts; she was afraid of his response.

"Oh, most definitely," Astaroth replied.

"Will I…?"she began, as if not sure she wanted to ask the next question. "Will I do that again? Hurt someone, I mean?"

"Do you expect me to know your future?"

"If you're an angel, then you probably do. I'm not asking you to tell me who I will hurt, or when it will happen. I just need to know. Will I ever hurt someone like I just hurt Jasmine?"

Astaroth gazed at her for a long moment, then silently nodded his head.

"Yes, child. You will."

Julianna's face twisted with sorrow.

"I'm evil, aren't I?" she asked, struggling to say the words as her throat tightened.

"Do you think you'd be here if you weren't?" Astaroth replied.

Though the look in his eyes said he wasn't giving her the whole truth, the parts that he did share were more than enough for Julianna to believe the answer was clear.

"I want to go home," she blurted out, her stomach starting to turn.

"All in due time, child. All in due time." Astaroth said, maliciously.

"I want to go home!" Julianna repeated, this time more intently than before. "You can't keep me here!"

"Oh, but I can!" Astaroth replied, suddenly looking more dangerous than he previously had.

Julianna froze. Her face turned ashen white, and her palms began to sweat.

"Please!" she begged. "I just want to go home."

Astaroth sighed, the sound resembling the hiss of the espresso machine at the coffee shop where Julianna and her mother sometimes went.

"Very well. But know this. If you choose to call my name in the future, I will return. I can teach you how to use your power, though, for now you must hide it from others so no one will know. Luckily, I was there to help you tonight. I was the one who closed that door, guaranteeing that no one but Jasmine would see what you are capable of. And trust me, she will never tell a soul. They'll think she's crazy, and she knows that.

"Still, beware of what she will do. Once she recovers, she will seek her revenge. She will try to make you use your powers again, this time where others will see. She will want others to see you as a freak, a monster, and she won't be satisfied until your life is ruined. Though she does not have powers like you, her heart bears the same darkness within. In a way, the two of you are now more like each other than you were before.

"Know this, Daughter of Eve, Jasmine will turn the world against you. And when she does, you must let her."

Julianna was caught off-guard.

"What do you mean?"

"Right now your best defense is to appear weak, at least until your powers fully develop. So, let your friends turn against you. Let them tease you, and harass you. Let them bully you as much as they want. When they hurt you, swallow the pain. Bury it deep in your heart. Let them believe that they've won."

"I don't know if I can. I don't know if I can be strong like that," Julianna admitted as she wiped her eyes.

"Would it be better if people knew of your powers? Would it be better if they labeled you a freak? Called you a monster? Is that what you want?"

"Am I?" she asked tentatively. "Am I a monster?"

Astaroth shrugged and waved his hands. A moment later, Julianna felt the cavern begin to spin, and she fell to her knees.

"Am I a monster?" she repeated, much louder than the first time now.

Her vision began to blur as the image of Astaroth started to fade. In the gloom, she thought she saw him nod his head. As her tears began once more to fall, the cavern began to have a transparent look.

"Keep your powers secret, child," Astaroth reminded her again. "Do not let anyone know! When you need me, call my name."

With that, he was gone.

The cave grew dark as it continued to turn, spinning faster and faster until Julianna no longer knew which way was which. She felt sick, and closed her eyes as she tried to keep from throwing up. The dizziness inside her felt even stronger, and she knew it was a fight she wouldn't win. Opening her eyes once more, she turned her head to the side and emptied the contents of her stomach all over the floor; the dusty, wooden floor of Eagle Hall.

CHAPTER EIGHT
THE AFTER PARTY

Small flecks of white and gray dust floated in the air before her, and a slight breeze tiptoed past her ears. The draft carried with it the smell of burnt metal mixed with the scent of the vomit that decorated her dress and the nearby floor. The unmistakable smell of refried beans was in there, too, and she wondered if they were still clinging to her hair or her back. Occasional sparks from the sputtering electrical panel were the only light in the hallway. The sporadic flashes gave an eerie sensation of movement as the shadows came and went in time with the display.

At first Julianna considered perhaps her most recent experience had been nothing more than a dream. Maybe what had really caused the chaos was just a random lightning strike, or some form of power overload. The fact that she and Jasmine had been in this hallway when everything went crazy could have been a coincidence. It had to have been. Anything else just seemed too weird. There was no way her life had just become like those characters in the superhero movies her brother always watched. Stuff like that didn't really happen, did it?

A slight movement to her right caught her attention. She turned in that direction, peering into the darkness, but saw nothing. She waited for another round of sparks to light the hallway. When it came, Julianna saw Jasmine's body lying crumpled on the floor; she couldn't tell if Jasmine was moving or not. At times it appeared she was, but with the flickering light, it was hard to tell. A low groan emanated from the limp form, telling Julianna that Jasmine was alive, but she was hurt, and hurt badly. Still, that didn't prove Julianna was responsible for Jasmine's injuries. She could have been hurt in a dozen different ways. But Julianna knew the truth. As much as she wanted to believe it wasn't her fault, the memories of the event were far too real.

Outside the hallway, Julianna could hear voices shouting, and a few screams. She could hear panic as the party guests stampeded for the doors, trying to get to a safe place outside the hall. She wondered if they would make it out. Some, she thought, might get knocked over, or stumble over a table, or a chair. Then, defenseless, they might get trampled, perhaps even killed. All because of her special power. She pressed her palms against her ears, trying to drown out the noise.

As she fought against the sounds of chaos, a new thought came to mind. How long had she been with Astaroth in that cave? It had seemed like at least half-an-hour. How could she have been gone that long, and yet it seemed as if, here in the hallway, no time had passed at all? Was that another part of her powers? Could she manipulate time? If so, maybe she could go back and change what happened? Make it all go away? Maybe she *could* make the terrible memories into nothing more than a bad dream?

Something told her that wish would never come true. It was not going to be that simple. This was not something she could just walk away from, or pretend never happened. This was something that had already changed her life, she just didn't know how much. The only thing that remained was to figure out what to do next. Slowly, she began to crawl towards Jasmine, moving with care in the flickering light. The turmoil that had exploded from her hands had not only thrown Jasmine down the hallway, but had scattered all of the items that had been stored there as well. Wooden stools and step ladders that had been carefully placed out of the way now created a maze for her to negotiate. Wishing she hadn't left her cellphone on the table where she had been sitting with her friends, Julianna continued forward in the darkness, using her hands as a guide.

When she was about halfway to where Jasmine lay, she could hear what sounded like softly spoken words. Shortly after, Jasmine began to stir. It was still too dark to see, though in the periodic flashes, it looked like Jasmine had landed with her face turned away from Julianna. There was no way to know if she was awake, or still unconscious. Unless she could somehow get the light to shine from her hands again.

The flames had been bright enough to cast shadows even when the lights had been on. If she could get them to ignite again, she should be able to see well enough to provide Jasmine with aid, perhaps get her out of the building to a safer place. The only thing was, she had no idea how her powers worked. She definitely hadn't been in control of them before, they had just randomly appeared. She didn't know if it had something to do with her emotions at the time, or if the strange feelings she had in her stomach were involved.

As she picked her way through the debris, her thoughts traveled back to the moment she had first brought her powers to life. Astaroth had told her that she had had help that first time. She recalled hearing a voice speaking to her, urging her to focus her fury, to let her anger flow through her, and to not try to control it. But that path had led to what she was dealing with now. There was no way she wanted to go back down that road again. There had to be another way.

Suddenly, she remembered the cloak Astaroth had given her when she had been with him in that cave. He had said that the cloak would help her focus her powers, giving her the ability to turn them on or off as needed. Reaching behind her head, Julianna searched for the fabric of the hood, but it wasn't there. Nothing was there. No fabric, no hood, no cloak. Again Julianna considered that the visions she'd had in the cave had been no more than a dream. She knew the truth, though.

By now the sporadic flashes from the sparking electrical panel had all but ceased. Julianna had made it to within a few feet of where Jasmine lay. She reached forward, her hands touching something soft, and she unconsciously let out a shriek. It had felt like a spider. After taking a moment to calm down, she considered it was probably nothing more than Jasmine's hair, Julianna reached forward again. This time, when she felt the same sensation, she didn't pull away.

"Jasmine? Are you awake?" she whispered, gently stroking her friend's hair.

There was a muffled response, but no more than that. Though it sounded like words, Julianna couldn't understand what Jasmine said, if she had said anything at all. She traced her hands down Jasmine's neck and along her back, her hands moving slowly. A sudden spark flashed out of the electrical panel, giving Julianna a look at her barely conscious friend. Jasmine had turned her head towards Julianna, and her eyes were looking directly at her. They were filled with fear. The panel sparked once more, and Julianna saw that Jasmine had raised her head off the floor. Then, she heard her speak.

"I…hate…you," Jasmine mumbled in low, barely discernable words.

"Jasmine, please don't say that. We both did something we shouldn't have tonight. I know you're sorry, you already said it. I am too. Can we just go back to being friends?"

Jasmine grunted and moaned. With her hands still lying on Jasmine's back and side, she could feel her friend trying to move. Again, she heard Jasmine trying to speak, and she leaned down closer, hoping to pick out the words.

"You…," Jasmine began, obviously in pain, "…are…," a few more gasping breaths, "…a freak!"

Julianna sat up. Her insides began to twist as she realized what Jasmine's words meant. Astaroth had been right! Jasmine would never again be her friend. She would, however, do whatever she could to make sure that no one else was, either. It wouldn't be long before everything would turn out just as Astaroth had predicted, leaving Julianna with only one choice. She had to make sure Jasmine never told anyone what had happened; what had *really* happened.

The empathy she had felt for her injured friend filtered away, replaced by a sensation Julianna hadn't felt before. It was like a hard shell closed over her heart. She became distant, emotionless, and callous. Moving one hand back up to Jasmine's shoulder, she squeezed tightly as she leaned in close. Jasmine hissed in pain.

"You better keep your damn mouth shut, Jazz. You know what I can do. One word from you about what happened in here tonight, and I'll burn you again."

Without warning, the hand that was squeezing Jasmine's shoulder burst into flame, and Jasmine cried out. The violet-blue light was not bright enough to illuminate much more than a foot or so of the inky blackness, but in that light Julianna could see the look in Jasmine's eyes. Even with the pain she was feeling, Jasmine's eyes no longer held fear. Now, they held nothing but hate. With a final squeeze, Julianna let go, and the fire in her hand ebbed away. Jasmine grew silent, once more lying still.

A loud noise erupted from the darkness behind her. Someone had broken through the door. Voices called out. She could hear Mr. Murphy—Heather's dad—and Stacey's voice as well.

"Jasmine? Jules?" Mr. Murphy called out. "Are you two in here? Are you okay?"

"Julianna? Where are you?" Stacey echoed.

"I'm okay, but Jasmine's not," she answered back. "Be careful if you come down the hallway. There's stuff all over the floor."

"Okay. Stay where you are. I'm coming to you," Mr. Murphy called out, then, in a quieter voice added, "Stacey, go back into the main room. See if you can find someone with a flashlight, or a lighter. Anything we can use to help see in this blasted darkness.

"You got it Mr. Murphy," Stacey said, the sounds of her feet thumping on the floor faded as she moved further and further away.

"What happened to Jasmine? How did she get hurt?" Mr. Murphy inquired.

Julianna could hear him moving towards her, bumping into the same debris she had just crossed over a few minutes ago. He would reach her soon.

"I...I don't know what happened. She just...fell," Julianna lied.

"Don't move her! We don't know how bad she's hurt. Just wait, I'm almost there."

The sounds of his shuffling feet grew closer, and then Julianna heard a *thump*.

"Oof," Mr. Murphy exclaimed as he bumped into something that had to have been large, probably hard, and most likely heavy.

A moment later, he *oofed* again. This one was followed by an expletive.

"Mr. Murphy?" she called out.

"Yeah?"

"It helps if you get on the ground and crawl. Use your hands to feel your way forward."

"Thanks, Jules," he said. "I'll try that."

An hour later, most of the guests were gone. The band had loaded their instruments away and were standing in a tight circle in the rear parking lot, smoking cigarettes and talking about the strange happenings in hushed tones. An ambulance and two paramedic vans were in the front parking lot, their lights were flashing, but their sirens were off. The EMT's were working on a final few party guests who had only minor injuries. Luckily, there had been only a few guests who had suffered anything major.

One of those who had obtained more significant injuries had been the DJ. One of the stacks of amplifiers had crashed down on his console, smashing half of his equipment and shattering his arm. Though he had been in considerable pain, his main concern had been for the equipment he had lost. He refused to let the paramedics even examine him until he was certain that the salvageable items were properly packed away. One of the band members had helped with that while the DJ sat holding his crushed arm against his chest.

Another of those with major injuries had been Jasmine. She had to be carried out on a stretcher, unconscious from the pain she was in and the medications they had pumped into her. From what Julianna had overheard, Jasmine had two dislocated vertebrae, a broken clavicle, and a cracked occipital bone. They also said she most likely had a concussion, too, but without the equipment to check, it was too early to tell. One of medics had speculated, though, saying that if the impact had been just slightly harder, Jasmine might not have survived. She had been taken away in the first ambulance that had arrived on the scene, and was by now at the hospital.

Julianna had left the hallway when the paramedics showed up, waving off any support for herself. Now, she was sitting on the edge of the stage watching the food vendors pack their equipment away. A cup of water was on the stage next to her, and a damp washcloth lay beside that. One of the paramedics had wiped the dust from her face and had quickly checked her for injuries, but had found none. She was waiting for her parents to arrive to take her home, but Mrs. Murphy was having difficulty reaching them, and Julianna was starting to worry.

As she sat there—sad, silent, and alone—a female police officer approached.

"Mind if I join you?" the officer inquired.

Julianna just shrugged, and the officer sat down next to her on the stage.

"Your name's Julianna, right?"

Without lifting her eyes from the spot on the floor she was intently staring at, Julianna replied.

"Yeah."

"Good to meet you, Julianna. Mrs. Murphy says she calls you Jules. Would it be okay if I did that as well?"

Julianna nodded.

There was a pause, one that dragged out longer than Julianna cared for. Finally, the officer continued.

"Well, Jules, I'm Officer Benavidez. You can call me Maria, though. Okay?"

"Sure," Julianna mumbled.

"Can you tell me what happened here tonight?"

Julianna looked up. She felt the icy grip of fear crawl up her spine. It was obvious she wasn't the first person the officer had spoken with. Though, who Officer Benavidez *had* talked to and what they might have said were two things Julianna didn't know, and wasn't sure she wanted to.

"I...I don't know," she managed to get out, cursing herself as she heard her own voice; the words carried no conviction at all.

"No? You don't know anything? Nothing at all?" the officer probed further.

"No. Not really."

She heard the officer sigh.

"Well, what about your friend, Jasmine? Did you two have a fight? Maybe about a boy? Devon, perhaps?"

Julianna looked up and met the officer's stare. Someone *had* said something. She looked into the woman's eyes for a moment, then turned her head away.

"Yeah, I guess. It wasn't really a fight, though."

"But you were pretty angry with her, right?"

"I guess. I mean, she knew I liked Devon, but she still kissed him."

"Yeah," Officer Benavides said, laying a hand on Julianna's shoulder. "I get that. One of my friends stole my boyfriend back when I was in junior high, too. And you know what I did?"

Julianna shook her head.

"I punched her right in the nose. That's how mad I was. I didn't want to. I mean, we had been friends for a long time, best of friends, actually. But I was really, *really* angry. Is that what happened to you tonight? Did you do something you didn't want to do? Maybe hurt your friend without realizing it?"

"No," Julianna said, a bit abruptly.

As far as she knew, the only person who could refute what she just said, had left the building unconscious, and she had been that way before the police had arrived. If the officer had been told something, Julianna couldn't see how she would prove it. Plus, even if Jasmine did tell the truth, would anyone even believe it? Julianna hardly believed it herself, and she had been one of the two people involved.

"I didn't do anything," she repeated, defiantly. "We were just arguing. You know, just yelling at each other. Then there was that explosion, and the lights went out. I must have fainted or something. When I woke up she was against the wall."

"So, you don't know what happened to her? You don't remember if something fell on her, or if maybe someone pushed her really hard?"

"No. It was just the two of us in the hallway. No one else was there. It was just us, and we were arguing, not fighting. Then that box blew up, I think Mr. Murphy said it was...rogue lightning. Something like that. Then the lights went out, and, like I said, when I woke up she was against the wall."

Officer Benavides sighed, pausing for a moment.

"Okay. If that's what you say happened," the officer got up off the stage and turned as if she was about to walk away, then suddenly turned back. "I guess I'm just wondering..."

Julianna waited for the officer to continue. When she didn't, Julianna looked her way.

"Wondering about what?" she asked.

"Wondering why Jasmine would tell the paramedics that you did it. That you pushed her into the wall. Why do you think she would say that?"

Julianna shrugged, hoping the officer didn't see the fear that had suddenly flooded her heart.

"I don't know," she mumbled after a moment. "She was hurt pretty bad. I heard someone say she hit her head. Maybe she was just confused?"

Officer Benavides nodded her head.

"Yeah, maybe she was," the officer stated, then after a pause, continued. "Tell me, are your folks here yet? Mom or Dad? Are they coming to get you?"

"Mrs. Murphy said she can't find them. They aren't answering their phones."

"Oh, I see. Well, will you do me a favor?"

"What's that?"

"When they get here, make sure to introduce them to me. I'd like to meet them before you go, okay?"

"Yeah. Okay."

"Good. And, if you think of anything...anything at all...about what might have happened to Jasmine when you two were arguing, you'll come to tell me, right?"

Julianna nodded once more, then looked away.

For what felt like an interminable moment, Officer Benavides didn't move. Julianna could tell the officer was looking at her, perhaps watching to see if she did anything strange, so she kept her face turned away and focused her eyes on the same small spot on the floor while she waited for the officer to leave.

"Hey, Benavides," a man wearing a Sheriff's badge suddenly called out.

"Yeah?" Officer Benavides said, turning to look back over her shoulder.

"You're gonna want to be in on this."

"What'cha got Bill?"

"Uh...this ain't something you want to share in front of the kid."

After a brief pause, Officer Benavides said quietly, "I'll come back and check in on you again soon, Julianna. You keep thinking about what you promised. See if there's something you forgot to tell me, okay?"

Julianna nodded, but wouldn't look up.

Chapter Nine
The Monster Within

"What's going on, Bill?" Officer Benavides asked when she and Sheriff Dunn were alone.

"Just took a call from dispatch. That kid you were just talking to, is her last name Berenike?" he said, struggling to pronounce the last name.

"Yeah, that's her," Officer Benavides replied. "Why? What'cha got? Did they find her parents?"

"Yeah, you can say that," Sheriff Dunn replied, shaking his head. "Mom's on the way to the hospital. Dad's being held downtown. Sounds like he did quite a number on her."

Officer Benavides frowned as she heard the news, then turned and looked back at Julianna, who was sitting motionless, staring at the floor.

"From what it looks like, violent acts must run in the family," she said.

"What do you mean?" Sherriff Dunn inquired, looking a bit puzzled.

"You know that girl, Jasmine, the one they took out on the stretcher?"

"Yeah," Sheriff Dunn said, then nodded in the direction of Julianna. "She the one responsible?"

Officer Benavides shrugged.

"I'm not certain of anything yet, but based on the evidence so far, it looks that way. Of course, by the time I got here, Jasmine was pretty well doped up, so I couldn't question her. Plus, I don't know how much of what she told the EMT's to believe. Something about Julianna using some sort of magic?" Officer Benavides frowned, then took a breath and sighed.

"Maybe we should take her in for questioning. She can share a cell with her dad," Sheriff Dunn said, his very dry attempt at humor making Officer Benavides grimace.

"I don't have enough probable cause to do much more than ask a few questions. You know how quick the State will jump in once they learn we're dealing with a minor. Plus, even if it turns out I'm chasing ghosts, since neither parent is able to claim her right now, she'll end up spending the night in a group home. You want to send a sweet young kid like that to one of those places?"

"No, I don't. Heck, I don't even like sending the not-so-sweet kids there. Nothing more than a schoolyard for tomorrow's criminals," Sheriff Dunn admitted, shaking his head. "She got any family nearby?"

"Not according to Mrs. Murphy," Officer Benavides said. "She does have an older brother, three years older I think, but he's on some church retreat. Won't be back till tomorrow."

"Well, we gotta do something. We can't leave her here all night."

Maria gave Sheriff Dunn a sideways glance.

"Tell you what," she said. "Why don't you head downtown and talk to her Dad. Maybe he knows a relative we don't know about yet. I'll check with Mrs. Murphy again, see if she can take the kid for the night. I highly doubt this kid's a flight risk. I think we're okay holding off till the morning.

"Then, I'll visit the Mom tomorrow, and I'll check in on Jasmine, too. Maybe she'll be lucid enough to fill me in on what really happened here. You wanna hit the church and talk to the brother when he gets back from the retreat? You could take that Social Services lady with you. You know, the one you got a crush on?"

"Are you talking about Maureen?" Sherriff Dunn said, his cheeks blushing.

Maria nodded.

"How'd you know that I liked her?"

Maria shook her head, "I've not met a guy yet who's subtle enough to hide a crush like that."

Sheriff Dunn grinned, and blushed even darker.

※

Julianna was sitting in the back of Mrs. Murphy's car, waiting for Heather's mom to load a few final items in the trunk. Heather was in the front seat, but neither girl was talking, which was just fine with Julianna. Her heart was torn, and for so many reasons, too. She was struggling to come to grips with the newfound power she had, and the peculiar conversation with that curious looking creature, Astaroth, too. To top it off, she had just learned that her parents weren't going to be picking her up tonight. From the little bit that Officer Benavides had told her, something bad had happened to her mom, and her dad was being held in jail. Julianna didn't need anyone to explain the details. She already knew. She had known this day would come. She had known it for a while now. In her mind, it had just been a matter of time.

When the officer had told her about her mother, Julianna had done her best to appear alarmed, as if she had never thought something like that would happen. She tried to look even more alarmed when the policewoman explained that her father was in jail, too. She didn't want anyone to know what was really going on inside her, as the wild emotions surging within were begging her to do to her father what she had just done to Jasmine. When she had started crying after she asked if she could see her mom, those emotions, however, had been real. Mrs. Murphy had promised to take her there just as soon as she could, which is where they were about to go, as soon as the trunk was packed.

"Hey, Jules?" Heather asked from the front seat.

"Yeah?" Julianna replied quietly.

"I'm really sorry about your mom," Heather offered, compassionately.

Julianna said nothing at first, just let the silence linger. Then she replied with just one word.

"Thanks."

The silence flowed back in, each girl returning to the activity they typically engaged in during difficult moments. Julianna picked at her nails, and Heather twirled her hair. Julianna could tell Heather wanted to ask her another question, and she knew exactly which question it would be, so she beat her to it.

"You want to know what happened in the hallway, don't you."

"Kinda...?" Heather meekly replied.

"Honestly, Heather, I don't know."

"People are saying..." Heather began, then paused, perhaps not wanting to share rumors.

"What? What are they saying? That I hurt Jasmine? Do you think I have the ability to throw her fifty feet like that? Really?"

"I don't know, Jules. I mean, maybe if you were mad enough. And you were pretty mad after she kissed Devon and all."

"Don't forget the refried beans she threw at me. I was ready to call it even after I threw my drink at her. She's the one who kept it going."

"Yeah, I know. I was pretty mad at her, too. I mean, she shouldn't have kissed Devon. We all know you put dibs on him. She just did it so she would win again. Everything with her is just about being first."

Julianna took a deep breath. At least Heather still seemed to be on her side. They had been friends the longest of the four. Jasmine had been the last to join.

"Yeah, I know. And trust me, I'm tired of her always challenging me all the time. I just never said anything," Julianna admitted.

"Yeah. I don't know why it's always been you. She doesn't do that with me or Stace."

The conversation lagged once more, and Julianna went back to staring out the window at Eagle Hall. She watched the employees cleaning up the building, which was still without power. They had set up generators and lamps throughout. Some of the employees were returning the tables and chairs to the large storage closet, while others were sweeping the floor. Mrs. Murphy had finished packing the car, and was now having a conversation with one of the employees, a conversation that appeared to be a little heated. Julianna tried to make out what they were saying, but they were too far away.

"Jules?" Heather said, breaking the silence again.

"Yeah, Heather?" she replied.

"Well, if you're telling the truth, then we can still be friends," Heather quietly shared, her eyes glossy and wet as she turned towards Julianna. "I've been getting tired of how competitive Jasmine has been lately, too. Just so you know."

Julianna gave her a brief, strained smile. She wondered why Heather hadn't said or done something to stop Jasmine, if she had really been that upset. Maybe if Heather *had* stood up for her, tonight would haven't turned out the way it had.

"But if Jasmine says it was you that hurt her like that," Heather continued, pausing for a moment, perhaps to gather the courage for what came next, "then our friendship is pretty much done."

Julianna grimaced, her stomach twisting in knots. Part of her felt like crying, the rest just wanted to scream.

Nothing else was said. Julianna knew her fate was sealed. If Jasmine talked, even after she had threatened her, then there was nothing Julianna could do. At that moment, Mrs. Murphy climbed in the car with a sigh. She said they would go to the hospital, and then went silent. For the rest of the ride, no one spoke. It was the longest and most painful silence Julianna had ever known.

Once they arrived, they learned that Julianna's mom was in surgery, and the nurse had no idea how long it would be. They waited in the lobby outside the surgical wing for nearly two hours, still in their dresses but no longer wearing their heels. Heather had put on a pair of Finding Nemo slippers, and Julianna was wearing a thin pair of socks. It didn't matter that her feet hurt with every step, or that her toes were cold. She couldn't stand another minute in those tight, wobbly heels.

Finally, just as Julianna was starting to fall asleep, a handsome young doctor came out and pulled Mrs. Murphy to the side. The two had a quiet conversation, then the doctor went back through the double doors into the surgery center. Mrs. Murphy came and sat by Julianna. A tear was in her eye.

"What's wrong?" Julianna asked after waiting a moment for Mrs. Murphy to settle herself. "What happened to my mom? Did she die?"

Mrs. Murphy shook her head, then breathed out a large and sorrowful sigh.

"What did the doctor say?" Heather said, a little louder than Mrs. Murphy liked, drawing a look of warning from her mom.

"Please, Mrs. Murphy," Julianna asked in a much quieter voice, "what did he say?"

"He said she was hurt bad, Jules. They're moving her to Intensive Care, and they have her sedated."

"So, can I see her?"

"Not yet. But soon. I promise. Keep in mind, she's going to be unconscious. She might not even know you're in the room with her."

"I don't care," Julianna said. "I want to see her."

Mrs. Murphy gave Julianna's hands a quick squeeze, then wiped at Julianna's eyes with her thumbs.

"You sure? We can come back tomorrow. Maybe she'll be awake by then."

Julianna thought about it for only a second or two.

"No. It has to be tonight. I have to see her tonight."

Mrs. Murphy nodded, then stood up.

"Come on. Let's go ask what room they moved her into. Maybe they already have her all set up."

Julianna took one of Mrs. Murphy's hands in her left hand, and one of Heather's hands in her right. Strengthened by their presence, she let them lead the way through the double doors and down a long, cold, antiseptic hallway. Eventually they reached a semi-circular nurses station. A small sign that said 'Intensive Care' was attached to the front, and another one hung above the desk. Two nurses in colorful scrubs were seated behind the counter, typing on computers. They each had a stack of patient files next to them while they worked.

"Hello," Mrs. Murphy said, wearing a pleasant smile. "Can either of you two tell us where Angela Berenike's room is?"

"Are you family?" the first nurse, who was wearing scrubs decorated with Snoopy cartoons, asked as she looked up from her work.

"I've been her friend since grade school, and I was the Maid of Honor at her wedding, if that counts."

"Sorry, we only give information to family," the nurse replied, turning back to her computer.

"I'm her daughter," Julianna said impatiently.

The nurse looked at Julianna for a few seconds.

"How old are you, sweetheart?" the nurse asked.

"I'm twelve," Julianna replied, wondering why that was important.

For a moment, the nurse didn't blink, then she turned to Mrs. Murphy.

"Is her father available? If we could talk to him, get his permission…"

"You know why she's in here, right?" Mrs. Murphy interrupted, swapping the pleasant smile she had been wearing for a more than irritated look.

The nurse just nodded.

"Well, where do you think the asshole is?"

"Mom!" Heather exclaimed with a surprised look.

"Sorry, dear," Mrs. Murphy said, then turned to face Julianna. "I didn't mean that about your father. I'm just angry at him right now."

"Yeah, you and me both," Julianna mumbled quietly, and then looked away.

Mrs. Murphy turned her attention back to the nurse, who had pushed her keyboard tray back under the counter and was now standing up. She leaned towards her co-worker for a moment and whispered, "Maybe you should get a cup of coffee, Evelyn. No use both of us getting in trouble."

The second nurse, whose scrubs were bedecked with Wonder Woman logos, stood up, gave her co-worker a smile, and then walked away.

"Cream and sugar?" she asked over her shoulder.

The first nurse didn't reply. She simply waited until Evelyn had disappeared around a corner, and then turned to Mrs. Murphy.

"Come with me. If anyone asks, say you're her sister," she instructed.

Mrs. Murphy nodded, then followed the nurse to the other side of the station with Julianna closely behind, her stomach buzzing like a nest of wasps. She gripped Mrs. Murphy's hand tightly, as if it was the only thing keeping her from running away. When they got close enough, Julianna could see that curtains blocked half of the room. Her mother's feet, dressed in light blue hospital socks, were the only part of her mom that she could see. They looked perfectly fine, however, and she relaxed a bit. A bit too soon. As she moved further into the room and was able to see the rest of her mother, Julianna burst into tears, doubling over in a heap on the floor as her legs refused to stand.

Mrs. Murphy knelt beside her, grasped her under her arms and helped her to her feet. The nurse brought over a chair, which Julianna collapsed in.

"Maybe this wasn't the best idea..." the nurse admitted, a bit callously.

"Would you prefer we denied this child the chance to see her mom?" Mrs. Murphy whispered harshly, then, lowering her voice even more, she added, "What if this is her last chance?"

The nurse simply stared at Mrs. Murphy, then turned and walked away.

"You've got fifteen minutes," she said.

"No wonder she works the night shift," Mrs. Murphy said under her breath, then knelt down beside Julianna and wrapped her arms around the young girl's shoulders, pulling her in tight.

"Maybe the nurse is right, Jules. We should come back tomorrow. You've had a rough night as it is."

Julianna squirmed out of Mrs. Murphy's grasp, pushing her away gently, then took in a deep breath and let it out in a sigh.

"It's okay," she said as she regained control of her emotions. "I want to do this now."

After a moment—which she spent by taking three more deep breaths—Julianna stood and again walked towards the room. She paused at the doorway, gathering courage and strength. The distance between the door and her mother's bed seemed so far, and each step she took barely closed the distance, making the next step that much more difficult to take. From every direction she was surrounded by the sounds of machines: the beeping of the heart rate monitor, the puffs and sighs of the breathing tube, and the occasional clicks and hisses from the machine that measured blood pressure. Each machine had a monitor, the light from which gave an eerie blue-gray tinge to the dimly lit room, making the situation even more surreal. Yet, Julianna persevered, eventually arriving at the side of her mother's bed.

"Mom? Can you hear me?" she asked peevishly, small tears sliding down her cheeks.

There was no response, though she thought she saw her mom's swollen, bruised eyes flicker.

"It's Julianna, Mom. I don't know if you can hear me or not, but I'm right here. The nurse is only letting me stay a few minutes. She said you're not strong enough for visitors. But I know you, Mom. You are strong. You're stronger than you ever give yourself credit for," she strained, her voice cracking under the weight of her sorrow as she buried her face briefly in a heap of linens that were gathered at the side of the bed. "I know you'll pull through, Mom. I know it."

Julianna felt a slight squeeze from the hand she was holding, and when she looked up at her mom's face again, she saw a small tear shaking as it fought to break free. Julianna smiled. Her mom could hear her; she knew her daughter was there.

"Just get better, Mom. Take your time, but get better, okay? I want you there when I graduate, when I get married, when I have kids. You can come live with me, and I'll take care of you. I promise you that," Julianna whispered, squinting out a few tears that refused to fall.

As she gave her mother's hand a gentle, loving squeeze, she felt a stirring in her stomach. A knot of anger began to form that twisted as her mind flooded with memories of the way her father had treated her mother over the years; the way he had treated them both, as if their feelings meant nothing. As if *they* meant nothing; no more than objects for him to control.

Julianna had seen something like this coming, and it pained her that she had never spoken out. She had hid behind false beliefs; believing she was too young, or that she wasn't powerful enough, or that she wasn't supposed to speak out against her own father. But now, she realized, those had all been lies. Lies she had told herself because, when it all boiled down, Julianna had been afraid.

No more.

Closing her eyes to fight off the tears, she felt the seeds of her anger crack open, then turn into something more powerful, and dark. Her fear became determination; her anger became her fuel. Down deep inside the pit of her heart, every time she had believed that she wasn't good enough, or strong enough, or brave enough, was now just one more ember. Though each cinder on its own was not enough to change Julianna's heart, together, they were. The memories from her past mixed with the memory of her fight with Jasmine, and she again saw the image of her hands burning with unquenchable fire. It was then that Julianna realized how much she was just like her father, how incapable she was of keeping her anger in check. That moment was all those embers needed to burst into uncontrollable flames.

A loud screech suddenly filled her ears as alarms began to sound. Julianna's eyes burst open and darted around the room as she tried to find the source of the alarms. Every machine was flashing and blinking as they reported that something was wrong with her mother. Unaware of what was going on, Julianna took a step back, letting go of her mom's hand. As she did, she glanced down and saw her own hands were once again engulfed in brightly colored flames. With a look of fright and shock, Julianna turned and looked at her mother, only to find her mother's eyes were open, and were staring right at her. Now, those same eyes that used to look at her with the gentlest love held only fear. It didn't take long for Julianna to realize what was making her mom so afraid. She knew there was only one thing in the room that it could be. That thing was herself.

A moment later, the door to the room slammed open, and 'Snoopy' nurse rushed in, followed shortly by Evelyn and two other members of the medical staff. Julianna tucked her hands into her armpits, clamping her arms down tight. The flames, though white hot in temperature, did not physically burn her or her clothing, it just felt as if they did. Luckily, in the confusion, no one stopped long enough to look at the tall, thin, frightened girl as she snuck into the corner of the room.

Julianna had always believed that monsters were hiding in the shadows of her bedroom, but never in her life did she think she would be one of those monsters. Yet, here she was, hiding in the shadows in the corner of the room. Tonight she realized, *she* was the monster. Of that, there was no doubt.

CHAPTER TEN
THE SCENT OF RED HOT METAL

For Julianna, the four years that followed that night had been a living hell. Every time she found the strength to move forward, her demons threw another challenge her way. The memory of Astaroth's words to her in the cave became distant and vague, until she could hardly remember them at all. Still, the words he had spoken had found a home deep within her mind, and they whispered to her in the darkness of her heart.

"Let the people turn against you."

"Let the world tease you, and harass you."

"Let them bully you as much as they want."

"When they hurt you, swallow the pain."

"Bury it deep in your heart."

"Let them believe that they've won."

As she did as he instructed, the shallow walls of her self-esteem stretched dangerously thin, until she became comfortable with the darkness inside.

The first of the challenges she had faced, had come the day after Heather's party, as Julianna's mother had gone from bad to worse. Already weakened from the physical trauma she had suffered, the emotional trauma of seeing what her daughter had become had torn her apart, and her heart had failed. When Julianna had been informed of this, she had known it wasn't a heart attack like the doctors claimed. She knew that her mother's heart had broken, and that she was the reason it had. She knew it had all been her fault.

Her mother had been rushed back into surgery, where the doctors had fought desperately for hours to save her life. Though they eventually were successful, the result of the new trauma had left her mother in a coma, one that would keep her stuck in limbo for the next several months to come.

Two days later, Julianna had moved in with a foster family, where her brother, Thomas, had already moved in. She would end up living with them until her mother finally did recover, nearly a year later. During the few months that she and Thomas lived with Ben and Terri Thomson, she had tried in vain to find some solace in the relationship with her brother, but his mind and heart were miles away. Not only was he facing his own spiritual battles, but he had also fallen in love. Ben and Terri had a daughter, Lily, who was two years older than Thomas, and was a beauty to behold.

Julianna had immediately been drawn to Lily's positive energy. She had always wished she'd had an older sister, someone to turn to when no one else was there. She had never developed that kind of a relationship with her mom. At first, Lily had been a saving grace for Julianna, providing her with an outlet to express the confusion of becoming a teen. Unfortunately, Lily had not always been available, as her brother had usurped most of Lily's time, leaving Julianna feeling like an outcast, unwanted, and once more alone.

The day after Julianna moved in with the Thomson's, Jasmine recovered from her injuries long enough for Officer Benavides to question her about the events of that night. This time, no longer weak from pain, nor under the influence of medication, Jasmine's story changed. Rather than confess that she had been bested by a girl with superpowers who threw magic balls of electric fire at her, she told the story that her demon, Sitri, had placed in her mind. Her new story matched the one that Julianna had claimed; the girls had argued in the hallway, but they had never gotten into a fight. The explosion of the electrical panel was nothing more than a random coincidence, one in which Jasmine had paid the price.

Officer Benavides had eventually been forced to drop the issue—there just wasn't any evidence—but Jasmine never did. Though she never did tell anyone what it was that she had seen that night, she constantly looked for ways to push Julianna into using her powers again. Jasmine didn't just turn her back on Julianna, but worked tirelessly to ensure everyone else at school did the same. Julianna had found herself shunned not just by the rest of the Four Winds, but by all of her other classmates, too.

The bullying had started right away. Though it had begun as simple teasing, like most youth at that age experience at one point or another, the longer it had lasted, and with no friends to stand up for her, the teasing had soon escalated to harassment and threats. Now, Julianna had not only lost her ability to turn to her mother, her brother, and her friends, but she began to feel like she was losing touch with herself.

The aftermath of the fight between her parents did have one positive outcome, at least in Julianna's mind: her father had been kicked out of the house. After spending six months in jail for the vicious assault on his wife, Mr. Berenike had fallen from grace faster than anyone ever had. Due to the constant pressure the demon, Raum, had continued to place upon the man, Julianna's father entered a dark depression, unable to face the man he had become. He was also unwilling to take the steps necessary to find healing and peace. From being a productive, active member of his community, and a frequent volunteer at his church, Julianna's father had found himself unable to hold down even the most basic jobs.

A couple of years later, her father passed away. Though the official medical report claimed that his death was due to cancer, Julianna knew that the cancer had not been in his physical body, but in his soul. Even with the strict rules he had forced her to live under, she still felt as if she had lost the man who should have been there to protect and comfort her through those challenging years.

After his death, the challenges had escalated quickly. Thomas had moved away to college, leaving Julianna and her mother to fend for themselves. With few practical skills and no work experience outside of the home, Julianna's mom had only been able to find low-paying retail jobs, which soon meant she was unable to afford the family home they had lived in since Julianna had been born. Though the move meant Julianna had to switch schools, it had also meant all of her ex-friends—the ones responsible for the bullying—were left behind. The only problem was, her new school was more dilapidated and rundown than the inner-city apartment they had moved into; but it had been the only place her mom could afford. Integrating into the rough-edged school hadn't been easy, and there had been days when Julianna had found herself missing her old school, even with the harassment and bullying she had endured. At least at her old school she had known who her enemies were.

And then, at the end of her sophomore year, an opportunity had come her way. Father Dominic, who by now had become a good friend of the family, was looking for young adults to help out at a mission project in

Panama that coming summer. For Julianna, this was more than just an opportunity to escape her problems for a while. In reality, it had been her last chance to end the nagging feeling that she had finally run out of strength. Though she had had to lie and deceive her mother in order to take advantage of the opportunity, she felt no shame in doing so. As far as she was concerned, she had been lying to and deceiving her mother since the day they had moved out of Julianna's childhood home.

Whenever her mother had asked how Julianna was doing, how she was fitting into her new school, or if she was making any new friends, Julianna had lied. In her mind, her mother had enough burdens just trying to pay the bills and put food on the table. She didn't need to worry about what was going on in Julianna's life.

When the Panama trip first presented itself, Julianna knew it wasn't going to be easy for her to attend. She would definitely need some help, and she was going to have to do something she had promised herself she wouldn't let happen again; she was going to have to open up and let someone in behind the walls she had built specifically to keep the world out. But, if she was going to survive long enough to graduate, let alone make it through the next two years, it was the only chance she had, and she knew it. Luckily, the help she required didn't take long to find.

Amanda—the Youth Minister at the church Julianna attended—helped her craft a plan to ensure Panama would become a reality. Amanda was one of the few people in Julianna's life who not only knew about the troubles the young woman had endured, but was always looking for ways to help. Father Dominic was another of those who still held Julianna's confidence. They were both convinced that the mission would be a place where Julianna could be with people she could trust. People like Beth, one of the young adult volunteers in Amanda's youth program; or Theresa, who was the only person from Julianna's old school who hadn't bought into Jasmine's web of lies. The two had found an instant connection the first time they had met, and they tended to stay close to each other at all the youth group events.

Julianna felt there was something special about Theresa, something that set her apart from all of the other girls their age. She felt the same way about Beth, too. From the moment Beth had been assigned to be her small group leader, Julianna had felt more confident and at peace. Amanda had told her she hoped the two weeks together in Panama would provide a chance for Julianna to get to know both Beth and Theresa much better. Perhaps even to a point where Julianna would feel comfortable sharing some of the pain she had been carrying for nearly four years, pain that Julianna had admitted to Amanda during her freshman year retreat. Amanda had also been the one who had arranged the finances for Julianna, making sure that there would be no reason for Julianna's mom to say her daughter couldn't go.

The day Julianna packed to leave was by far the happiest and most excited she had been in a long, long time. It had seemed like a perfect opportunity to start over. Plus, there was one other reason she had been so excited. Thomas would be there as well. She hadn't seen her brother for nearly a year. The college Thomas attended was twenty-five hundred miles away, and he hadn't been home over the winter holiday. With nothing but great expectations in her mind, Julianna had left for Panama with Theresa and Beth.

The first few days at the mission had been just as she had planned. They went swimming under a waterfall in the jungle nearby, and she had spent hours on the flight and at the camp talking to just Theresa and Beth. Thomas arrived the second day, in the company of a young woman named Gemma, who Julianna had never met; bringing back memories of how she had once felt she had lost her brother to Lily. Though Gemma had been nothing but nice to her, Julianna hadn't treated her the same. She was aloof and distant, mostly ignoring her older brother's new friend. Julianna didn't know why she acted the way she had, and, if she was honest with herself, she really didn't care. She didn't know Gemma. She just saw her as one more person who was getting in between the life Julianna still wanted, and the life she now had.

But those feelings quickly went away. For starters, on the third day they had been joined by seven other young adults, all of whom were people Julianna felt could easily be the new friends she had so longingly desired. It wasn't long before Julianna was laughing again, and truly enjoying the feeling of being alive.

Then, right at a time when Julianna was feeling the most at ease, tragedy had struck. Here she was in the jungles of Panama, just as planned, only, as far as she was aware, her brother was dead. Shot by a low-life thug who had shown no more emotion in killing Thomas than if he had just swatted a fly. That same low-life thug hadn't stopped there. No. He had the gall to take her and the rest of her group hostage, tying them up like cattle and marching them for hours through the sweltering jungle. At some point during the kidnapping, Theresa and Gemma had disappeared, and Julianna could only think that the worst had happened to them.

Every time the man who had killed her brother spoke, Julianna would cringe. She couldn't bear to look at him, or the three other men he commanded. Right now, she could hear them, standing just a few feet away, smoking cigarettes and laughing as they stole quick glances at the captive teens. Julianna knew, if her hands weren't tied behind her back right now, she would lose it, and the four men with the scandalous smiles and disturbing gleam in their eyes would pay.

Had the men known she was plotting revenge, that she was simply waiting for them to become comfortable, make a mistake, or find a reason to get them to untie her hands, she knew they would shoot her just as easily as they had already shot her brother. Yet, that was exactly what she was doing. In the core of her being, in the depths of her soul, the same sensations Julianna had felt when she had used her powers for the first time were beginning to return.

But there would come a time. She knew there would. She just had to be patient and wait, hiding her emotions behind the thick wall she had built, brick by brick, over four long years. Though inside she seethed with rage, and her heart was swollen with a desire for revenge, on the outside she looked defeated and weak; the perfect place from which to launch her plan.

From the corner of her eye, she saw the leader of the kidnappers pick up his backpack and sling it over his shoulders. He gave a few terse commands to his men, who immediately forced the captive teens to their feet, and the march continued on. The only sound the group made was the scuff of their feet on the soft, loamy soil, and an occasional sniffle or sigh. How far they'd marched so far, and how much longer they had to go, Julianna had no idea. All she knew was what she'd do to the four cowardly men who hid behind the power of their weapons once her hands were free. Somehow she knew, that chance would come soon.

PART TWO

God created shadows to better emphasize the light
– St. Pope John XXIII

INTERLUDE
BETH

Beth McConnell was unable to distinguish the difference between the drops of moisture that were trickling down her forehead, and the tears that were dripping from her eyes. The ones that found the corners of her mouth all tasted the same: salty. Those that didn't find her mouth, either ran down her neck, soaking the collar of her shirt, or they dripped off the edge of her chin, leaving a part of her forever ensconced in the soil of the jungle she wished more than anything she could leave, and quickly, too.

She suddenly recalled the last time she had felt like she did now. Just like the events of the past few hours, that day had been one of the strangest days of her life; at least up until now. This one could quite possibly top that one, by far.

It had been nearly five years ago, at the start of the fall semester of her junior year in high school. She had been out for a quick five-mile jog, trying to improve her stamina for cross country, her favorite sport. Tryouts were to be held the next week, and she was gloriously out of shape. The loop she was running had been chosen for the nearly constant changes in elevation, something that had always been a challenge for her in the past.

Her plotted course followed an old fire road that wound through the foothills, just outside the subdivision where she lived. She ran it several times before, and other than scaring a few cows, she hadn't had many encounters along the way. The path had always made her feel safe, even after dusk. That night, however, everything changed.

She had just entered her third mile when she heard a rustling in the sparsely wooded area on the left of the path. A burst of fear flashed through her gut, warning her to turn around, but she was at the point on the trail where she was closer to the end than the beginning, and decided to continue on. It was only after another fifty yards or so when she realized she should have listened to her gut.

Though she had heard rumors about a pack of wild dogs that roamed the hills around the subdivision where she lived, no one had ever seen them this close to the homes. The previous winter had been an exceptionally dry one, followed by a warmer-than-normal summer. There had also been a few wildfires out deeper in the hills. All of this combined to make the dogs usual food and water sources scarce. Though, none of that mattered to Beth. She was worried about only one thing: getting away.

There were eight of them in all, ranging in size from the smallest at around twenty pounds, to the largest that was eighty pounds at least. Three of them looked like pit bulls, and the rest were all mixed breeds. All except for the largest one, which was so mangy and covered in filth, it was hard to tell what it was. It looked like it was part wolf. It was definitely the alpha wolf.

Beth's first instinct was to turn and run—she had become frozen in her tracks when the first dogs had appeared from behind a thicket—but somehow she knew that was what the dogs were waiting for. The moment she turned her back on them, she knew they would charge, and there was no way she could outrun them for two full miles. She would have to come up with another plan.

Softening her voice, Beth tried speaking to the dogs, hoping she could win them over, and they would let her go. But they were far too hungry, and far too wild for that. They looked like they hadn't eaten in weeks. Their eyes all had a strange, yellowish tinge to them, and their ribs were showing.

As the animals approached, the largest dog was on the path, with three others on its left, and four on its right. Beth continued stepping backwards, slowly, not wanting to give the animals any reason to pounce. Then, when she was at the height of fear, she remembered the story of Daniel in the lion's den, and she began to pray.

A moment later, she heard a voice from behind her. It seemed to be whispering right in her ear.

"Strike the ground."

At first, she thought it was only her voice that was speaking to her, though she had no idea why it would say what it did. She also wasn't sure how she was supposed to strike the ground, or where, or with what.

"Strike the ground," the voice repeated.

Beth decided to do what the voice was suggesting, and stomped her foot hard on the ground. All except for the smallest dog, none of the animals even flinched.

"It didn't work!" she called out.

"Kneel down, then strike," came the voice.

The last thing Beth wanted was to put herself in a position where she felt vulnerable, and kneeling on the ground would definitely make her feel that. But she had no other ideas at the moment, and so she complied. Keeping her eyes locked on the largest member of the pack, she lowered herself until her left knee was on the ground. She kept her right leg bent, just in case she needed to rise quickly, and try to run. Then, she balled her hand into a tight fist, and gently punched at the ground. Though at first she thought she heard a fizzling sound, nothing else occurred.

"*Strike hard!*" urged the voice.

"How hard?" she yelled, a bit franticly.

Before the voice could answer, the leader of the pack leaped forward, growling and snarling as he began to charge. The look in his eyes changed, taking on a feral gleam. The animal had been about twenty yards away from her, and he was closing ground fast.

Beth screamed, then raised her hand above her head, and drove it onto the hardened dirt path. If nothing else, she hoped the sound would stop the dog's attack, or ever better, perhaps drive them away. Neither of those happened, but what did come next was something even she never would have dreamed. From the point where her fist had struck the ground, a fountain of golden light spouted forth, rising six feet into the air, then, spreading open like an umbrella, it cascaded back to earth. Beth was surrounded on all sides by a brightly shining, golden dome.

The pack leader slid to a stop, and then cautiously approached, sniffing and pawing at the air. The other dogs sat in place, or lay down, and a few began to whimper. Beth watched as the lead animal came up to the dome and sniffed at it carefully. Then, it stuck out its tongue, and licked at the edge of the light.

A bright cloud of golden sparks exploded towards the animal, which made the dog promptly tuck its tail between its legs. It bolted away, whimpering as it ran. The rest of the pack followed closely behind. A moment later, when the dogs were a sufficient distance away, Beth felt a strange pulling sensation in the palm of her hand. It felt like a cramp, coupled with the tingling feeling one gets when a part of the body 'wakes up' after having gone numb. She tried rubbing her hands together, but the feeling only increased.

Opening her hand, Beth looking first at the palm, then flipping it over to look at the back. The moment her palm faced the ground, the edges of the golden dome lifted from the dirt pathway, retreating and folding back in on themselves until the entire circle reached the top, leaving only the center post. Beth was mesmerized as she watched the remaining shaft of light diminish back into the ground, leaving only a disc the size of a Frisbee. She could tell the disc was spinning by the small plume of dust that it was kicking up.

Curious, Beth reached towards the disc, wondering if it was something she could pick up. The moment her hand touched it, the disc split in two, then each of those split once more. All four of the glimmering discs rose into the air, formed into pairs, and then each pair began to circle around Beth's hands. The tingling sensation grew stronger, but not enough to cause pain. Still, Beth flapped her wrists gently in an attempt to shake off the discs. The discs followed every movement of her hands, always staying just a few inches away.

Beth continued to move her hands, moving them in unison at times, and at other times raising one while lowering the other. Regardless of what she did, each pair moved in the same direction and speed as the hand they revolved around. She was unsure what to do or how to remove the discs, and there was no way she wanted to return home with the tiny UFO's. She tried one last idea. Getting back to her knees, Beth struck the ground once more, but nothing happened this time.

Frustrated, she sighed, and stood back up. As she did, she moved her arms behind her back, clasping her palms together as if she was about to stretch. The moment her palms touched, the tingling sensation Beth had been feeling disappeared. She threw her hands out in front of her, and saw that the golden discs were finally gone. Where they went, and if they would ever return, Beth had no idea. Confused, she simply stared at her hands, and then the ground, and then the point in the woods were the dogs had disappeared.

"Okay, that was weird," Beth said aloud with a shake of her head. "Like don't-ever-tell-anyone-about-this kind of weird."

Continuing to glance between the ground and the woods, she spent another few moments stretching out her lower back and legs. When she was ready, she took one last look at the ground where the golden dome had sprung forth, then shook her head once more.

"Really, really weird," she commented again, then started down the trail at a slow jog, and then gradually picked up speed, eventually sprinting the last half-mile to her house. If nothing else, the event she had just experienced had done one positive thing; Beth felt stronger and more in shape than she had in months.

Over the course of the ensuing five years, Beth never did tell anyone of the event, even when her gut instinct told her it would be okay. Brother Thomas was the one person she had come closest to confiding in, but for some reason, she held back. It wasn't until that Saturday night on the retreat when she had met Thomas—and Theresa, too—that Beth learned what her powers were, and how to use them. That explanation had come to her in a dream.

Now, her gut instinct was telling her that the time for her silence was over, and that she was going to have to do more than tell other people about her strange gift; she was going to have to show it to them, too.

CHAPTER ELEVEN
A DEAL WITH DEMONS

Several miles behind the captive and their guards, three young adults sat huddled in a tight circle on the side of a dirt road. A rust covered, dirty hatchback was parked close by, all five doors open. On the other side of the vehicle from where the three sat, a dark stain on the ground showed the place where Thomas had recently died, and where Gemma and Theresa had worked together to somehow bring him back. None of the three wanted to look at that stain. The memory of how close death had come was still too powerful an emotion.

Their circle was tight, close enough for the three to be holding hands. Thomas sat with his back to the jungle with Theresa on his right, and Gemma on his left. They all had their eyes closed, focusing on their spiritual superpowers that were becoming more familiar with each use. A dim blue light encircled the group, casting eerie shadows in the darkness.

During their trip into Gemma's spiritual realm, they had learned to share their powers, as they were doing now. In that alternate realm they had fought against—and defeated—a demonic force that had threatened Gemma's faith. Now, they had returned to the physical realm and were ready to find their friends; Beth, Julianna, Terence, Brendan, Adriana, Francis, Sam, Jennifer and Jeremiah; as well as the four men who held them captive. The only problem was, they had no idea where that group was. Too much time had passed.

They had a general idea of which direction the captors had led the prisoners; the footprints on the dirt road and the trampled foliage of the jungle floor weren't that hard to spot. And they had tried making a first attempt at rescue by simply following that path. Unfortunately they soon lost the trail and had to backtrack to where they were now.

Now their plan was for Thomas to try and pick up the emotional signatures of the group, which was one of the powers he had; the ability to see things as they truly are, not as they appear. Reading others' emotions was like having a window into their soul. Regardless of how many times a friend might say 'I'm fine,' Thomas could tell the truth. He was becoming fairly adept at reading the signs, which appeared as shapes of various dimensions and colors, and at times, also carried pungent smells. The only problem was, he had never extended his reach farther than a half-mile or so. The three were betting on the chance that their ability to share powers would fix that.

Theresa had the ability to boost another hero's power, as she had done for Gemma when they had brought Thomas back from the dead. However, since boosting another hero's power meant she had to give away some of her power, she could only maintain it for brief periods of time. This is where Gemma came in. One of the powers of *The Paladin*—Gemma's chosen superhero name—was the ability to heal; therefore, as Theresa began to weaken, Gemma restored her to full strength. Though this meant that Gemma was depleting some of her own strength, which is where Thomas' powers came in.

His job was to watch the emotional symbols of the other two, ensuring they didn't expend too much energy or they could become depleted. They all knew that finding their friends would only be the first part in their plan, and that they would still need to defeat the armed gunmen to rescue them. They had to save as much of their strength as they could for the eventual battle that was certain to come. Therefore, Thomas only allowed himself to search until either he found the trail, or until he could sense Gemma's energy flicker towards exhaustion. Then they were forced to take a break. Hopefully they would find the trail quickly. Fear, he knew, was one of the strongest emotions he had ever felt, and it was certain to be the emotion his friends would be experiencing right now. To him, the emotion of fear looked like a rough sphere covered in spikes; it smelled vaguely like scorched metal, with a slight tinge of vinegar, or ammonia.

Now, as they tested their new plan for the first time, Thomas tried to block out not only the emotions of his two companions, but his own emotions as well. Luckily, there were two people in the group he searched for whose emotions he had felt on several occasions in the past: his younger sister, Julianna, and his college roommate, Terence. He had also briefly felt the emotional energy of the man who had shot him, but he believed that brief moment had been enough to stay with him for a long, long time. There would be no way he would miss it if he ever felt it again.

Several minutes had already passed since the three had begun their search, and Thomas still hadn't picked up anything that felt out of place. The jungle was a place of constantly changing emotions, and every new flicker of emotion had to be examined. The creatures themselves gave off subtle energy vibrations as they went about their nightly tasks; hunting, feeding, and chasing or being chased. And though the animals' energy vibrated at a much lower level than any human emotion would, there were still countless ebbs and flows to filter through. This slowed the process down quite a bit.

But Thomas didn't need to find where his friends were right now, he only had to find where they had been. Emotional energy left footprints behind. The stronger the emotion, the deeper those footprints would be, and the longer they would last. Even a slight familiarity in any of the emotions he was currently sensing would provide a better idea of which direction the group had traveled than what they had to work with right now.

And then, just as Thomas felt Gemma's energy begin to weaken, he smelled it: the scent of red-hot metal. There was no mistaking it, this was what he had been searching for. Fear. Human fear. Visceral, harsh, mind-altering fear. Thomas knew which way they needed to go.

"Find something?" Theresa asked, sensing a change in the power she was helping to boost.

"Yeah," Thomas said, opening his eyes and breathing in deeply. "I don't know where they are, but I know where they were. Let's go!"

Jumping quickly to his feet, Thomas reached down to help Theresa and Gemma stand. He was about to ask them how they were feeling when he remembered he didn't have to ask. All he had to do was look. Gemma's current emotional energy looked like the calm before a storm. It was gentle and at peace, but Thomas could sense deeper emotions building behind that calm. She was not only ready for a fight, she was looking forward to it. Theresa, on the other hand, was perfectly calm. Either she was not thinking of the danger they were heading towards, or the confidence she had in the powers of the trio was stronger than her fear.

"Any idea how far away they are?" Gemma asked, brushing off and adjusting her clothing.

"No. When I can pick them up without Theresa's boost, then I'll know we're close. Until then, we need to move as fast as we can, and hope we reach them before they reach wherever it is that they're headed. Who knows how many more armed men they might have out there in these woods," Thomas said, holding Gemma's gaze.

A moment later, Gemma blushed, and bashfully turned away. Thomas watched as the emotional signature above her changed, matching the energy currently flowing through her. Even in the warm jungle night air, Thomas could feel heat rising in his cheeks, and he turned quickly and walked away, hoping neither of his companions noticed. With his sister and friends in trouble, the last thing he needed was to deal with his own conflicting emotions. Silently, he whispered a prayer of thanksgiving that Gemma wasn't able to read his emotions like he could read hers. A moment later he entered the jungle, then took off at a fairly brisk pace.

※

While Thomas was engaged in the search for his friends, Furcas was searching for something as well. Revenge. He had waited four years for a chance to prove himself once more. Four long years. Four years spent planning, preparing, watching, and waiting. Four years of scratching together the resources he would need; one eye always on Thomas, and the other on Father Dominic.

From the moment Astaroth had banished him from Hell, the only concern that had plagued Furcas' thoughts was how he might earn his way back in. Since his banishment had come after he had failed to turn young Thomas' heart towards the world of evil and deceit, Furcas thought the best way to regain his position would be to finish that mission, even if it took him the rest of eternity to complete it.

Early on in his self-assigned vendetta, Furcas had learned one important fact; wherever Father Dominic went, Thomas was never far behind. He knew if he kept close to the mentor, sooner or later the protégé would show up. He also learned that the one place Father Dominic spent the greatest amount of time—outside of his assigned church—was at a mission project in Panama.

The project was located near Boca de Cupe, a small village near a section of jungle known as the Darien Gap, one of the most remote, isolated, and dangerous places in the world. Inside its borders one could find: poison-dart frogs, ninja-like jaguars, vampire bats, jungle scorpions, deadly snakes, and palm trees lined with bacteria-filled spines. And on top of the challenges nature provided, there were also drug smugglers, gun runners, Coyotes, slave traders, and paramilitary guerrillas. A perfect place for someone to get lost, as unwary and unskilled travelers often did in 'The Gap.'

The first part of Furcas' plan had been to control the section of the Darian National Park between Riosucio, Columbia and Yaviza, Panama. Even with his demonic powers stripped the moment he was banished, the effort had only taken Furcas two years to complete. For hundreds of generations of humanity, Furcas had watched as conquerors and tyrants rose to power, and he had learned that there were always only two forces that determined the conquerors success: persuasion, and fear. Furcas was comfortable using both, and he did so with artistic skill. It wasn't long before he had established himself as a competent ally with the forces on both sides of the delicate balance of power that existed in The Gap.

As he had once done to gain Astaroth's attention and trust, Furcas began with small missions at first; missions which had been easy to exceed expectations, and he had risen quickly in both notoriety and demand. The leaders of the various cartels that ruled the Darien had learned to trust him, to rely on him, and to expect him to always produce results. They didn't care how he achieved the results as long as they were the ones who profited, and Furcas had used every foul, underhanded, evil and wicked trick he could to ensure that they did. Equipped with the freedom and ability to use persuasion and fear like no mere human could, Furcas' name was well known wherever he went, and he was always greeted with the honor and privileges a man of his notoriety demanded.

Once his power and reputation was established, all he had to do was wait for the right time to strike. He didn't have to wait long. Early in the fourth year of his exile, he had heard a rumor that the mission was scheduled for a large project that coming summer. A few well-placed bribes had been all that Furcas needed to obtain copies of the paperwork Father Dominic's charity had filed; papers requesting travel visas for one-dozen Americans for a period of up to two months. Though the request hadn't listed the names of those being granted the visas, Furcas had known whose name would be at the top of the list: Brother Thomas Berenike.

From that moment on, finding a way to finish the assignment he had failed four years ago was the only thought Furcas had. To assist, he had hired one of his most reliable operatives, a man whom he had used for several other assignments before. This man, who had been given the name Juan Carlos by his parents, but earned the nickname *El Salvaje* by reputation, was not only reliable, but was nearly as evil as Furcas himself.

Furcas had given Juan Carlos specific instructions to bring Thomas back alive, if possible, but if not, then he was permitted to end the young man's life. He had trusted those instructions would be followed, and had believed his request was clear. And yet, several hours ago, Furcas had a wavering sensation in the pit of his stomach. He knew what that feeling was. At some point during Furcas' first encounter with Thomas, he had developed some form of psychic bond with the young man. Even over thousands of miles, Furcas could feel Thomas' power. The moment Thomas died, that feeling had disappeared, leaving Furcas with an empty longing, as if a part of him had been taken away.

Somehow Furcas had known Thomas' death wasn't necessary. He knew Juan Carlos had gone beyond the purview of the mission, making the decision to kill Thomas for no reason other than he could. How he knew this meant one of two things. It had either been no more than what humans called 'intuition', which was in reality one of the few spiritual powers available in the physical world, or it had been something else, something Furcas hoped was true: his demonic powers had returned. Either way, the message he had received was simple: Thomas was dead, and Furcas hadn't been the one to deliver the killing blow. The rage that had filled every cell of his being was the catalyst for the revenge he now planned.

After gathering his thoughts, Furcas had gone to the stables and saddled Gauerdi, and then rode out to seek that revenge. The distance from Riosucio, Columbia to the camp Juan Carlos used was about thirty miles, most of which was through dense, unpredictable, and dangerous jungle. The trip took nearly six hours, and Furcas had let his anger stew for every minute of that ride. By the time he and Gauerdi rode into camp, his fury was at the breaking point. It took every ounce of strength to keep from killing the men that Juan Carlos had left behind to guard the camp, a situation that the hired thugs had been able to sense. They had kept their distance, avoided eye contact, and only spoke when questioned. They were more than aware of who Furcas was and what he was capable of. Furcas could feel their fear, and he greedily swallowed every morsel of that delicious emotion.

It had been about an hour since he had arrived at Juan Carlos' camp, and once more Furcas felt the sensation that his demonic powers had returned. This time the power that he felt was one that demons used to communicate over great distances. The more powerful the demon, the greater the distance the communication could be sent, and from the way the incoming message made his head buzz, he could tell the message had traveled a long, long way. Furcas found a dark corner of the camp where he would not be disturbed, and opened his mind. A moment later, he was face to face with Ose, a demon with whom Furcas had once shared the same rank.

Ose greeted him with the customary salutations used between demons, and Furcas replied in kind, though he was more than a little suspicious to be greeted as an equal and not as one who had been banished.

"I see the four earth-years since your exile have been productive," Ose said after the introductions.

"What is it you want, Ose? To delight in my current misfortune?" Furcas sneered.

"Not at all, my brother. I assure you, my intentions do not follow that path," Ose stated in a failed attempt to assure his fellow demon.

"Then speak your mind. I have important tasks waiting," Furcas sighed.

"I have an…opportunity for you," Ose said after a brief moment had passed.

Furcas knew any opportunities offered would most likely not be in his best interest. No resident of the underworld ever offered help to another demon unless the one making the offer stood to gain something even more valuable in return. It was simply the way things worked in Hell. Furcas had done the same in his past, and would continue to do so every chance he had. However, the fact that the contact had been made at a time when Furcas was just starting to feel his demonic powers return had to be taken into consideration. If nothing else, it meant Ose was the one behind the powers return. The challenge Furcas faced now was to not listen to what Ose was about to share, but to determine which details his brother demon was leaving out.

"I'm listening," Furcas finally said, hoping his expression was placid and unreadable.

"Here is what I propose. I know you want the rest of your powers back, and your rank in the Dark Kingdom as well. You know that I have always wanted more power; what demon does not? To gain the power I seek, I need demons willing to take a risk. Swear to me your allegiance and the legions you control, and I will have enough power to usurp Astaroth," Ose stated plainly.

Furcas considered the situation carefully. Having his full powers returned would be of significant value, but losing his entire army would place him near the lowest ranks of Hell…though at least he would *be* back. Even if it took ten thousand generations for him to climb back up the ladder, there would at least be a ladder to climb, which was more than he had now. Still, there was something in the request that he knew Ose was not saying, a deeper truth known only to Ose himself, and one that Furcas would need to discover, and soon. Only then could he twist the advantage Ose held for himself.

Of course, Ose would be anticipating Furcas to do exactly that, and would be prepared. No demon ascended to the level that Ose now held, a level that Furcas had once enjoyed, without anticipating the moves of their rivals. Furcas knew that. In Hell, the game of subterfuge was like playing chess with pieces made of loosely stacked rice. Even well-conceived plans would fail if one moved his own pieces too carelessly.

"You know as well as I do, that Astaroth would already be prepared for such a move. How do you plan to succeed?" Furcas questioned, merely biding time, knowing any response Ose gave would reveal very little of the actual plan.

"Astaroth has become distracted. He has been spending most of his energy pursuing one single human soul," Ose said, causing Furcas to grant a look of surprise at the freedom with which his fellow demon gave this information away.

There were only two reasons to give away information as freely as Ose had just done. The first was that the information was of little to no use, as it was already, or would soon be, publicly known. And the second, was that the knowledge shared protected a secret even more valuable than what was given away. For now, there was no way for Furcas to know which of these two categories this information belonged, and he made a mental note to keep the discovery of what Ose was hiding at the forefront of his thoughts.

"If I agree to this, you know I must request a few accommodations," Furcas offered, attempting to distract Ose from what he was truly thinking about.

"Of course. I expect nothing less," Ose replied.

"First, I want my powers returned now, not after you are successful, for there is always a chance that your attempt will fail. When you strike, Astaroth will know which armies you lead, and should you fail, then I will have lost everything. I will not only be a banished knight, but a knight with no army. Any chance I have of being reinstated will disappear."

"Consider it done. Any other requests?"

Furcas grinned.

"I have one assignment for which I will need my troops before they can be yours," he said, already desirous of using his demons against Juan Carlos and his men.

There was an interminable pause while Ose considered, then replied with a single word, "Agreed."

Furcas felt a stirring in his gut at the ease with which Ose appeared to have acquiesced, a feeling he hated. It seemed so...human. As the intensity of the sensation increased, he could taste bile rising in his throat. This was a sensation he relished, and a wave of pleasure washed over him as every inch of his skin began to burn. He knew all residue of his banishment was being purged, and his demonic nature was taking over once more. Furcas braced himself, not wanting the moment to end. With each passing moment, he felt as if he would burst. Still, he held on, allowing the flames of Hell to burn away what he had been forced to become. Behind him, Gauerdi began to trot in a tight circle, neighing and snorting and tossing his head. He, too, had powers that had been torn away at the banishment, and were now his once more.

Finally, the sensation grew to where Furcas could hold it no more, and with a thunderous yell he leaped into the air, then crashed back down, landing on one knee and driving his fist deep into the ground. The earth responded by belching an explosion of dirt, rock and flora into the air. A wide circle of jungle was instantly transformed, with Furcas at the epicenter. The force of the blast rushed outward through the jungle as the destructive shockwaves spread, announcing to man and demon alike that Furcas' powers had returned. With a sneer and a devilish laugh, Furcas looked around.

The camp was gone.

Men, equipment, weapons, drugs. All of it. Gone.

All that remained was a midnight-black stallion, and a demon-knight in armor of ebony steel.

The first indication that they were getting near their destination was when the four armed men began to relax. Julianna became aware that the guards weren't swiveling their heads around as often, and their eyes were no longer darting from object to object in a constant search for danger. The tension in their shoulders disappeared soon after, and a mile or so later, they began to joke and laugh. Where most of the night had been spent in near silence, now there was a persistent buzz.

As the captor's mood improved, however, Julianna's mood became even more despondent. She knew that once they reached their destination, it would mean more men, and more guns. She had to do something, and soon. Escape seemed impossible, especially while there was a rope securing her to Beth, who was in front of her, and Jeremiah, who was behind. Still she considered every possibility that she could imagine, but each idea came up empty. There was always some reason it wouldn't work. Until her hands were free, she would never be.

And then a memory flashed through her mind, one she had discarded years ago believing it had been no more than a dream. The memory was shadowy and uncertain, as if she was seeing it through a mist, or a veil. Though, the longer she focused her attention on the memory, the more real it became.

She recalled the stalagmites and stalactites that had been interspersed throughout the large, dank cave; and she saw the thick, luminescent fog that had clung to the cavern's floor as if it was around her even now. She even swore she could hear the steady pattern of water dripping from the ceiling.

Plink.

Plink.

Plop.

A flash of shadow to her left made her head spin, bringing her back to the present moment. Her eyes began searching the darkness. Was that the beastly creature with the dragon's wings moving in the shadows? Had he come to help her? Julianna fought to remember his name. Astral? Astrid? No, those weren't right. Then, she heard his final words, as if the heavy, damp, jungle air itself was whispering the words.

"Keep your power secret, child. Do not let anyone know! When you need me, call my name."

It was then that she recalled his name, and as she did, she spoke it out loud.

"Astaroth..."

A low, rumbling clatter sounded in the distance, followed by the cacophonous chitter of birds and primate howls. Somewhere nearby, a jungle cat growled. Julianna saw the man who had been leading the group suddenly turn back, his eyes wide with fear. Behind her, one of the teens raised their voice in alarm. As Julianna tried to figure out what was going on, the rope around her neck tightened, pulling her off balance. Then, the ground itself began to rise and fall. With no way to counterbalance the shifting earth, Julianna fell.

More voices cried out as the weight of her body dragged down those next to her, but Julianna didn't hear their cries. All she heard was a deep rumbling sound, like that of an earthquake. Then that sound, too, began to fade as the rope tightened further, strangling her windpipe and causing blood to swell in her ears. Her body began to convulse as her hands desperately tried to reach the rope around her neck, but she couldn't break the bonds. Julianna knew she was choking, and there was nothing she could do. She tried to scream for help, but the words died before they left her mouth. Her last thought was the memory of her hands, bathed in violet-blue electric flames. With that, Julianna's world faded to black.

CHAPTER TWELVE
AFTERSHOCKS

In her position at the front of the line of captives, Beth had been the first to feel the earth move as the quake rolled through, though she was the last one to fall. By the time the weight of the teens in the line behind her had pulled her to the ground, she had already been aware of one important fact; what she had felt had been no mere quake. She'd experienced earthquakes more than enough times back home to know that this one felt different. With this one, Beth had felt something not quite normal. If her intuition was right, the earthquake had not been created by nature, but by a supernatural force, one that she had been warned would be coming.

As she lay on the ground waiting for the rolling of the earth to subside, her mind flashed back to the retreat where she met Brother Thomas, only a few months back. That was the day she had first learned of the role she would play in The Guardians' quest. And now, as she waited for the supernatural quake to pass, she knew that the moment was near. Beth steadied herself, then slowly got back to her feet.

※

For nearly two hours Thomas had led the way, keeping a brisk pace. Gemma and Theresa followed close behind, though they were showing signs of fatigue.

Thomas would run for fifteen minutes or so, and then the sensations he was tracking would fade and he would stop, allowing Gemma and Theresa to catch up. As soon as they did, Theresa boosted Thomas' power while Gemma healed them both, giving them back as much energy as she could afford to provide. Once their brief respite was done, Thomas would race ahead as fast as the thick undergrowth would allow, following the sensations once more; though it was no longer the sensation of fear that he chased. His friend's emotions had degraded beyond fear, and Thomas was now registering feelings of exhaustion, futility, and despair. The further they had been driven into the jungle, the less hope his friends had been able to maintain. In their minds, no rescue was coming, and they had all but given up.

He wouldn't, though; give up, that is. It simply wasn't an option. Regardless of what happened, regardless of what risks he had to take, he would see this through. Besides, he had a few things in his favor. First, not only did his friends think he was dead, but so did the kidnappers. Surprise was on his side. And he also had his faith. Over and over again he silently repeated the words, *'If God leads you to it, He will lead you through it'*, using the phrase as a mantra to continue on. The final advantage was the spiritual superpowers that he and his two companions held. If nothing else, once they caught up to the group, their powers would help offset the weapons the four kidnappers had. At least, that was what Thomas was hoping for.

Pushing through a knot of tightly bunched palms, he came to a small clearing with a stream flowing nearby. Reaching out with his powers, he knew Gemma and Theresa were only a few minutes behind.

"This is as good a place as any, I guess," Thomas said aloud, though no one was near enough to hear him. He then searched for a dry place to sit.

He relaxed as he waited, stretching his tired legs out before him as he focused on slowing his breathing, counting down the seconds until he could hear Gemma and Theresa approach. When they were close enough, he called out, directing them to him with the sound of his voice. A moment later, they emerged through the same palm fronds he had come through. Theresa immediately knelt down beside him, panting as she wiped the sweat from her brow.

"Take a moment, Theresa. Steady your breathing," he instructed, feeling her emotions ease as the young woman relaxed.

Gemma took a seat on his right side, while Theresa moved to a sitting position on his left. Then, they joined hands, breathing deep as their powers interlaced, and Thomas began to search. This time he picked up the trail almost at once. His friends were close. Really close. The distance couldn't be more than a few miles now. Perhaps four, maybe five miles at the most. Although he had found them and knew which way to go, Thomas paused for a moment. He was close enough now that he could pick out the individual fluctuations in the emotions of the group. Those individuals he had known for a longer period of time stood out right away. He recognized the way Terence's energy buzzed inside him, and could feel the lighter energy that belonged to Beth, and...

Julianna!

Though he could feel her energy, it was very faint, as if it was barely there.

Something was wrong...

※

Julianna's eyes flicked open, only to be confused with what she saw. Rather than the shadowy darkness of the jungle, she saw a pale, misty-yellow glow. As her mind cleared, she realized the temperature had changed, too. The oppressive heat and humidity were gone, replaced with a damp chill. The faintly glowing mist collected in droplets on her hands and face, and she wiped at them with the sleeve of her shirt to clear the moisture away. As the fabric touched her cheek, she suddenly realized what that meant.

Her hands were no longer tied!

With a gasp of surprise, she moved her hands to her throat. The rope that had been rubbing her skin until it was chafed and swollen was gone! She was free! With a breath of relief, Julianna leaped to her feet and looked around, realizing at once that she was back in the dimly lit, fog-filled cavern. And she was not alone. Without turning, she knew who she would find.

Astaroth.

She heard his familiar chuckle behind her, and slowly turned around.

"Hello, Daughter of Eve," Astaroth said, bowing low to the ground. "Welcome home."

Julianna looked around. Surely this cavern was not the home he referred to.

"This," she said with disdain, "is not a home."

Astaroth feigned an astonished look.

"No?" he questioned with a feigned look of surprise and shock. "Why not? Where I come from, this place would be considered a paradise."

"Paradise? It's an empty cave!"

"Ahh…would a more…familiar setting help?"

Julianna just shrugged.

"Depends on why I'm here, I guess."

"Well then, why don't we first fix where *here* is, then we can chat. Think of the place where you are most comfortable, the place you feel most at home."

For Julianna, that was easy, and the moment it came to mind, she found herself there. Her old bedroom, in the house she had lived before her life had been torn apart. Looking around at the familiar room, she saw her old bed, the blankets tossed in a haphazard heap, as was her norm. At the foot of the bed she saw the bean bag chair where she would sit and read, and next to that was a neatly stacked pile of books, just like she expected to find. On her right was the dresser where she had kept not only her clothes, but the secret jewelry box, too. Sliding the top drawer open, she saw that the box was still there.

Feeling more joyous than she had in years, she crouched down low, then, giggling loudly, launched herself into the air and landed in the middle of the bed. The bed responded by bouncing her back up a few times as her giggles turned to laughter. As the bouncing settled down, and with a tear in her eye, she breathed in deeply, savoring the familiar smells.

"Oh, Astaroth, this is perfect!" she exclaimed, closing her eyes as she let the experience embrace every part of her being.

"Well then, I'm so glad that you approve," a familiar voice responded.

Julianna's eyes popped open as her heart leaped into her throat. Standing in the doorway was someone she never thought she would see again. Her father.

"Dad?" she hesitantly inquired, fearing the answer she might receive.

The image of her father smiled, and his soft laughter met her ears.

"Is this not what you expected to see?" her father's image said with a grin. "It is the image you were holding in your thoughts."

Julianna thought for a moment. It was true that she had always imagined her father standing in the doorway, smiling at her. It was rare that he would do so. Usually, when he came to her room, it was because she was in trouble for something she had done, or hadn't done, and he was there to lecture or reprimand. Her elated emotions suddenly dropped.

"I would rather never be reminded of that man again," she groaned.

"Fine," replied her father as his voice changed, and his image became ghostly as it swirled and shifted for a moment until Astaroth's body appeared once more. "I much prefer to be myself, anyway."

"Thank you," Julianna replied, a bit timidly, then, in a more questioning tone, asked, "So, what are we doing here? Why did you call me back?"

Astaroth shook his head in disappointment, a gesture that reminded Julianna of her dad.

"It was not I who called you, but you who called me," he informed her. "As you recall, when we last spoke, I informed you that you had but to speak my name if you were in need, and I would be there."

The statement made Julianna feel as if she had her own personal magic lamp.

Astaroth's eyes narrowed as he asked, "Has something in your world gone wrong?"

Julianna's eyes popped open wide and her jaw dropped in surprise.

"Are you kidding me?" she said, her words thick with disbelief. "What hasn't gone wrong?"

She felt her throat tighten and her eyes swell with tears, and she reached over to find the box of tissue she always kept on the nightstand by her bed. Pulling out three tissues, she wiped at her eyes. Astaroth said nothing and so she continued on.

"My brother is dead, my friends and I were kidnapped, and we've been walking for hours tied together like cows! Where have you been?"

Astaroth grinned at her, apparently enjoying her frantic, expressive behavior.

"You are far from my primary responsibility, Daughter of Eve. I cannot be everywhere."

Julianna looked away, composing herself.

"Might I ask why you did not call sooner?" he questioned, a bit smugly.

Shrugging her shoulders, Julianna looked down at the familiar blankets upon which she sat, then gathered them around her shoulders, a habit she had developed whenever she had felt scared, or sad, or lonely.

"I don't know. It all happened so fast. After my brother was shot, I think I just kinda went numb."

"Well, now that I am here, what can I do for you?"

Julianna raised her eyes to meet his. She paused, taking in a deep breath.

"I want to know more about this power that you said I have. I want to know if it will help me, if I can use it to get free…to get my friends free."

Astaroth looked at her, studying the expression on her face. Finally, he spoke.

"Is that all you want the power for?"

Julianna looked down at the blankets on her bed, then, after a long pause, she shook her head softly. When she looked back up her eyes were glossy and wet, but they held a determined glare. In her mind, images of faces flashed by, faces of those who had hurt her in the past; made her feel inferior, or worthless, or weak. Faces of people she hadn't realized she hated as much as she now realized she did. Suddenly, Julianna realized, it wasn't just freedom from the four kidnappers that she wanted. She wanted something more.

"No," she sighed as angry tears began to fall. "I want revenge."

Having admitted out loud what she knew she had been feeling inside for years, Julianna stared at Astaroth, waiting for his response. Behind the fragile wall of tears, her eyes were now dark and foreboding.

"The road to revenge is a hard one to travel, and one from which you may never return. Are you certain you know what it is you are asking of me?" Astaroth questioned, the tone of his voice was compassionate, but the devilish grin on his face betrayed his true thoughts.

Julianna choked back her tears, swallowing hard as she gathered her resolve. Steeling herself, she threw her legs over the side of the bed and stood.

"Yes," she said confidently. "I know what I ask."

For a long moment, Astaroth didn't move, a brief twinkle in his eyes was the only indication of the thoughts on his mind. He stepped over to Julianna's dresser, reached into the top drawer, and pulled out the jewelry box she knew so well. Immediately her thoughts turned to Grandma Berenike and she wondered why Astaroth was drawing forth the gift her grandmother had given to her years ago. Were the two events connected? Is this what Grandma Berenike meant in her letter when she said the jewelry would one day have a hidden value in them?

She watched as Astaroth slowly opened the lid, and then drew out the jewelry that lay inside. He then held the necklace up to the light, whispering in a language she did not understand. As a wispy fog began to swirl and condense around the edges of the room, the necklace began to glow with the same violet-blue light that Julianna had seen burn from her hands the night she had attacked Jasmine at the party.

"Then, come, child," Astaroth said as he extended his hand to her. "Today you will no longer be a Daughter of Eve. Today you will join The Fallen."

Though a small part of herself shouted desperately to refuse to take his hand, Julianna stepped forward, grasping for his outstretched arm as if she was about to fall from a cliff, and his hand was the only support within reach. Though, once their fingers touched, she did fall, and from a much greater height than any she could have ever imagined. Somewhat unknowingly, she gave herself to Astaroth, putting her future into his trust. The life Julianna had been born to live began to crumble to dust, and with it, every part that had made her who she was, changed. Julianna didn't just *choose* evil over good. At that moment, she *became* it.

※

Thomas felt a palm frond scratch against his face, leaving behind a small cut that burned fiercely. It was most likely the hundredth frond to have scratched him since he had started his headlong dash through the jungle.

His arms, face and legs were covered with a glossy red sheen from the countless small cuts, but he didn't care. He had only one concern; finding Julianna before her emotional signature disappeared for good.

Somewhere behind him, Gemma and Theresa were struggling to keep up. They couldn't match his speed, nor the on-again/off-again ability he had to see the future. The first time this uncontrollable power came to him, Thomas had been in a fight with a group of kids his age, kids who had tried to steal his bike. With the help of his future-sight, he had been able to see their attacks before they launched them, allowing him to set himself in the perfect place to counter every strike. The fight had been over quickly, as he had methodically eliminated one assailant after another. Now, this intermittent power was on, and he was seeing images of trees, rocks, and other dangers, allowing him to change his path to avoid them.

Along with this power, he was also using his ability to sense emotional energy, and had locked his attention on two images, one of which he knew belonged to his roommate, Terence. The other he knew in his gut belonged to the man who had shot him. There was no way Thomas would ever forget the spinning, vicious vortex of negative energy that sucked every ounce of goodness it came near. It made his stomach turn every time the sensation flushed through him. He would do his best to save the man if he could, but the dark energy that lived within the man had to go.

Thomas had been running at this accelerated pace for nearly five minutes now, and he had cut the distance between himself and his sister by half. If he had been in the open, without all of the trees, rocks, plants and other dangers of the jungle, he would have already reached her.

But with the hazards, he could only run at about twice normal speed. He knew he was capable of speeds of at least three to four times what he was running now.

Suddenly, rather than a bright, blinking image of a tree or rock ahead of him, letting him know an obstacle was approaching, the entire horizon flashed brilliant white as a powerful force stretched across the full field of his vision, rushing towards him. A moment later, the power of the force crashed into him, and he fell. The force sent Thomas tumbling uncontrollably, his body rolling like an avalanche, smashing through the undergrowth, exploding smaller plants like they had been struck by lightning, and ricocheting like a pinball between the larger, harder obstacles in his way.

Finally, he struck the base of a giant banyan tree, smashing through the smaller and less densely grouped outer trunks. Then, his inertia spent, Thomas stopped fast. His body was bruised and broken, and he lay in a twisted and chaotic mess. Pain flooded in. He knew he would be unable to fight the pain for long. With the last moments of consciousness, he reached out with his powers. This time he was not in search of his sister, but of the two friends who were somewhere back the way he had come. He needed healing, and Gemma was somewhere behind him. He only hoped she could hear his wordless cry.

※

"Theresa! We need to hurry! Thomas needs our help!" Gemma called out, hoping that her younger friend would have enough stamina to continue at the pace they had been traveling. The reply from Theresa came in a series of gasps.

"You go ahead...go...help Thomas...I'll catch up..." Theresa panted, swatting at palm fronds as they got in her way.

Gemma slowed her pace, then stopped, allowing Theresa to catch up.

"I'm not leaving you behind. You might never find us," Gemma replied.

Theresa had also stopped, and was standing bent over at the waist, her palms were pressed hard against her knees and her chest was heaving as she gulped in oxygen. Gemma sighed. She knew she couldn't rush off to rescue one friend and at the same time leave another one behind. She pointed at a spot on the ground.

"Sit," she commanded.

Theresa didn't have to be asked twice, and she quickly lowered herself to the ground, her backside thumping hard against the dead foliage that littered the jungle floor. Gemma knelt beside her, placed one hand on Theresa's arm, and another on her leg. Closing her eyes, Gemma began to channel energy through her body, sending it like a wave of cool water washing over her exhausted friend. She could hear the change in Theresa's breathing almost immediately.

After a few moments had passed, Theresa's face relaxed, and then, she smiled.

"Ahh..." she sighed contentedly, letting her muscles relax along with her breath. "Do you have any idea how amazing your powers feel?"

Gemma smiled to herself as she continued to pump Theresa full of healing energy, even though the cost to her was nearly equal to that which she gave away. She knew she would recover at a faster rate than Theresa ever would, even if she completely drained herself. As soon as

Theresa was healed, all she would need for herself would be a few minutes more, and then the two heroes would be able to press on. As long as Thomas was alive—which he still was, she could feel his life-force—she would know where to find him. She knew he was in terrible pain, but as long as she held power in her veins, even just a small amount, she could bring him back to health. Even if he died, she could heal him. She had already done that once, after all. She just had to get to him while his soul still clung to his body.

CHAPTER THIRTEEN
REVIVAL

"Theresa, do you feel that?" Gemma asked loudly, grasping a hanging vine for support as the ground began to surge and swell.

"Yeah, I do," Theresa said, taking a stance like a surfer riding out a wave. "Feels like a quake. We get them all the time where I'm from. Don't worry. It will pass."

A few moments later, it did exactly that, and, after a few words of encouragement, Theresa was able to coax Gemma from her stranglehold on the vine.

"So, that's what an earthquake feels like?" Gemma said, still a bit shaken.

"Yeah. Either it wasn't a strong one, or we're pretty far away from the epicenter," Theresa responded, then crossed her arms over her chest and leaned against the trunk of a large tree. "You ready to continue? Still got a lock on where Thomas is?"

Gemma stood tall and straight, and closed her eyes. She began to spin slowly to the left, paused, and then spun back towards the right.

"The feeling I'm picking up was coming from this direction, but it's faint now. Really faint. Like maybe that quake wiped out the trail or something?"

Theresa walked in the direction Gemma was currently gazing towards.

"Well, we might not need your power after all," Theresa said as she pulled a palm frond close enough for Gemma to see. It was splattered with blood.

"You think that's Thomas' blood?" Gemma asked.

Theresa took a few steps forward, grabbed another frond and pulled that one close as well. It, too, had splashes of the sticky, dark liquid scattered across it.

"If I had to guess? Yeah, it's his. It's leading in the direction you pointed. Look," Theresa said, pointing ahead as she released the palm frond, "there's another splattered leaf up ahead."

The two moved forward to the leaf Theresa indicated, they examined it for a moment, and then looked deeper into the jungle once more.

"You said he was injured, right?" Theresa asked.

"Oh, yeah, he's injured. I don't think he'll die, though. Not if we get there in time."

"Okay, you keep checking with that power of yours, and I'll keep my eye out for more bloody leaves."

"By the way, how can you see so well when it's this dark?" Gemma inquired.

Theresa shrugged.

"When I go invisible, it's like the world becomes negative; blacks are white, and vice versa. I don't have to be fully invisible for that to occur, just my eyes."

Gemma turned to look directly at Theresa. She hadn't focused on the young woman's face for some time. Sure enough, her sockets were empty. Not hollow, as if Theresa's eyes weren't there, but empty. No whites, no colors, no empty socket...nothing.

"Sometimes I wish we had a training manual for these powers of ours. We seem to keep finding new ways to use them," Gemma said, shaking her head and waving her hand forward, motioning for Theresa to lead the way. "Come on, let's keep moving. You first. I'll let you know if you go off course."

The two moved forward at a moderate pace, Theresa leading, while Gemma constantly checked that they were heading the right way. Nearly thirty minutes passed before they came upon the banyan tree where Thomas' body lay. Gemma rushed to him and immediately knelt at his side. Theresa was right behind her, and when she saw the way Thomas' mangled body lay, like a discarded, broken doll, she gasped with shock.

"Oh no," Theresa moaned. "Not again!"

"Help me straighten him. He's not dead yet," Gemma said, glancing up at Theresa urgently.

Together they moved Thomas into what looked like a more comfortable—and more normal—position, then Gemma went to work, kneeling near Thomas' feet and placing her hands over his left ankle, which was twisted in an unnatural way. Her hands began to shimmer with a pale, blue light, and a slight humming sound could be heard. As she stitched the bones back together and repaired the ruptured and torn muscles, his foot moved, lining up with his leg like it should. Gemma moved her hands to his other ankle.

"At least this one isn't broken, just sprained," she said as the blue light continued to glow.

She spent only a moment relaxing the sprain, and then moved up his legs, her hands always hovering about six inches above Thomas' unconscious form. She explained each injury to Theresa as she went along: both femurs shattered, a dislocated right hip, three broken ribs, a bruised sternum, fractured clavicle, ruptured disc, and a shattered jaw; along with multiple contusions and lacerations. Theresa watched in awe as the red and purple splotches faded away, and the edges of the lacerations stitched themselves together, leaving not even a scar.

Finally, after the last wound was healed, Gemma opened her eyes and shook out her hands. She breathed deeply, then gave Theresa a quick smile.

"Thanks for boosting me a moment ago. My energy was starting to fade," she admitted.

"Oh, yeah. Not a problem at all. So, is he healed?" she asked, glancing at Thomas.

"As best as I could; he's still a bit in shock, though. He was smashed up pretty bad, like he hit a brick wall or something." Gemma said.

"Why isn't he moving, then?"

"Give him some time. He'll come around."

"Yeah, that's the thing. I've got a feeling *time* is something we don't have a lot of."

※

Juan Carlos wasn't a superstitious man. He didn't believe in higher powers, or ghosts, or even bad luck. It was early in his youth when he learned the truth about the world; the truth that life was dangerous and unforgiving. In fact, it was the morning of his fifth birthday; the day he lost his mother. They had gone into town, as they did at least once a week. The only difference was, this time, neither of them made it back. His mother was gunned down, an innocent victim of a turf war between two rival factions, both vying for the right to rule over the small town. All it had taken was one random bullet—just one—to forever change Juan Carlos' world.

At that moment, he had become homeless, orphaned, and alone. Eventually a young priest found him wandering the streets; dirty, hungry, and tired. The priest took Juan Carlos to an orphanage where he promised the boy that he would be safe; though that had not turned out to be the truth. When the nuns who ran the orphanage weren't looking, the older kids had their way, hitting and kicking the younger ones, stealing the best parts of their meals, and always threatening what would happen if they cried out. For five years Juan Carlos had endured their punishing ways, until, at the age of ten, he finally fought back.

Three of the older boys caught Juan Carlos on the way back from Mass, cornering him on a stairway. They had only meant to make him cry like they had a thousand times before. But this time was different. After five years of being picked on and teased, Juan Carlos struck back. When the biggest of the three started poking him, Juan Carlos bit the boy's finger as hard as he could. The boy's eyes had gone wide with surprise, and then he had taken a step back. Juan Carlos had stepped towards the boy, his fists raised to strike again, and the boy stepped back a few more times, only to find he had run out of floor. The boy lost his balance and tumbled down the stairs, striking his head so hard against the landing it cracked.

The other two bullies had turned and ran to get help, yelling that Juan Carlos had killed their friend. In a panic, Juan Carlos had jumped through a small window and ran along the crest of the terracotta roof. He had found a small hiding spot in the shadows where two roofs came together, then hid until dark. After the moon had set, he had snuck back down, climbed over the wall of the courtyard, and disappeared into the streets.

While living on the streets had been nearly impossible for Juan Carlos at the age of five, he found doing the same at age ten was much easier. It hadn't taken long for Juan Carlos to be initiated into one of the many gangs of street kids that roamed the downtown area, gangs who made the money they needed to survive by running errands for the criminal organizations of Panama. Two years later, at the age of twelve, Juan Carlos was given an assignment that had placed him in contact with a man of significant influence, a man who had taken him on as his own errand boy and began to give him larger and more important jobs. Eventually Juan Carlos had gone from being a runner, to a bag-man.

He found that he was good at the collections job: Very good. His methods of getting people to pay what they owed had been so violent that he had quickly earned a reputation, and a nickname as well.

El Salvaje - The Wild One.

It was this reputation that had put Juan Carlos in front of yet another of Panama's most dangerous men; a man whose reputation was equally as vile as Juan Carlos considered himself to be. This man, whose name was Furcas, was always accompanied by a midnight black steed. It was Furcas who had hired Juan Carlos and his men for the assignment they were currently on, saying it would be one of the most urgent and important tasks that Juan Carlos would ever complete. When Juan Carlos heard what the task was, he had internally denied that it could be as important or urgent as Furcas claimed, but it paid extraordinarily well with very little risk, a combination that Juan Carlos rarely refused.

He accepted the task eagerly, establishing a base of operations not far from where he was now, with nine of the original twelve young Americans that had been his target now his captives, and one other dead—and by his own hand, too. Juan Carlos was beginning to relax. The job was nearly done. Within another hour or two he would deliver the captive Americans, collect his pay, and then perhaps take some time off. He was tired of the constant demands for his skills.

While in the jungle, in the midst of these reflective thoughts, Juan Carlos found himself suddenly on his back, staring up into the deep, penetrating gloom that clung to the upper branches of the canopy above. Though he had experienced earthquakes several times in the past, the one that had just ripped through the jungle had felt nothing like any of those he previously felt. The quake had carried with it an ominous feeling; one that chilled him to the bone.

Rising into a seated position and grasping his rifle, he quickly called out the names of the three men who had accompanied him on this mission, receiving a verbal response from each. Mixed in with those responses were grunts and groans from his captives, and Juan Carlos scrambled to his feet to check on his prize. Just as he and his men had been knocked off their feet by the quake, so too had their captives, and they now lay in a jumbled mass of bodies. He watched as they struggled to rise from the jungle floor. Two of them were sitting up, and a third — Terence — was already up on his knees. Suddenly, one of the older females became frantic, shouting for help.

From where he was, Juan Carlos was unable to understand what she was shouting about, and he turned to one of his men, who was closer to the frantic woman.

"Why is she shouting?" Juan Carlos asked.

"She says the rope is choking one of the girls," Matias informed him, putting both his hands around his own neck and showing a strained expression, mimicking the look they both had witnessed on the faces of those the men and women they had strangled.

"Oh? Which one?" Juan Carlos asked casually, his face showing no emotion.

"The one who you almost shot," Matias said, this time holding his hand in the shape of a gun and pointing it at his head.

Juan Carlos knew the one Matias meant. He *had* almost shot her. Had come very close to doing it, too. The only thing that had stopped him was knowing how much a girl like her was worth to him. Though he would rather have simply killed all nine hostages, he knew he could use the extra cash. In the dark world of human trafficking, young adults—and especially Americans—claimed an especially high price.

"Well? What are you waiting for?" he finally said, turning his attention away from Matias. "Go help her! If she dies, you will owe me what she is worth!"

Matias didn't hesitate. He rushed to the captives and began to pull on the ropes to try and lessen the tension. As the rope loosened its grip, the color in Julianna's face returned, but she still continued to choke.

"Untie me!" Beth urged. "I know CPR!"

Matias turned to get permission from Juan Carlos, quickly translating what Beth had said. Juan Carlos waved his hand dismissively, giving his okay, and Matias grabbed for his knife. Rather than waste time undoing the knots, he pulled Beth towards him, then cut the rope around her neck, and finally, the rope tying her wrists.

Juan Carlos watched Beth move to Julianna's side, straighten the younger girl's body, and then check her windpipe for blockage. She said something to Matias, and once more the man translated it back to Juan Carlos.

"She says it would be more helpful if we were to untie the injured one."

Juan Carlos waved his hand again, then motioned for his other men to stand guard. The replied quickly, pointing their rifles in the direction of the group. Juan Carlos knew the two young women that Matias had just freed would not be a match for his men, but he had learned to take the cautious route whenever possible. If this was some form of ruse and the two women tried to escape, it would be the last act they ever took.

Chapter Fourteen
A Knight Returns

Julianna felt the rope go slack, and she began to gasp for breath. Though she was fully conscious and aware of everything around her, she continued to act as if she was still couldn't breathe. While she hid behind this deception, she was also waiting for an advantage, something that would allow her to act without being watched. A moment later, she heard Beth ask to be cut free, pleading with their captors to let her help. They complied, and Julianna was soon aware of Beth's hands pulling on her arms and straightening her legs. Julianna knew the moment was close. Soon, she would create a distraction, perhaps something that involved Beth as well, and definitely something that would force her captors to look away, if even for just a moment. When they did, she would strike.

She could feel Beth began to evaluate her situation, searching for the cause of her inability to breathe. Beth leaned her head back to straighten her windpipe, and placed two fingers on the side of her neck to check her pulse. Julianna continued feigning as if she couldn't breathe. Then Beth plunged two fingers down her throat, and she nearly lost the deception, along with whatever remnants of her dinner earlier that night were still in her gut. Finding nothing, Beth began to administer CPR, but with Julianna's arms tied behind her back, it was ineffective. Then, the unthinkable happened; Beth asked the captors to cut Julianna free, too. And they did!

As the cords fell from her wrists, and Beth moving her arms from behind her back, Julianna's anticipation grew. That disgusting coward who had shot her brother would pay for what he had done. She would kill him, and not gently, either. He didn't deserve mercy, and even if he had, it wouldn't come from her. Mercy was not a part of her world anymore. She was done being kind. The world owed her, and these men would be the first to pay.

Once they were gone, then Julianna would disappear, too. She had nothing left to keep her here. Her brother was gone, and she had no friends. Not even the small group she was currently held hostage with were really her friends. They were just being nice for the past few days while they worked together on the mission project. Once that was over, and they all returned home, their friendship would end. There was no reason for it to last beyond this trip. They treated her okay; they hadn't teased or bullied her like everyone at her school had, but she had sworn she had seen a few of the boys looking at her with side-eyed glances. And hadn't she heard them whispering to each other as she walked past? She couldn't have imagined all that.

※

The first thing Thomas recognized as his vision began to clear, were the faces of his two friends. Gemma and Theresa smiled at him, their eyes glistening with tears as they did. He smiled back, then raised his right hand and gave them a thumbs-up.

"You know, Brother Thomas," Theresa said as she wiped tears from her eyes, "you really need to stop dying. It's getting a little out of hand."

Thomas smiled at her. He opened his mouth to reply, but found his throat was too dry for words. After trying unsuccessfully to clear it a few times, he gave up, and just smiled again.

"Can you sit up yet?" Gemma asked, moving her hands beneath his back for support.

Thomas pushed himself up onto his elbows, then tried to sit forward, but after feeling a bit faint, he fell back again, shaking his head.

"Okay, one more good boost should help out," Gemma said, placing one hand over his forehead and the other over his heart.

Thomas could feel a warm, soothing sensation flow through him, and as it entered into his body, the last vestiges of weakness began to flow away. Soon, he felt much more like himself, and this time, when he tried to speak, it worked.

"Thanks, Gemma. That really is quite the gift you have," Thomas said, blinking his eyes a few times as he sat up. "How long was I out?"

"Not long. I think it took us…maybe thirty minutes to find you?" Gemma informed him. "But we got you healed pretty fast."

Now in a seated position, Thomas stretched out his arms, and then his legs. Satisfied that there was no longer any pain or injuries, he stood up.

"What happened? There's no way that earthquake was enough to do that much damage," Theresa stated.

Thomas shook his head.

"That was no earthquake. There was emotional energy attached to whatever that was. I could feel it," he told his friends. "Are you two are okay, though? You didn't get hurt, did you?"

Gemma placed her hand on her stomach. "I felt nauseous for a while, but other than that, no. We were farther away though."

"What do you think it was?" Theresa asked.

"I'm not sure. I know I've felt something like it before," Thomas explained, rising to his feet and preparing to travel. "I just don't remember where."

He paused, giving both of his friends a confused, hopeless look, then continued on.

"Whatever it was, I'll be able to detect it sooner next time, now that I know what it feels like. Maybe there's a way for us to avoid it, or deflect it somehow."

"Hopefully it won't happen again." Theresa said, and the other two nodded in agreement.

"Come on," Thomas urged, taking a step towards his captive friends. "We're not that far away now."

"Are you sure you're ready?" Gemma asked, the look in her eyes showing her concern.

"Probably not," Thomas admitted, giving her a half-smile. "But I don't think we can afford to wait."

Thomas moved ahead quickly, but this time he kept at a pace which allowed Gemma and Theresa to stay close behind. It didn't take long to reach the clearing where his friends were being watched by three of the men. The fourth man, he knew, was just out of sight. He could see the man's emotional signature slowly moving, though he could not see the man.

The three companions took a position behind a large fern where they could see into the clearing, but were fairly certain they would not be seen. Thomas knelt down. Theresa did the same on his left side, and Gemma, likewise, on his right. For close to a minute, no one spoke. They simply watched, and waited.

Though there was still a few hours until dawn, the moon was riding high and the captives and captors had come to rest in a large clearing with little tree cover overhead. It was far from what daylight would show, but the bright moon and thousands of stars provided plenty of light. As Thomas looked around at his friends, he saw someone that looked like Beth, administering CPR to another of their group. Since Beth's back was currently facing towards Thomas, he was unable to see who it was that was requiring help. Glancing around quickly, he did a silent roll call in his mind.

At one end of his tightly-grouped friends, was Brendan; his jet-black hair hanging limply over his eyes. He watched as Brendan tried in vain to toss the damp, dirty strands out of the way, but they just fell back where they had been before. To the outside world, Thomas could see that Brendan looked as if he had given up hope, but using his superpower, Thomas could also see the truth behind the mask, and the image that he saw hanging over Brendan's head appeared stalwart and secure.

Next to Brendan, was Terence, who also appeared physically and emotionally drained at first glance, but Thomas knew that this, too, was a ruse. The shape and color of Terence's emotions appeared like a dark storm cloud over his head, leaving Thomas with only one feeling; Terence was plotting revenge. He could see a patch of dried, caked blood clinging to Terence's long, blonde hair; the leftovers from when he had been struck by the butt of a rifle back when this whole nightmare had begun. Thomas knew that was more than enough reason for Terence to want payback from the man who had struck him down. Having seen Terence angry, Thomas did not envy the target of his roommate's ire.

Adriana was next in line, and again, from what Thomas could see, Adriana seemed to be handling the situation fairly well. Her emotions registered in his mind as a still, quiet pool, and the look in her hazel eyes was bright and serene. Next to her, Francis appeared to also be quietly accepting what the future might hold. As Thomas watched, he saw that Francis was moving his lips, just barely enough to be seen. He wondered if Francis was whispering to one of the other captives, or silently praying. His emotional state registered in Thomas' mind like a pale-yellow balloon.

Jennifer was beside Adriana, and from what Thomas could see, it appeared as if she was wearing just the slightest of smiles, though, at this distance, he couldn't be sure. He also believed that her smile appeared just after Jennifer had turned and looked his way, making Thomas wonder if Jennifer could see him. He realized that if she could, then the bandits might be able to as well, and he pulled back even more into the shadows of the fern. Jennifer's smile grew for the briefest of moments, then quickly faded away, though her emotions appeared to be still filled with hope. They looked like a small fire, in colors of deep crimson, orange and gold.

"That's weird," Thomas whispered.

"What is?" Gemma asked.

"Well, most of our friends look surprisingly peaceful and calm, considering everything they've been through so far tonight," he replied.

"Hmm…that is strange. Any idea why? Maybe they're just holding onto whatever hope they can?"

"Yeah, could be. But…I don't know. It feels like something else is going on," Thomas said, turning his attention to the next captive in line.

This time, it was Sam. His expression was devoid of emotion, but the image that Thomas saw above him looked like a solid pillar of granite. It was incredibly dense and immobile. Sam had his eyes closed, but his lips, too, were moving, just as Francis' lips had been. Thomas was certain now that his friends were preparing for something. But what?

The last three captives were partially blocked from his view. He already knew that the person with her back to him, was Beth. Next to her, with only about one-quarter of his body in view, had to be Jeremiah. Thomas was able to determine that through the process of elimination; Jeremiah was the only male he hadn't yet counted. This left only one person, the one lying flat on the ground and currently being assisted by Beth. Again, since he had counted all the other women, so this one had to be Julianna. From what Thomas could see, he knew they would have to make a move soon. Taking a deep breath, he stepped back, then turned to his right.

"Any ideas, Gemma?" he asked worriedly.

"I just wish we could do something about the guns," Gemma responded.

"Maybe we can," Theresa said, flashing a quick smile, then promptly disappearing from view.

A slight rustle of the undergrowth indicated Theresa had moved away, but where she was going and what she was doing, Thomas could only guess.

"You know, I really wish she would stop doing that," Thomas grumbled softly, then rose to his feet. "Come on, Gemma. I bet I know what she's going to try, and I think I know how we can help."

Thomas reached out a hand to Gemma and helped her to her feet.

"So, what? We just storm into the clearing screaming our heads off or something?" she asked.

"No, nothing like that," Thomas replied, smiling. "But if I'm right about what Theresa has planned, we probably won't have to. You know when she's invisible, I can still see her, right? At least, I still see her emotions."

"No, I didn't know that. So, what's she doing?"

Thomas peered out from behind the fern once more, watching the image of Theresa's emotions as it moved slowly across the clearing.

"You see the three men who are guarding our friends?" Thomas asked, pointing.

"Yeah, I can see them," Gemma replied.

"Okay, there's the two on this side who are holding their rifles up, pointing them at our friends. And there's one more just on the other side of where Beth is. We can't see him from here, but trust me, he's there. I thought at first that his emotional image was just part of one of the shadows or the plants, but he's there."

"Oh, yeah. I can see a part of his camouflage jacket," Gemma shared.

"So, that leaves the final gunman, the one who shot me. And he's right over there," he said, pointing a different way. "See him? He's sitting sideways from where we are, but you can just make out his face."

"Okay, I got him."

"Look down a bit. See his hands?"

"They're empty," Gemma said after a moment. "Where's his gun?"

"It's resting against the trunk of that tree, close enough that he can grab it if something were to happen, but right now, he's trusting his men to stand guard, and he doesn't know that we're here."

"So…Theresa's going for his weapon?"

"That's what I would do if I was invisible."

"Okay, so what do we do?"

"If she is going for that guy's rifle, once he realizes it's not where he put it, I'm sure he'll call out to his men. When he does, all three of them should turn to look his way. And when they do, that's when I'll strike."

"You're not just going to run in there empty-handed, are you?" Gemma asked.

"Gemma, trust me. When I was younger, I got into a fight against this group of kids, five of them, all my age. They had tried to steal my bike. It was the first time I'd been in a fight like that. Something…strange happened. I think it's another part of these powers we have, I don't know. Anyway, I was able to see things happen before they did. Like, I knew when one of the kids was about to throw a punch and I knew exactly what to do to block it or get out of the way. I'll be fine," he said.

"So, what do I do? I'm not going to just sit here and watch!" she whispered harshly.

"No, you're not. You're going to untie our friends. We might be outnumbered right now, but once Theresa gets that rifle, and if I can knock one or two of the others out of the fight, I'm sure they'll surrender, especially if you can get a few of our friends free."

Gemma looked at him for a long moment.

"It sounds dangerous, Thomas."

"Yeah, of course it is. But I don't think we have much choice. We can't wait. We don't know how far it is to their camp, or wherever it is that they're headed. And we don't know how many more men with guns they might have waiting. Plus, we still don't know what was behind that earthquake! We have to do this now!"

After another moment of silent contemplation, Gemma nodded.

Thomas reached up and grasped her shoulders, giving them a gentle squeeze. He waited until she looked him in the eye, and then he poured as much confidence into his gaze as he could, hoping some of it would soak into Gemma, too.

"Okay, I want you to sneak over as close as you can get to our friends. Just be careful. Don't let the kidnappers see you, and whatever happens, don't leave the safety of the brush until you see me come out of the jungle on the left. I'm going to try and swing around so I can come up from behind that gunman on the far side," Thomas said, turning back to check on Theresa's progress. "We gotta move quickly, though. Theresa's almost reached her man."

CHAPTER FIFTEEN
THE BATTLE BEGINS

Theresa inched closer to her target. Her entire body was tense and alert. Her heart was beating so hard she could hear it. She hoped the man she was approaching couldn't. Though her footsteps made no sound on the lush, grassy ground, she still took them tentatively, moving like a jungle cat stalking prey. Just a few more seconds and she would have his rifle in her hands. She counted them off silently.

Five...

Staying in the shadows of the foliage, Thomas had circumnavigated the clearing, and was now on the opposite side of his captive friends. From this angle, the only one who was facing in his direction, was Beth. Thomas wasn't worried about Beth seeing him as he crept closer. Her focus was on helping Julianna. He watched as she poured water from a canteen onto a piece of cloth and gently wiped it over his sister's forehead and neck.

To his right he could see a twisting shape made of dark colors and sharp edges. That, he knew, was the emotional signature for Gemma. From his interpretation, he could tell she was nervous and tense, but not afraid. Across the clearing, he could barely make out the shadowy form that let him know where Theresa was, and from what he could tell, she was only a step or two away from the rifle. It was time for him to strike.

Four...

It was one thing to fight against shadowy demons in the depths of the spiritual realm, it was another to face a real, physical, human threat; one that could damage more than just the strength of her faith. Gemma was nervous, but she was also resolute. These were her friends, and she owed it to them to do everything she could to set them free. Besides, she trusted Thomas. If he told her the risk was worth the effort, she had to believe that he was right.

As soon as she saw Thomas make his move, she would make hers. She let her mind drift just for a moment, picturing herself back in the castle she had built deep in her heart, the place where she kept her faith. In the safety of her dream-world, she donned her armor, once more taking on the role of The Paladin. Her only goal now was to defend, protect, and to heal, but if she had to take the life of one of the kidnappers in order to save her friends, she would. Gemma took a deep breath, knowing she was ready to do whatever was required of her.

Three...

Julianna was breathing comfortably, but she had yet to open her eyes. Whatever had happened to place her in the catatonic state she was in, Beth was unable to determine. It might have been the stress of watching as her brother was killed mercilessly, or could be nothing more than the exhaustion from a long day of work in the oppressive heat and humidity followed by the strain of this forced march they had been on. At least her vitals appeared to be normal, or as normal as Beth could tell without medical equipment to measure them. All she could do now was provide as much general aid as she could, and hope her young friend would recover soon.

She could tell the men were getting anxious to be on the move once more, and, to be honest, so was she. When they were up and moving, the four gunmen were spread apart, taking positions to the front, rear, and each side of the shuffling group of teens. The further their captors spread out, the better chance she had of protecting herself and her friends. But when they were standing at random positions, some very close to the teens and some much farther away, it would be harder for her to do what she was planning. Even so, at some point, she would have to take a risk. What she needed was something to distract the four men, even for just a moment.

Then, a slight movement at the edge of the jungle caught her eye. There, in the shadows of the forest, she saw Gemma unexpectedly appear, stepping cautiously away from the protection of the foliage, and moving directly towards the closest gunman she could reach. Though Beth couldn't be certain, it looked like Gemma was bathed in some form of phosphorescent light. At that moment, Beth knew the time had come. Laying aside the wet cloth she had been using to keep Julianna cool, she prepared to fight.

Two...

Her moment had come. Julianna could feel it. There were so many subtle changes in the energy surrounding her that she had trouble determining what was going on; she only knew that something had happened, something she could take advantage of. The act she had been playing had provided her with the opportunity to feed her power with every ounce of anger she had ever buried deep within her soul. If she fed her power even an ounce more, she would run the risk that her power would spill over, and her hands would begin to glow. She couldn't risk that. It would not only prove she wasn't as invalid as she was pretending to be, it would also give her captors time to respond, and possibly even strike first. Julianna wouldn't let that happen.

As she began to open her eyes, she silently thanked Beth for the help she had provided. The cold, water-soaked cloth Beth had placed on her forehead had helped her stay calm and focused. She would need that when she released her power on the man who killed her brother. Though she knew she would kill him, she didn't want to do it right away. She wanted him to suffer as much as she had before she would let him die. If it was up to her, he would be sent to his grave with the knowledge that it was a teenage girl who had sent him there.

At that moment, she felt Beth's energy become tense. Her eyes flickering open, Julianna began to move.

One...

Juan Carlos froze, his entire body becoming anxious. Something, or someone, was coming; he could feel it. Danger was something he had always been able to sense. Knowing where an attack would come from before it arrived had kept him alive more than once. This time, the danger he felt was different than anything he had felt before. There was more than one threat, and they seemed to be coming from all around.

The most imminent danger, Juan Carlos knew, was from directly behind; and it was close, way to close for comfort. Moving just his eyes, he checked that his rifle was still within reach. It was. The weapon was resting against the trunk of the tree exactly where he had placed it, and it was well within his reach. From his current position, he knew he could grab the rifle, stand up, aim, and fire; all within a span of fewer than two seconds. That much, he was sure of. He had practiced the maneuver over and over again, until he believed there was no way he could be any faster. He would be ready when the attack came. His only concern now was, which threat should he take out first?

The battle begins…

Theresa reached for the rifle, her hands grasping the stock a mere second before Juan Carlos grabbed the barrel. With lightning speed the man leaped to his feet, not even loosening his grip, then planted his feet as he began to claim the weapon for his own. Theresa, too, set her feet, then tightened her grip and threw all of her strength into making the rifle hers. The two began pulling and twisting the weapon savagely, trying to wrench it free from the other's hands.

※

Thomas moved at incredible speed, rushing out from where he had been hiding, his powers feeding him images of the future that was soon to come. He saw Beth stand and raise her right hand, grasping at something in the air above her, then slam her fist back down on the ground. A circle of golden light spread out from where her hand struck the ground, spreading rapidly as it encompassed his captive friends.

※

Julianna leaped to her feet, her hands glowing violet-blue and her eyes seeking the one target she wanted most of all. A moment later, she saw him. He was halfway across the clearing, standing with his back towards her. She could see his hands were wrapped tightly on the barrel of his rifle, but it looked as if he was struggling to wrestle the weapon away from someone, but Julianna could see no one there! She wanted to watch a moment longer, just to see what he would do, but her power begged to be released, and she complied. With a primal scream, she released a blast of energy at the man for whom she felt nothing but hate. The two gunmen closest to her heard her scream and raised their rifles, their eyes wild with fear.

※

Thomas took out the closest gunman, the one called Matias, by diving feet first towards the man's left leg. At the speed he was moving, the full weight of his body crashed into the man's knee with a sickening crunch. Matias' leg dislocated and bent as both the tibia and fibula bones shattered. He began to fall, but then, with the skill and reflexes of a trained soldier, Matias spun in midair, pointing and firing the rifle in the direction Thomas had come from. But Thomas wasn't there, and the bullets flew harmlessly into the jungle.

After sliding through Matias' leg, Thomas dug his feet into the ground, providing enough leverage for his body to pop upright, like a baseball player stealing a base. Once vertical, he spun in a half-circle, ending up behind the gunman as Matias had spun and fired his weapon as he fell. Thomas kicked his right leg forward, connecting with the back of Matias' head. The gunman went limp, his rifle falling uselessly away.

Across the clearing, Theresa was losing the struggle against Juan Carlos. The man was just too strong. Just as she was about to give up, a glowing, violet-blue ball of flame slammed into Juan Carlos' back, lifting him off his feet and launching him through the air. Though he landed hard on the ground, Theresa watched him climb quickly back to his feet. She changed her grip on the rifle, becoming visible as she did, and then turned his way, aiming the rifle at his head.

The moment Theresa reappeared, holding Juan Carlos' rifle like she knew what to do with it, Julianna froze, unsure that she had witnessed what she believed she had just seen. A moment later, a curtain of golden light washed over her, then spread quickly until it covered half of the clearing. The light was so bright and dense that she was unable to see anything on the other side. Somehow she knew, if she stayed where she was, she would be safe. But she wasn't done. She knew the blast had struck Juan Carlos, but she had restricted her power for that first assault, sending only enough energy to knock him from his feet. There was more she wanted to do to him, and the golden dome was in her way. Julianna set her shoulders, and walked out of the dome with the confidence of a prizefighter entering the ring.

Thomas had spun around and was heading towards his next target when he caught the sight of Julianna walking away. He stopped for just a moment and called out her name, but she either didn't hear him, or she didn't care. Her energy was darker than Thomas had ever seen it before and he was suddenly afraid, but before he could go after her, he heard his own name called. He turned towards the sound to find Beth kneeling nearby, her right fist pressed on the ground.

Thomas looked at the spot where Beth's fist had struck the ground, realizing that was the point where the mysterious golden light was coming from. A thin pillar of light shot straight up, about ten feet in the air, then it cascaded back to earth like a fountain, creating a perfect circle that was growing even wider as he watched. He looked at Beth, and she at him, her face twisting with a look of confusion and surprise as her mind wrestled with the fact that he was somehow still alive. He smiled at her, and casually winked.

"Long story, Beth. I'll explain later," he said loudly over his shoulder as he spun back around and rushed towards the next foe.

※

Beth watched Thomas as he moved with incredible speed towards one of the two remaining gunmen, both of whom had spun their rifles his way. Before the first gunman could take aim and fire, Thomas was on him. She watched him jump high in the air, spin a full summersault, and then come back down, both feet striking the man on his left shoulder and chest. The gunman grunted as the air was driven from his lungs, the impact twisting him sideways and knocking him backward at the same time. She saw Thomas land in a crouched position, and quickly chop his right hand down on the side of the man's head. Beth could see the man go limp, and she knew he was out of the fight. Thomas stood up, then turned to face the final opponent.

From where Beth was standing, it didn't look like Thomas could make it in time. She could see the man's finger pull the trigger, and she started to scream. But before the sound crossed over her lips, the strangest thing happened. A knight in glowing armor came crashing through the side of the protective dome. The shimmering cavalier slammed into the back of the gunman, knocking his aim off just enough to send the bullet whizzing past Brother Thomas' head. Though the bullet caught the edge of Thomas' ear, drawing a thin red line that began to ooze blood, the gunman had missed!

For a moment, Beth just stood there, gaping at the scene, with a dozen questions running through her mind. Where had the knight come from? How was Thomas still alive? What were those blue fireballs that had shot forth from Julianna's hands?

As the questions continued to flood in with no answers forthcoming, the knight, who was rising back to its feet, raised its head, and Beth burst with joy.

"Gemma!" she exclaimed, her mouth stretching into a wide smile.

Gemma smiled, pushing her long, raven-black hair from her face. She gave Beth a friendly wink, then walked over to the gunman she had just knocked to the ground and placed her foot on his back.

"Nice work, Gemma. I'm glad you didn't have to bring me back from the dead again," Thomas quipped with a grin as he walked up and disarmed the man Gemma was holding down.

"Oh my God, right?" Gemma playfully joked, "Twice in one day was enough!"

"Well, technically, I don't think the second time counts. I wasn't dead. I was *mostly* dead."

"True!" Gemma laughed as she drew the Sword of the Spirit from its sheath at her side and placed the tip on the back of the man she was holding down, about where his heart should be.

"You got 'em, Gemma?" Thomas asked, tossing an assortment of weapons he had collected near the center of the golden dome.

"Yeah, I got this. Go help Theresa."

Thomas nodded, starting to turn away, then quickly looked back. "And, seriously, thanks again."

"Don't mention it," Gemma replied.

With that, Thomas darted out through the walls of the golden dome and was gone.

※

"Hey, Jennifer," Gemma called, knowing that the young woman could translate what she wanted to say to the man she was guarding with her sword.

When Jennifer didn't respond, Gemma turned to look over her shoulder. Seven faces looked back at her with a mixture of expressions. Shock, amazement, surprise. Strangely, though, none appeared in disbelief, even with the display they had just witnessed.

"Jennifer?" Gemma called again, this time capturing the young woman's attention.

"Oh, sorry. I was just thinking," Jennifer replied.

"Yeah? About what?" Gemma inquired.

"Where in Heaven's name you found that outfit!" Jennifer said, grinning.

"Oh, you like it? Just something I picked up," Gemma replied, then with a more serious tone, asked, "Can you translate something for me?"

"Yeah, sure. What do you want me to say?"

"Let this guy know if he moves, even blinks, I'll drive this sword straight through his heart."

"Are you serious? You'd do that?" Jennifer inquired, obviously a bit taken back.

Gemma turned her head so Jennifer could see her face, then gave her a quick wink.

"Of course not," she whispered, "but he doesn't know that, right?"

"Oh, yeah, right!" Jennifer responded with a mischievous twinkle in her eye. "I'd be more than happy to translate that."

After Jennifer translated, Gemma turned her attention to Beth.

"Any way you can come check him for weapons? He's gotta have a knife on him somewhere. We can use it to set the rest of our group free."

CHAPTER SIXTEEN
A HERO FALLS

Thomas stepped through the wall of the golden dome, wondering what he might find on the outside. The moment he crossed to the outside, he froze, not at all expecting what he found. There, a few yards away, the Endlessly Dying Girl was lying on the ground, writhing in pain. Standing over her and blasting her with bolts of violet-blue electric fire, was his sister. From what Thomas could see, Julianna was more than upset; she was absolutely livid. Her eyes were wild with fury, and her mouth was twisted in a snarl.

"What happened to her?" Thomas wondered as he rushed to Theresa's aid.

When he was close enough, he could make out the words Julianna was growling as she continued to blast Theresa's thrashing body.

"If I say he's going to die…"

Another blast of electric fire leaped from her hands, and Theresa screamed.

"…then he's going to die!"

Another blast. Another scream.

"No one can stop me."

Blast.

"Not you…"

Zap.

"…not Thomas…"

Crack.

"…not even God!"

With those words, the flashes of violet-blue flames began to flow in a constant stream, and Theresa's screams became desperate as she writhed in agony on the ground. Thomas could tell that Theresa was fighting for her life.

"Julianna!" he screamed, trying to capture his sister's attention.

"He killed Thomas! He killed Thomas!" Julianna was shrieking again and again as she poured even more power into the stream. Thomas saw Theresa's eye roll back in her head, and her body go limp.

Thomas breathed in deeply, and then bellowed as loud as he could, "Julianna! Stop!"

Julianna froze, then turned her head his way. Thomas saw the emotional shape above her change rapidly, going from one that appeared like a tornado, to one that looked jumbled and confused. Shock, relief, surprise, and elation all seemed to spill forth at once. Julianna's expression changed, too. The desperate, angry glare in her eyes melted as she stared at the brother she had thought she had lost.

"Thomas?" she asked skeptically, her eyes reflecting a hint of disbelief. "Is that you?"

"Yeah. It's me," Thomas replied, holding his hands at his sides. "Please, Julianna, leave Theresa alone. She's not the one you're angry with."

Julianna stared at him as he began slowly moving towards her. From the corner of his eye, he saw Juan Carlos' body lying still, and considered that the man might already be dead.

Suddenly the look in Julianna's eyes changed from disbelief to fear.

"No!" she screamed. "It can't be! It can't be you! You're a ghost! I watched you die!"

"I know you did. And I'm sorry you had to go through that. But I'm not dead. I promise you. Gemma saved me. She has a power, just like you do, Julianna. And like Theresa does, too."

Julianna took a step back, her eyes darting from Thomas, to Theresa, to Juan Carlos, and back. Thomas could tell by the fiercely twisting shape of her emotions that she was close to a breakdown. Somehow, he had to get her to calm down.

"I have a power too, Jules. We're the same. You, me, Theresa, Gemma, Beth. We're all the same."

"I don't believe you. You're dead. You're dead," Julianna muttered as she continued to back away, her fingers clawing at the skin of her arms, leaving deep crimson scratches behind.

"I know that's what you saw, and I did die, but I'm not dead anymore. I swear to you. It's me. It's Thomas!"

Julianna began a wild, cackling laugh as the emotional shape above her split in two, then sputtered and spun, showering invisible sparks into the air. She raised her arms, her hands bright with electric flames, and her eyes locked on Thomas' face.

"You're...not...REAL!" she screamed, sending two balls of electric fire at her brother.

Thomas flinched, preparing for the pain about to come; but it never did. Slowly, he cracked one eye open. The twin balls of violet-blue fire were inches away. He flinched again, but again, there was no pain.

"Don't worry, Brother Thomas," he heard someone say. "I got 'em."

Thomas turned towards the voice, seeing that the golden dome Beth had created—shielding herself and her friends—was gone, and all of his friends were now free.

Brendan and Terence were carrying one of the unconscious kidnappers. The other two gunmen were sitting with their backs to each other, their hands behind their backs. Thomas noticed his friends had also bound the gunmen's feet. Francis and Adriana were guarding the two who were sitting up, and Thomas could see they were using the same weapons the men had been pointing at his friends not more than five minutes ago. Jeremiah, whose voice it was he had heard, was slowly walking forward, his hands extended out, palms to the front.

Thomas turned to look at the violet-blue fireballs his sister had thrown. His curiosity got the better of him, and he reached out to touch them.

"I wouldn't do that, Brother Thomas. They may not be moving right now, but they're still just as powerful," Jeremiah said. "Maybe you should move out of the way, and I'll let them go."

Thomas took a few sideways steps, not once taking his eyes off the two flaming balls. When he was no longer in their path, Jeremiah dropped his hands, and the fireballs sped off towards the jungle. A moment later an explosion of vegetation burst into the air.

"By the way, welcome back," Jeremiah said, stretching out his hand.

Thomas took the offered hand, but rather than just shake it, he pulled Jeremiah in close, wrapping his arm around the young man's shoulder and hugging him tightly. He held him for a moment, then let go, but kept his hands on Jeremiah's shoulders.

"So, you're a superhero, too?" he asked.

"Yeah, I guess so," Jeremiah replied.

Thomas smiled, then turned back towards his sister. Julianna was staring at him, still in disbelief.

"It's really you?" she asked again, her eyes twitching unconsciously.

"Yeah, Sis. It's me," he replied, opening his arms as if to give her a hug.

Julianna's face broke into a smile, and she began to slowly move towards Thomas. Then, a sound from behind her caused her to stop, and she quickly glanced over her shoulder. The sound had come from Juan Carlos, who was slowly climbing to his feet, obviously wracked with a great amount of pain.

"Oh no! You're not going anywhere!" Julianna growled, her smile fading away, only to be replaced by a venomous, evil grin.

Stumbling weakly and dragging one obviously broken leg, Juan Carlos hobbled towards the potential safety of the trees. He wouldn't get that far. Thomas saw the jumble of confused emotions spinning in the air above Julianna rapidly become like a tornado once more. Then, her shoulders dropped and her hands clenched into fists. She flexed her arms in a powerful, downward thrust, and her hands again burst into flames. Julianna raised one hand high, thrusting it forward and sending a blast of violet-blue fire at Juan Carlos. The blast slammed into the ground by his feet, lifting his bruised and broken body ten feet in the air. He slammed back to the ground with a crunch, the air in his lungs escaping in a loud gasp.

"Jules! Don't! Trust me, it's not worth it!" Thomas yelled after her.

"Don't stop me. This is the guy who killed you. It's his turn to die!" she replied.

"No, Jules. That's not what we do!"

"Maybe it's not what *you* do, Brother," she said with a sneer, "but I'm not you."

Thomas moved quickly, hoping to get between Juan Carlos and his sister before Julianna reached the injured man. He knew words would no longer make a difference; her tornado of emotions told him that Julianna was no longer in control.

As he moved her way, he heard Brendan shout, "Jeremiah! Can you freeze people, like you just froze those fireballs Julianna was throwing?"

"Yeah, but not for long," Jeremiah said, taking a few steps forward and raising his hands, his palms facing Julianna, who was nearly on top of Juan Carlos.

"When I say, freeze Julianna," Brendan said.

Juan Carlos was cowering on the ground, his hands held out in front of him as a last measure of defense. From the few words that Thomas was able to translate, he could tell the man was pleading for his life. Still, his sister raised her arms, the flames in her hands leaping and crackling with unbridled power, and her face twisted with fury as she prepared to deliver the final blow.

"Now!" Brendan screamed, and Julianna froze.

A half-second later, Thomas heard a *pop* and was surprised to see Brendan standing next to Juan Carlos. The young man knelt down and placed his hand on Juan Carlos' shoulder, and the two disappeared, making the same *pop* sound once more.

"Okay, Jeremiah. We got him," Brendan called out from somewhere behind Thomas.

"Should I let Julianna go?" Jeremiah asked.

"Yes, that's fine," Thomas replied as he turned to face his sister once more.

Jeremiah lowered his hands, and Julianna's arms slashed forward, fire belching from her arms as she cut a deep furrow in the ground…right where Juan Carlos had been. She took two steps before she realized her target was no longer there. Her arms dropped to her sides as she began to search around.

"What the heck?" she growled, turning to look at Thomas. "Where is he?"

"We moved him. I'm not going to let you hurt him any more than you already have."

Julianna spun around, her fury still demanding a target. She spied where Brendan and Juan Carlos had moved to, and she raised her hands, sending a stream of energy their way. A moment before the blast struck, the pair disappeared again, and the blast struck empty ground, causing an explosion of dirt and grass. Julianna screamed, her head swiveling back and forth while she searched for where the pair had moved. Spotting them again, she fired once more, and again she watched them disappear, the blast striking the empty ground. Julianna howled with rage.

Thomas stared at his sister, wondering what had changed her into the monster she now was. He had never seen her behave in this way before, and it scared him.

"It's over, Jules," Thomas stated. "Please, calm down so we can talk."

She spun in his direction.

"I don't want to hurt you, Thomas, but if you don't let me do this, then I'll kill you, too!" Julianna threatened, turning towards Juan Carlos once more.

She raised her hands, her power was overflowing, and sparks were showering to the ground.

"No, Julianna, you won't. I won't let you hurt this man, or your brother, either," Brendan stated flatly. "I can teleport as often as I need to protect them. Your brother is right. This isn't what we do."

"Fine. Then you can die with your new friend!" she shouted, blasting forth a stream of energy once more, only to see it strike bare ground for the third time.

"I'm serious, Jules," Brendan said from somewhere behind her. "We don't murder."

"Who is this *we* you're talking about?" she snarled, turning towards the sound of his voice.

"I think he's talking about me," Adriana said as she stepped between Julianna and Brendan, then crossed her arms over her chest as a soft, pink halo appeared, floating just over her head.

"He's talking about me, too," said Jennifer, her eyes now glowing a brilliant blue as she moved to stand next to Adriana.

"I don't want to fight you, Julianna, but I know your brother and Brendan are right," Sam stated as he took a spot on the other side of Adriana.

As soon as he did, Thomas saw bright green tendrils, like roots, extending from Sam's legs near his knees. The tendrils thrust downward into the dirt, securing him to the ground.

"It's the same for me, too, Julianna," Francis announced, his entire body cloaked in a shadowy mist as he joined the group. "It's one thing to fight for our freedom, or in defense, but it's another to seek revenge. I haven't known you long, but I honestly don't believe this is the real you."

"Sorry, Jules, but you know they're right," Beth said as she, too, joined the group.

Two pairs of golden discs were revolving around Beth's hands as she added herself to the wall of people that were now standing between Julianna and the man she wanted to kill.

Terence was next, his entire being bathed in bright, white light as he stood next to Beth.

"I agree, kid," Terence sighed. "If we act like them, then we're no better than they are."

Jeremiah was the eighth hero to join the group, saying, "You'll have to count me in, too."

And Gemma was the ninth, though she said nothing, and simply took her place in the line, letting her actions speak for her.

Behind the wall of heroes, Brendan now stood up. He came around to the front of the group, then stood at the center. The rest of the group closed around him, each one placing a hand on his shoulder or arm.

"So, what's it going to be, Julianna? You're either with us, or you're against," Brendan plainly said. "You can't blast us all."

Julianna stared them down, her breathing heavy and slow, and her face twisted with anger. Thomas could tell she was wondering if Brendan was telling the truth, and if he could teleport the entire group away if she attacked. Then, before anyone moved, a rustling sound came from Thomas' left, and he turned to see Theresa rising slowly to her feet.

"Theresa!" he called out. "You're okay!"

"Of course I'm okay, Brother Thomas," Theresa said, walking slowly over to join the group. "I'm the Endlessly *Dying* Girl, not the Oh No, She's *Dead* Girl."

Thomas smirked as Theresa limped over to take her place in line, then she turned to face Julianna.

"Please, don't do this, Jules," Theresa pleaded, her voice weak and shallow. "I haven't known you long, but I know enough about you to know that this isn't you. Please, Jules. Stand with us, not against."

Theresa stretched out her hand, her eyes begging Julianna to take hold of it. A moment later, Beth stretched out her hand as well, followed by Terence, Adriana, Jennifer, and Sam. Then, the last four did the same.

"We're here for you, Jules," Beth quietly said. "Come, join us. Let us help you figure this out."

Though none of the others spoke, the look in their eyes shared a similar message; they were concerned for Julianna, and they wanted to help. Thomas smiled as he looked over the group of ten young men and women standing before him. These were the Guardians he had been sent to find. He wanted to stand with them, but he knew he had to help his sister first. He knew he was the eleventh Guardian, and deep down, he knew that Julianna was the twelfth. She just had to be. If only he could figure out a way to get her to see that.

When he turned back to face his sister, the emotional symbol above her was changing shape and color so fast it was impossible to read. He knew she was struggling to reach a decision, and he knew there was nothing that he could do. It was up to her now. She had to be the one to make the choice. Julianna would either join them, or she would stand against them. He prayed she would join them, but his heart told him that his prayer might not get answered. At least not tonight.

※

Julianna fumed. She hadn't expected this. She thought the group gathered before her would want to see the kidnappers pay for what they had done. She thought that they, too, would want revenge; for shooting Thomas, for slamming the butt of a rifle into Terence's face, and for knocking her violently to the ground. But they didn't want revenge. In fact, they were so far on the other side of where she thought they would be, that they were choosing to support their kidnappers, rather than one of their own. Even Theresa, the one person she felt like she had developed a friendship with, had stepped up to defend the four despicable, horrible, evil men.

Rage filled her as she growled, "How can you do this? These men hurt all of you just as much as they hurt me! How can you want to protect them now?"

No one spoke at first, though a few began to shift positions as if uncomfortable with her questions. Finally, Beth stepped forward.

"Like Brendan said, Julianna, we don't do this. It's not what our powers are for," she began, speaking softly. "Sure, we needed to use them to escape, and in so doing, our captors got hurt. But we can heal them now that we're free. Besides, we're not protecting the men; we're protecting ourselves."

Julianna huffed, showing her immaturity, then turned her eyes away as they began to flood with tears. She blinked a few times, trying to drive the tears away, then turned back.

"How?" she squeaked.

"How?" Beth echoed, looking confused.

"How are you protecting yourselves?"

She watched as Beth took in a deep breath, steadying herself for a moment.

"You're right to be angry at them. And it's normal to want revenge, but think what you would be doing if you acted on those feelings."

"I'd be giving them exactly what they deserve," she groaned, clenching her jaw.

"Maybe," Beth said, still keeping her voice soft. "Maybe they do deserve it. But is that our choice to make? Are we the ones who are meant to judge?"

"If not us, then who?" Julianna asked, feeling like she was losing control. "And don't you dare say God!"

She turned away for a moment, her hands balling into fists. When she turned back, the anger and hate had returned to her eyes.

"When my father beat my mother nearly to death, where was God? If He's the only one who can judge, then He must have hated my mom if He let that happen to her. I don't care what you say, I can't believe in a loving, kind, forgiving God. Not when he lets something like that happen. He doesn't care, and he sure as hell isn't going to do anything to these men for what they did. So why shouldn't we be the ones to judge them?"

"Because that would make us just like them, and we're better than that, Jules. You're better than that, too. You know you are," Beth said, barely whispering.

Julianna locked eyes with Beth, seeing nothing but compassion and concern. Yet, as hard as she tried, she couldn't see the truth in Beth's words. She couldn't see how hurting these men who had hurt her would make her like them. In her mind, it would make her better than them; more powerful, too. And why was her brother just standing there, saying nothing? Why was Beth the one who was trying to convince her?

Suddenly, she looked at her brother, for the first time realizing how much he looked like their father. At that moment, Julianna no longer had the ability to care for herself, or for others. Her compassion had been pushed so far deep inside her, she couldn't reach it anymore. It was the same with her kindness, her generosity, and her ability to love. Everything good vanished. All she had left, was hate. And though she wanted nothing more than to obtain the revenge she was so desperate to have, she knew she was outnumbered. There was only one choice left.

"Fine. If you don't care enough about what those men did to us, then you can all go to Hell!" she screamed at the group, letting her power flood into her hands.

This time, rather than using her power against another person, she sent the streams of energy downward, blasting a huge chunk of dirt into the air, leaving behind an impressive crater. While her ex-friends turned to shield themselves from the shower of dirt and rocks, Julianna turned and ran the other way, heading towards the jungle. She didn't know where she was going, she just knew she needed to get away.

※

At the edge of the darkness, Furcas stood, watching and waiting as the events played out. There, in the midst of these spiritually powered young adults, was the man that he, too, wanted dead. Silently he had hoped the furious young brunette would succeed in her quest; he considered that it would actually be fun to see a man with a reputation like Juan Carlos, being bested by a tiny little thing like Julianna. It would be almost poetic.

But, she hadn't been successful, and now, the rest of the heroes had learned the secret that Furcas had been sent four years ago to stop; that they were The Guardians of Zion, a powerful force for the forces of righteousness in a world that was so close to tipping forever the other way. Earning his place back in Hell would be very difficult now. He had but one option left.

"Come, Gauerdi," he said, slyly grinning. "Looks as though someone is in need of a new friend."

The mighty steed tossed his head and whinnied, then stomped one hoof on the ground.

"Aye! This would be a good time to call forth the demons I command, before we lose them to Ose. Shall we see if they still answer?"

Gauerdi pawed at the ground again, tossing his head in affirmation.

Furcas grinned, then turned his head and spat at the ground. He watched the acidic fluid sizzle and foam, just as it had done four years ago. The difference this time, was that this ground had not been blessed. This was not good soil, not like that which had surrounded the retreat center, the place he had first faced off against a much younger, and a far less confident, Thomas.

A dark, black foam boiled out of the ground and began to gain shape, taking the form of a large shadow-sprite. As the foam continued to bubble, the sprite stood, stepped out of the slowly growing mud puddle, and then the sprite bowed to his Lord.

Furcas waved off the show of reverence, knowing there was no true respect behind the gesture. Shadow-sprites would just as soon turn against him if they believed he had become weak. Such was the way of the underworld. No creature was ever safe, not even from their own kind.

"So, you're The First?" Furcas questioned.

The title referred to the shadow-sprite who was granted an ability to lead other sprites, like those who were rapidly coming forth as the sizzling foam produced yet another sprite, and then a third. The First hissed an affirmative reply.

"Good, good. When ten thousand demons stand ready, you may attack. But, hear this, you worthless bag of vapor, do not kill the one who carries the cross. You are free to do as you wish with all of the others, but leave the cross-bearer alone. I want him distracted and despondent, not slaughtered. Understand?"

The First hissed again, bowing once more.

"Ten thousand only! Not one shadow more!"

Another hiss sounded, followed by another bow. Furcas turned to Gauerdi and grasped the horn of the saddle. He placed his foot in a stirrup, and then swung his other leg over top of the mighty beast. He drove his heels deep into Gauerdi's sides, and the horse lurched forward, quickly gathering speed. Behind him, the number of shadow-sprites was nearly a thousand strong, and increasing rapidly. Furcas knew it wouldn't be long before they launched their attack.

CHAPTER SEVENTEEN
SILENCE BEFORE THE STORM

Father Dominic glanced at his watch, his mouth sliding to the left side of his face in a half-frown.

"They should be back by now," he puzzled internally, wondering why Thomas and the rest of the group hadn't made it back to the camp yet. They should have completed their meal over two hours ago, and it wasn't that long of a drive back up the hill.

Rising from his cot, he took one more look at his watch, as if to ensure he had read the time correctly the first time, then looked around his room, which, though dim and dusty, was comfortable. What little light there was came from two lanterns burning in opposite corners of the small room; their flames casting shadows that danced along the bare plywood walls. Father Dominic stood still, listening more with his heart than his ears, seeking any sign of the young man that he had had the pleasure to watch mature over the past four years. Though he stretched the limit of his power, there was only the somber hum of the gas in the lamps being converted to light, and the shallow, barely-audible rumblings of a pending dismay.

The tiny hairs at the base of his skull began to twitch, and his half-frown became full. He moved to the center of the room, then paused, extending his arms out to the sides. With a quick breath, Father Dominic began to turn in slow circles as he waited for even the slightest twitch from the hairs on his forearms; his most trusted 'early warning system.' While he turned, he occasionally sniffed at the air, trying to detect any strange scent the slight breeze might be carrying.

There!

With his arms pointing almost perfectly east and west, the vibration of the hairs became a constant buzz, and a faint, foul odor met his nose. Father Dominic's lip snarled, and a low growl rumbled in his throat. He shook his head, clearing the sour smell. He could no longer deny it; something was wrong. But, then again, he had been expecting something like this would happen. He knew Satan and his army of demons were going to come sooner or later; he just wished that he and his young volunteers weren't four-thousand miles from home.

A violent shiver came over him, like a dog shedding water after a bath, and he felt a bit faint. He needed to get outside, clear the stench from his nose, and feel the light of the moon and stars. Checking his watch once more, he knew the adults in the camp nearby might still be awake, though none should be outdoors. The mosquitos were plentiful at this time of night, and the volunteers knew to avoid those pests as best they could. But with what Father Dominic had just sensed, he had no choice but to head outside, travelling deep into the jungle where the annoying, blood-thirsty insects would be the least of the dangers he would face. With a sigh, Father Dominic stepped into the night.

He walked the short distance to the spot in the road where he had tossed the set of car keys to Thomas. The twin tracks were still visible where Thomas had let the tires spin in the gravel before driving away. Again, he took a moment to sniff at the air, wondering if he could tell where the car was now. As he did, his ears perked up, straining to pick out any sounds that didn't belong in the symphony of the night. Nothing seemed out of place. He had stood in this same spot a hundred times before, listening to the world of nature around him. This was his most favorite time each evening, and, other than the gathering insects, one of his favorite places to stand. Though the air was not cool, it was not nearly as overbearing as it had been during the day.

With a frown, Father Dominic turned back towards his room. He was about to take a step when he felt a gentle tug, just at the edge of his thoughts. With a soft smile, he lowered himself to the ground, crossed his legs, and let his mind drift on the gentle evening breeze. Slowly, his consciousness reached for the source of the tug, and he closed his eyes. Almost immediately, his perceptions began to change.

At first there was nothing but an impenetrable darkness so thick he could feel it as it washed over him. Then, he and the darkness merged. Surrendering to the experience, Father Dominic focused on the one thing still connecting him to the physical world: his five senses. He felt the weight of his clothing against his skin, smelled the rich earth he sat upon, heard the soft breeze that brushed through his thinning hair. Though the darkness that was pulling at him felt as if it was coming from above, he knew that, too, was just a perception. Where he was going, none of the sensations of direction were real. They were only trappings of his mind, and as such, he knew how to control them. By changing his perceptions, he could change his world, allowing him to travel farther than he ever could in the physical domain. Through the power of meditation, he could enter any realm he wished, even one that only existed far beyond the most distant star.

Where he was heading was the one realm where true magic existed, the place where miracles were born. It was the realm of pure spiritually, the world of the angels and the saints. He had been here before, dozens if not hundreds of times, and yet, the feeling of awe and wonder that flowed through his veins would never become commonplace or dull. He always felt the same; like a young child on Christmas morning. It was his most favored feeling of all.

Dominic spent a few moments basking in the warm, inner feelings of the moment, allowing the sensation to wash away any worries or concerns. Every cell in his body tingled with anticipation and delight. Then, he let go, allowing his connection to the physical realm to fade away. In the depths of his mind, his consciousness now enveloped in his spiritual self. Father Dominic opened his eyes. The jungle was gone.

In its place was a world beyond description, a realm built from fantasy, and from dreams. A marvelous vista spread before him, filled with a golden light. A wide, azure stream flowed peacefully amidst gently rolling hills blanketed with grasses of green and gold, while colorful blossoms dotted the land like cupcake sprinkles. This was the place where life had first begun. It was the place where creation and love prevailed. Here, there was no death, no mourning, no sadness or despair. This was Paradise, Eden, and Heaven all in one.

"Welcome home, my son," a buoyant voice sounded from just behind him.

Father Dominic turned to find a small, stone bench, upon which sat a man that Father Dominic knew well. It was his namesake, his mentor, the man whose life he admired for the depth of faith through which it had been lived. A man whose deeds he knew well. It was this man who had been the source of the tug he had felt, and he bowed deeply to show his respect.

"Saint Dominic! Once again, you honor me with your call," Father Dominic said.

"Come, come. There is no need for praise, not directed towards one such as I. Save your praise for the Redeemer," Saint Dominic tendered, tapping the bench next to him. "Come. Sit. We have much to discuss."

The priest did as requested, moving slowly, and yet with purpose. As he lowered himself onto the bench, he took one last wonder-filled glance at the vista before him, then turned and faced the saint.

"Is it here? Is this the night you predicted would come? The Awakening; has it begun?" he asked with an urgent desire.

Saint Dominic nodded.

"It is, and it has," he responded, placing his hand on top of the priest's shoulder. "Are you ready?"

"Is one ever ready to answer God's call? I know, if left to my own devices, I would never be."

Saint Dominic smiled, "Then, let's be glad you have your faith!"

A quiet moment passed as the two locked eyes. Father Dominic allowed the trust he saw in his mentor's eyes to strengthen his resolve. He knew the gravity of what he was about to undertake, that this could be the last time he would see Paradise. If he failed in his quest, then the Guardians might fail, too. And, if they failed, it would launch the start of an era the world hadn't seen since the time of the Inquisitions and the Crusades, the era of Saladin and Genghis Khan, and the Albigensian threat; a time of great darkness and fear.

Though, it had also been a time of great triumph, for this was the era when the first Guardians were born. Led by Pope Saint Gregory VII, the original Guardians included pious and revered men and women, such as Francis of Assisi, and the sisters Agnes and Clare. Bernard of Clairvaux, Hildegard of Bingen, Albert of Vercelli, Bernard of Quintavalle, Margaret of Scotland, Angelus of Jerusalem, Elizabeth of Hungary, and Simon Stock had been members, too. And, of course, Dominic de Guzman, the man with whom Father Dominic currently shared the stone bench. The first Guardians were responsible for the crafting of religious orders and relics used to fight against the powers of hell. The Franciscans, the Carmelites, the Dominicans; even the rosary had been born from the work of the first Guardians, most of whom were venerated, and some who had been canonized as saints.

Now, nearly one-thousand years later, a new generation of Guardians had been born, and Father Dominic had been granted the most sacred honor of all; to be their spiritual guide. As he sat next to one of the greatest of all Saints, the mortal and fully-human priest felt unsure of his ability to respond.

"You've worked hard to prepare yourself for this moment," Saint Dominic interrupted his thoughts. "Trust that your faith will guide and protect you. And trust in the powers of those you've been asked to lead. Their path is the more dangerous and difficult one. Do not let your ego cause you to believe otherwise."

Saint Dominic rose from the bench and walked to the edge of the surrounding lawn, stopping to gaze at a bush filled with Bleeding Hearts blossoms. He paused, drawing a branch heavily laden with blooms up close to his nose, and deeply breathed in their perfume.

"I just love a garden in bloom, don't you?" the Saint inquired as he gazed lovingly at the flowers.

"It is one of my favorite things," Father Dominic replied as he, too, stood and approached the plant. "But, unfortunately, I am far too anxious to tarry."

Saint Dominic nodded.

"Yes. You have a long journey ahead of you. And you must arrive on time. There are powerful forces at work. Do not for a moment let down your guard."

"That, I can promise," Father Dominic pledged, then nodded his head, and turned away.

As the colors of the lush panorama began to pale and fade, he heard Saint Dominic's voice call out.

"Remember, young Dominic, your strength lies not only in your faith in God, but in your faith of others, especially the young. Trust they will make the right decisions when their time comes."

With that, Father Dominic closed his eyes, letting the silent stillness of the dream-like world slip away. Slowly, the sounds of the jungle returned. Dominic breathed in deep, then stood and walked back to his room. There, leaning against the foot of his bed, was a large backpack, already bursting with supplies. He knew his journey would be a long one, but he had packed well. He placed the backpack over his shoulders, then clasped the supporting belt around his waist.

Next, he moved to the plywood table he used as a desk and drew out a single sheet of paper. On the page were written instructions for what he wanted the volunteers to do until he returned. He knew the men and women he had hired to run the construction would know what needed to be done far better than he did. Still, he didn't want them to worry, even though he knew full well that they would. They had all heard the rumors of a ruthless new group of smugglers operating in the area, and they were all worried their mission had caught the attention of these unjust men.

Father Dominic knew criminals such as these smugglers were never fans of progress, especially when that progress brought either education or religion to the indigenous tribes. And, since this mission would bring both, that would only double the smuggler's disdain. He knew they wouldn't hesitate to take action against him or his project if they could. And though the local authorities had been on his side so far, it was a tentative relationship, one that could easily be swayed with the right bribe.

He placed the document on the pillow of his bed, grabbed his favorite walking stick, and headed out into the night. Outside once more, Father Dominic glanced up at the night sky. There was a bright halo surrounding the full moon. And, though the image looked magical, he knew there was a scientific explanation for what he saw. Ice crystals were forming in the upper atmosphere. When enough crystals gathered, clouds would come.

He sniffed tentatively at the air, his nose curling upward as he picked up the nearly undetectable ozone smell. A storm was coming. Father Dominic adjusted the straps of his pack, and then extinguished the lamps. In the darkness of his room, he sighed, knowing it was going to be a long, long night.

※

Ten pairs of anxious eyes locked on Thomas, urging him to speak. He could tell they needed answers. But unfortunately, those answers would have to wait, at least for now. He was having trouble digesting everything that had happened so far this evening, and he needed a moment to think. Though it had only been five or six hours since the group had sat together in the restaurant sharing a meal, laughing and joking as if they hadn't a care in the world, it felt like months had passed. Thomas definitely felt as if he had aged, and quite a bit at that.

Since that meal, he had been shot, killed, and subsequently resurrected. He had traveled with Gemma and Theresa deep within the world of Gemma's spirituality where they had faced off against a demon hell-bent on preventing Gemma from becoming the hero she was meant to be. They had learned how to join their powers together, creating new powers they couldn't access on their own. Thomas had used one of those new powers to dive even deeper, into the very core of Gemma's faith.

There, he had been given a few hints of what the future would hold for himself and those around him now. Then, after returning to the physical domain, the three had undertaken a harrowing and exhausting journey through the most difficult terrain he had ever traversed. Finally, he had not only rescued his sister and the rest of the group, but had learned that every single one of his friends was a hero, too. Now, when everything had just started looking up, when the darkness felt as if it was about to lift, his sister had disappeared.

"Thomas?" Gemma inquired softly. "Are you okay? I'm so sorry about Julianna."

He looked at her for a long moment, afraid of sharing the only answer that he knew would be the truth. He couldn't tell her what he was feeling, not what was really going through his mind. The ten pairs of eyes currently looking at him didn't want to know that his heart was filled with doubt, or that once more he felt like running away. Not now. Not after all that they had been through so far tonight.

They needed a leader, someone with conviction, and someone to tell them where to go and what to do, not someone who wanted to be anywhere else but here. Part of him wished he could surround himself in the strength of Gemma's faith, or that he had Theresa's power to disappear. But he had only himself.

At least none of those gathered around him had the ability to see hidden truths, not like he could. He could only imagine the shape and colors his emotional display would be right now. But since they couldn't see it, then they wouldn't know if he was truly being strong, or just faking his way through. Thomas realized that he didn't have to be fearless and bold, he just had to pretend to be. Maybe that would be enough. Besides, he didn't have to have everything figured out, and he didn't need all of the answers. He just had to deal with what was in front of him now; and then take the rest one step at a time.

Breathing deeply, he took that first step.

"Yeah, I'm okay. I mean, sure, I'm worried about Julianna, and I plan on going after her as soon as we can, but first, this is what we're going to do. Gemma, I need you to use your powers and get everyone healed. And I mean everyone. Those four over there, too," he said, nodding his head in the direction of the men who, until just a few moments ago, had been the ones in charge. "Theresa, help her out. Boost her powers if she needs, but only if she needs. I don't want anyone to spend energy that doesn't need to be spent. We may be out of the woods, but we're still a long, long way from home.

"As for the rest of you, I need to know what it is you can do; more importantly, what your powers are. Jeremiah, what was it you used to freeze those fireballs that Julianna fired at me? And Brendan, I know you can teleport yourself and others, but how many, and how far? And Beth, what is the purpose of that golden dome you created? Have you all known about your powers for a long time; or did they just recently appear?"

Thomas took a deep breath, and then sighed. He glanced over at Terence, who appeared about ready to say something, but stopped when Thomas shook his head.

"There are far more questions than we have time for answers right now, Terence, and far more important tasks, too. What those tasks are may not be obvious yet, but they're out there. What *is* obvious is that we have each been blessed, and from what I know, these powers are nothing like the kind we're used to superheroes having in movies and on TV. We didn't get our powers from a radioactive spider, or from an accident in some secret lab, and we weren't born with them, either. They were granted to us through the Fruits of the Holy Spirit. Why God chose us over all other Christians is not something we should worry about, or something that we should boast of, either.

"Right now I think the only information that is of utmost importance is to understand what our powers are and what we each can do. It's clear that we are here for a reason, and the only reason that stands out for certain in this moment, is that we're here to support each other through whatever comes next. Once we understand how to do that, then we can figure out where we are, where Julianna might be, how we can find her, and how we can get back home. *All* of us. Together."

Thomas paused, taking a moment to look at each of his friends in the eye.

"What about your powers, Brother Thomas?" Adrianna asked when Thomas looked her way.

Thomas gave her a brief smile, knowing she had every right to ask her question. If he was asking them to be honest with him, then they should expect that he would do the same. Just as he was about to answer, a bone-chilling screech splintered the stillness of the night. Thomas' eyes went wide as he darted a look towards the edge of the jungle where a sea of midnight-black shadows began to pour out from every side.

CHAPTER EIGHTEEN
WHEN DARKNESS FALLS

If plants could feel pain, then the section of the jungle that Julianna was thundering through would be screaming. Palms, ferns, hanging vines, even small trees; nothing was safe from her wrath. Blast after blast flashed from the flames that were steadily burning around her hands. Each flash that burst forth destroyed everything in her way, leaving nothing but a scar of devastation. And though a part of her urged her to return to the clearing and the safety of her friends, she no longer listened to that part. That was the part of her where feelings such as love, respect, kindness, and joy had lived, and Julianna no longer had use for emotions such as those. She would rather wander endlessly through the jungle than return to the group she once thought of as friends.

How could they treat her the way they did? How could they deny her the right to get revenge on the men who had caused her to feel such anguish and pain? Beth, Terence, Gemma and the others had not only kept her from causing those men to feel even just a fraction of what they had made her feel, but were protecting them, too. They were even planning on healing any injuries they had caused. That fact alone was beyond her ability to understand. It just didn't make sense. None of this did.

Discovering that she had been granted powers was a difficult revelation in its own. Discovering that she was part of a group of so-called superheroes who all held a gift similar to hers felt like something she should be reading about in a comic book, or watching on TV, not living out like some crazy dream. And, though she had spent a brief moment in which she had considered joining them, rather than going off on her own, she couldn't see how the power she had been given could ever be used for good. No, from every angle she looked at the situation, the choice she had made seemed to have been the only choice she had left.

As her anger continued to rise, her hands relentlessly threw blasts of energy, and each new blast felt stronger than the last. Though her powers were helping her to clear a path through the densely twisted undergrowth, Julianna was completely unaware of where she was going, and she had no plan on what she would do. For now, she was content simply destroying anything and everything she could.

※

Sitting atop Gauerdi, his faithful steed, Furcas trained his eyes on the trail ahead. It was no ordinary path he followed, but a dark, blackened scar that he knew had been left by the power that Julianna held, a power he knew to fear. Even if he didn't have the ability to see the lingering, inky stain that marked her power's path, he knew it wouldn't have been that hard to follow the young woman. The devastation she left in her wake was equally dark, and just as wide. Though he could tell Gauerdi wanted to run, Furcas held the horse to a walk. He was in no hurry to catch Julianna, and with the damage she was doing, there was no way he would lose her trail. As far as he was concerned, the more power she used to blast and damage the world, the less power she would have when they finally did meet. For his purpose, the weaker she became, the easier it would be to gain her support when he explained his plan to her.

Using demon-sight, a part of his attention remained on the shadow forces he had left behind. Though he knew that ten thousand shadow-sprites wasn't a large force, considering he commanded ten times that, it was certainly sufficient for the part of his plan he was using them for. He knew that Thomas and his spiritually powered superhero friends would eventually defeat the shadows he had placed in their way, but he hadn't put them there with the hope that his demons would win. Shadows-sprites were expendable. He could care less if they were destroyed. They were there only to distract and delay. The longer he could keep Thomas from going after his sister, the better the chance it would give the rest of his plans. Regardless of what else happened tonight, for his plans to work, Furcas had to reach Julianna first.

He nudged Gauerdi forward, letting his mount pick up the pace. Now that his trap had been set and the diversion had begun, he was free to focus on more important things. Furcas grinned a wickedly evil grin as he considered the layers of deceit he was about to unfold. Persuading Julianna to join him and his forces was just one step in that plan, but it would give him the advantage he needed to pull off the greatest ruse he had ever attempted. If successful, he would become the second most powerful demon in the Kingdom of Hell.

He couldn't wait to see the look on Astaroth's face the moment he knocked Satan's current second-in-command—and the demon who had banished him from hell four years ago—from his current position, and take his place. Becoming one of the three ruling members of the Dark Trinity would give him access to resources he had only dreamed of. Maybe, if he was feeling generous, he would allow Julianna to be the one to strike the final blow. That, he knew, would be a perfect revenge.

※

Already bathed in sweat and breathing fast and hard, Father Dominic quickened his pace, a difficult task with the heavy backpack he wore. He could sense the balance of power starting to tilt, and knew he was running out of time. He would have to hurry to reach the Guardians before the Awakening took place. It had been hours since he had left the comfort of his makeshift quarters, and he had already come so far. But he had still a few miles left to travel, and dawn was coming soon. He had to reach the Guardians before first light, otherwise all his planning and preparation would be for naught.

At least he had reached a point where his heightened senses could smell the gathering of demons, warning him that he was getting close. It was an acrid, distasteful smell. He also thought he heard, from time to time, a sound similar to that of lightning, but the pending storm was still some hours away. He wondered if one of the Guardians was wielding a power that would make a noise like that, yet somehow he realized that he already knew. He had been watching Julianna for some time now, sensing that she was hiding a dark secret behind her hollow smile. He had come to understand, especially when dealing with young adults, that regardless of how they appeared on the outside, their eyes never lied, and the story he had been able to read in Julianna's eyes told the tale of a young woman on the verge of despair.

Thomas had that same look in his eyes four years ago when they first met, and. Thomas had also suffered through most of the same life-changing events as Julianna. He had assumed Julianna would have been just as strong as her brother had been, and would have found her way safely through to the other side. Now, however, with the odors assaulting his senses, and the obvious stench of demonic interference, he wondered if perhaps he should have done something more to assist her, and he prayed for an opportunity to do so now.

As the priest pressed on through the tangled undergrowth, he could tell he was getting close. Any closer and the enemy he was sensing would be able to sense him as well. He knew it was time to take on his spiritual form. An immense growth of banyan trees to his right looked like the perfect place to shed his cargo, and he quickly headed that way.

Reaching the main, inner trunks, he extended his arm and grabbed one of the lower branches, then easily swung up. He repeated the process twice more until he was certain he was far enough above ground to deter any predators, then quickly shed the pack. Unzipping the top, he removed a section of rope and began threading it through the frame of the pack. He then wrapped one end of the rope around a branch just above his head, and tied it off securely.

The other end he tossed over a nearby branch, then jumped and caught that branch, hauling himself up into a sitting position. He wrapped the loose end around the branch a few times, then pulled the rope, effectively suspending the metal framed pack in midair between the branches. Finally, he tied the end of the rope to the branch he was on, and lowered himself to the ground. He looked back up into the tree, declaring the pack to be as secure as he could make it. He knew a curious, enterprising tree-dweller may still be able to reach the pack, but he had one last trick up his sleeve.

Kneeling on the ground, he removed a small aerosol can from a side pocket of his cargo pants and shook it vigorously. When he was satisfied, he removed the top, attached a small tube to the spray nozzle, and doused the pack with some of the liquid inside. He covered his face with his free hand to prevent any of spray from being blown back into his eyes. Satisfied that a sufficient amount of the spray had been applied, he set the aerosol can down. A faint whiff of leopard pheromones reached his nose, making it curl in distaste.

"That should be enough to frighten off even the most curious creature," he said to himself, knowing he was now ready to change.

Kneeling down on the soft earth, he placed his hands in front of him, then raised his head. His eyes went wild for a moment, and then shut tight as his face twisted in pain. His mouth opened in a silent scream as his limbs began to twist in strange ways, and his joints started to pop. When he could hold the pain in silence no more, Father Dominic sucked in a great gulp of air, then threw his head back and howled.

"Looks like our small group chat just ended," Terence said in a failed attempt at humor as the rest of the group moved to form a circle, their backs to each other as they faced the midnight-black shadow-sprites that were surrounding them from all sides.

"What are they, Brother Thomas?" Jennifer asked, her eyes once more burning a deep blue.

Thomas looked to his right. Jennifer was two places away from him, with Gemma standing in between. He could see only a part of her expression, but what he did see was filled with fear.

"Some form of demon, I believe. Gemma, Theresa, and I faced something similar, though not here in the physical world," Thomas replied as the murky creatures began to close ranks.

The shadows in the front lines hissed and spat and gnashed their teeth. They were eager for battle, and were more than willing to be the first to die. They knew that death, for them, would never be permanent. They were born from the darkest thoughts in the minds of men. As long as those thoughts existed, as long as selfishness and tyranny and apathy prevailed, they would be born again.

"How did you defeat them?" Beth asked, her eyes growing wide as the wall of shadow became thick and dense. "There's gotta be thousands of them!"

"There's only one thing I know that can defeat shadows such as these," Thomas said, doing his best to appear confident and strong. "Faith. Faith in your powers. Faith in the powers of those around you. Listen for the still, quiet voice in your heart, and let it guide you. When it speaks to you, don't doubt, not even for a moment. These shadows live on fear, and they feast on doubt."

He watched as the emotions of his friends continued to falter, and he knew he needed to do more to calm their fears. Looking through the force amassing around them, Thomas picked out one of the largest shadows he could find. It was a hulking, distorted creature that stood on short, squat, powerful legs that bent backward at the knee. Its torso twisted tightly, like the shaft of some nightmarish drill. Rather than just two arms, the creature had four, two that faced forward, and two that bent back. At the end of each arm was an abnormally large hand sprouting three, five-knuckled fingers that were tipped with razor-sharp claws. When the creature balled its hand into a fist, its hand became a solid sphere with claws, like spikes, facing in every direction.

As this creature marched before the front lines, it hissed and barked out commands. Thomas knew this was the leader of the demons. If he defeated this one, as they had defeated the Black Dragon in Gemma's spiritual realm, the smaller shadows might flee. Taking out this massive and thoroughly frightening beast might be the key to winning this battle. Somehow he knew that he would be the one that would have to face it; alone. Though he had never sensed the emotions of a creature of darkness before, he held his breath as he reached out with his powers and let their minds connect.

"That was a mistake," he thought as a jolt of the darkest, blackest, sin-filled emotions touched his heart, causing his knees to falter and grow weak.

Thomas had felt darkness like this before, but never so close, and never directed exclusively for him. This was the purest hate, the deepest loathing, and the most unbridled disdain he had ever sensed. It was pure evil. Just as he was about to cut the connection, he felt something else, just under the surface. Something that felt like disappointment, or frustration. It felt like the creature was viewing him from behind a thick pane of glass, as if it could see him, but for some reason, it couldn't touch him. Thomas suddenly realized he had found the advantage that he and his friends would need.

He was about to charge out to meet the beast head on, when another sound rang out, overpowering for a moment the snarling, gnashing and hissing sounds that the shadows made. At first the sound surprised Thomas, so foreign did it sound, considering the landscape that they were within. He froze, as did all of his friends and every shadow within view. And then, he heard it again, off to his left. This time, there was no doubt. It was a howl, like that of a wolf, or large dog.

Thomas turned in the direction of the sound, just as the mass of shadows on that side began to shift, moving quickly to each side, creating a wide berth. A moment later, a great wolf-like creature covered with bright metallic-silver fur burst through the gap, its mighty head snarling and snapping at any shadow that had failed to get far enough away. Once through the lines, the creature picked up speed as it bolted across the clearing, heading right for Thomas and his friends.

"What the..." Terence began, leaving the final word unsaid.

Thomas felt several hands grab at his shoulders and arms as the Guardians closest to him reacted to the beast charging their way. Behind the wolf-like creature, the chaos that its entrance had stirred among the shadows had stirred something else as well; the shadows began to break ranks, with some now charging after the animal in a wave of dark rage.

Thomas unconsciously took a step back, and then another, as his instinctive reactions were to get as far as he could from the large beast bearing down on him and his friends. Then, his eyes locked with the animal's eyes, and a wave of shock washed through him as the creature opened its mouth, and spoke.

"Guardians! Form a circle!" the creature shouted at them. "Quickly! Gather together, as close as you can!"

"What should we do?" Gemma gave voice to the question most likely running through everyone's mind.

"Hurry, my friends! Gather quickly!" the beast shouted again, now only a few yards away. "We don't have much time!" The animal finally came to rest, lying at Thomas' feet, panting hard and obviously exhausted. Its eyes, though, were still full of life. It flashed its bright steel-gray eyes from one Guardian to the next, then urgently asked, "Which one of you holds Goodness? Who among you can create the golden shield?"

"Uh...I think that's me," Beth admitted, pensively raising her hand.

"Do it! Now!" the beast demanded.

Thomas turned to look in the direction the beast had indicated and saw a wave of shadow-sprites about to crash into their group with a fury of claws and teeth.

"Do it, Beth!" Thomas urged.

Beth flicked her hands before her, and the twin golden discs appeared, one circling around each wrist. She raised her hand high above her head, then slammed the fist into the ground. Like before, a ray of golden-white light shot up from the point where she had struck the ground. The light rose ten feet into the sky, then burst open like a fountain and rained back to earth, creating a circle around the group. Everyone but Theresa was inside the dome, as she had been still outside, sitting alone as she recovered from Julianna's assault.

"Theresa! Get in here!" Jennifer shouted as Theresa began to limp their way.

"She's not going to make it," Francis said as the wave of shadows was nearly on top of her.

"Theresa!" Terence shouted. "Duck!"

Terence thrust his arms forward, and a wave of white light flashed out. Thomas watched as Theresa's eyes went wide, then she threw herself to the ground just as the wave of energy flashed past her and slammed into the shadow-sprites. The force of Terence's blast stopped the front edge of the wave, but the creatures behind continued to press, piling on top of their unlucky brethren as the wave began to grow in height.

"Brendan, can you get her?" Thomas asked.

A moment later, Thomas heard a familiar *pop* sound, and then Brendan appeared, standing by Theresa's side. Brendan reached down to help her stand as the wave of shadows behind them doubled in size. As she staggered to her feet, the wave had doubled again, and began to topple forward. Just as the crest started to fall, Brendan wrapped his arms around Theresa, and they disappeared. Another *pop* sounded behind Thomas, and he turned to see that they were both safe.

The wave of shadows continued to fall. Then, as the weight of it crashed into the ground, it spread forward, rushing towards the young adults as they held tightly to each other's arms. The wave slammed into Beth's golden shield, and she released a gasp, as if the force had slammed into her and not her protective barrier. The walls of her shield bent inward under the weight, and it appeared that her shield might fail. Theresa reached out and placed her hand on Beth's shoulder, sharing her energy and boosting Beth's power. The golden shield glowed brighter, then brighter still, and finally, the walls sprung back, pushing the wave of darkness to the side. For the moment, the group was safe.

CHAPTER NINETEEN
THE COLOR OF FAITH

For the next several heartbeats, no one spoke. All eyes watched as the ever-growing flood of shadows continued to flow around Beth's shield, until nothing existed outside the protective sphere but darkness. More and more shadows pressed in, forcing the evil to spread higher and higher up the walls. Thomas watched as the walls of the dome began to splinter and crack. He knew that even with Theresa boosting Beth's power, the dome would not hold.

Thomas had witnessed shadow-sprites—similar to the ones he now faced—in battle before. Their claws and teeth had torn their target to shreds. But that battle had been between two spiritual armies, and had taken place inside Gemma's spiritual realm. He wasn't sure if the sprites would be equally as deadly here in the physical realm, he only knew he didn't want to find out.

Thomas turned to look at Beth. He could see the struggle in her eyes. He knew she wanted nothing more than to protect her friends, but her power only went so far. From what he knew, his friends had only recently discovered their powers. They hadn't had four years, like he had, to practice and perfect their abilities. Suddenly, Thomas felt like he had failed. Though he had found the Guardians, as Saint Thérèse had instructed him to do, now he was afraid that they would die here in this jungle, smothered by a sea of evil that wanted nothing more than to crush their spirits, and their lives, too.

Thomas turned away, glancing towards the ground, only to find himself locking eyes with the creature lying at his feet. He gazed into the animal's eyes, seeking any sign of what the creature was, or where it had come from. Before he could ask, the creature spoke.

"Thomas, have you learned how to enter the spiritual realm of another hero?" it asked.

"Yes, I have," Thomas answered, suddenly feeling something very familiar about the beast.

"Then, quickly, we don't have much time. Beth can't hold this dome forever. Everyone, gather close," the creature commanded. "Form a circle around Theresa. Hands on each other's shoulders. Hurry! Link up!"

After only a moment's hesitation, they responded, forming two concentric circles around their friend. Brendan, Thomas, Gemma and Beth made up the inner circle, with Terence, Francis, Jeremiah, Adriana, Jennifer, and Sam on the outside.

"It's up to you, now, Thomas. Hurry, I can feel the dome beginning to fail," the beast urged.

Thomas looked up, seeing the creature was right. A large crack had begun to form on one side of the dome. Thin lines were spreading out in every direction, and a small amount of the darkness had begun to flow through. He turned to look at Theresa. She looked exhausted, frail, and worn down, obviously still weak from the assault she had endured from Julianna. Using her powers to boost Beth hadn't helped. She appeared ready to collapse.

"Gemma. Quickly. Heal her!" he begged, turning to face The Paladin as he spoke.

Gemma was already at work. Her eyes were closed, and the faint blue light that shown around her was as bright as Thomas had ever seen.

"Thomas, we don't have time!" the dog begged.

"Forgive me, whatever you are, but there is always time to heal," Thomas said confidently, not taking his eyes off the Endlessly Dying Girl's face.

The cracks in the dome continued to grow, as the shadows continued squeezing through the tiny cracks, spreading them apart as they picked and peeled the golden dome to shreds.

"Thomas, now!" the dog barked at him, roughly.

"One moment more!" he shouted back, watching the fatigue in Theresa's face slowly begin to fade.

Slowly, she opened her eyes, and Thomas sighed.

"Theresa, you remember what to do?" he asked as she breathed in deeply.

Theresa grinned. Thomas could see that she knew what he was asking her to do. With a flush of youthful pride warming her face, Theresa closed her eyes.

Above them the ceiling of the dome gave way with a sound like shattering glass, and the uppermost shadows began to fall. Several of the Guardians gasped, and Thomas felt their grips tighten on his arm.

"Okay, Theresa," he whispered. "Take us home."

The young woman breathed in deeply, then opened her eyes, locking her gaze with his.

"Brother Thomas," she said softly, giving him a warm smile, "I surrender my heart…"

With that, the jungle faded away.

※

The first sign Theresa had that they were no longer in the jungle, was the change in temperature. The next was the absence of hissing, spitting, and gnashing of teeth.

In fact, there was no sound at all. Just an overarching sensation of peace. Theresa smiled giddily. She knew where she was, and before she opened her eyes, she knew what she would see.

Purple.

As far as she could see there was nothing but red and blue blended a thousand different ways. Plum colored clouds floated through opal skies. Birds with feathers of eggplant, sangria, and hyacinth perched on violet branches under wisteria colored leaves. Mauve and lavender grass lined a royal purple path that led down from the knoll on which she stood, disappearing behind an amethyst hill. Everything was purple. It was, after all, her favorite color.

Theresa's smile widened. She had left the world of the physical domain, and was now within the spiritual world hidden within her heart.

Her heart!

Which, she suddenly realized with a giggle, meant that this was her faith.

Her faith!

Brother Thomas could have picked anyone from the group. But he hadn't. He had picked her. He trusted her; *believed* in her. It was the first time she had felt as needed, wanted, and valued as much as she did right then, and she cherished the feeling immensely.

The sound of something moving behind her broke the reverie of the moment, but she knew the memory would always be there.

"Wow!" Adriana sighed as she, too, blinked several times and opened her eyes.

A few of the others also gasped in amazement at the beauty of Theresa's world.

"Where are we?" Beth asked as she spun in a slow circle, taking in the full view.

"This…" Thomas began.

"…is *my* heart," Theresa finished with a grin.

He smiled back, warmly.

"Your heart?" Brendan inquired. "It's beautiful!"

Theresa's smile stretched to the full now, and a rosy glow warmed her cheeks.

"Thanks, Brendan. I'm glad you like it!" she said, blushing just slightly.

She felt a hand squeeze her shoulder, and turned to see Gemma giving her a knowing look. Out of everyone in the group, only Gemma would understand what it felt like to stand where Theresa did now.

"So, Theresa," Gemma said, grinning playfully, "would you like to lead the way?"

Theresa wanted to respond verbally, but could only nod, as she found her throat to suddenly be tight.

"Oh, yes. By all means," Thomas added. "You remember what to do?"

"Oh yeah. I got this," Theresa said after swallowing hard to choke back the overwhelming joy. She flashed the group a mischievous smile, and spun around, saying loudly over her shoulder, "Everyone, follow me!"

"Does that include worn-out old priests, like me?" asked the voice of the dog as it rose from its reclined position at Thomas' feet.

Suddenly, the animal began to spasm, its body twisting and contorting as its limbs began to lengthen and its head became round. Theresa watched as the hairs of the animal knit themselves together, becoming a fabric, and the fabric became that of a robe; a long, plain, brown robe with a white rope belt at the waist and a hood pulled up over the animal's head. Then, from the sleeve of one arm, one paw extended out. Each of the padded digits grew longer while the claws shortened and spread wide. It took only a minute for Theresa to realize the creature was no longer an animal, but had become human. By the size of the hands and feet, it had to be a man.

The man rested on the ground, still on all fours, then slowly began to rise. As he did, he brushed the robe's hood back from his head, then turned to face the group.

"Father Dominic!" Beth was the first to say, with a few others repeating her words.

"Father!" Thomas exclaimed, a warm smile growing. "I had a feeling that was you. How did you do that? And how did you find us?"

Father Dominic blinked his eyes a few times, then stretched his arms above his head as he laughingly said, "This isn't my first rodeo, Brother Thomas."

"I don't believe it," Jeremiah gasped. "Father Dominic, you're a *Domini Canes*!"

"A what?" Brendan asked.

"*Domini Canes*. It's Latin. Translated into English, it means ..." Father Dominic began.

"...The Dogs of God!" Jeremiah finished.

"Oh, yeah!" Sam announced, excitedly. "I remember that story from when I was researching confirmation names. It came from a dream that Blessed Joan of Aza had. She was Saint Dominic's mother."

"What was in the dream?" Adrianna inquired.

"She saw a dog with a torch in its mouth that ran around setting the world on fire!" Jeremiah explained.

"True, true," Father Dominic shared. "Some believe that is how his name was chosen, but no one can know the truth for certain."

"His first followers adopted the name, and to this day it is still used at times as a symbol to represent their mission." Jeremiah continued.

"Which is?" Father Dominic prompted.

"To sniff out all heresy and remove it from the minds of those whose faith has wandered," Jeremiah stated with confidence.

"Man," Terence said, "I should really have spent more time researching before I chose my saint name, 'cause that's a pretty cool story!"

"That it is," Father Dominic agreed, then turned to Theresa, "and one that I'd love to talk more on, Terence, but I believe we have some traveling to do."

"Did he just call me a moron?" Terence whispered to Thomas, drawing an exasperated sigh.

A few of the others smiled or giggled at the joke, and Father Dominic gently laughed as well.

"Yes, Father," Theresa said as she gave Terence a sideways look. "We do have some traveling to do. So maybe we should stop joking around and get started."

"Then, lead on, my dear. Lead on!" Father Dominic said, sweeping his arm in front of him, indicating that Theresa should take the lead.

With one last teasing look at Terence, a look that garnered her a playful wink in return, Theresa started off down the path. As she approached the first bend in the trail, she called over her shoulder. "First thing's first, Brother Thomas. Kill the birds."

"Kill the birds? What?" Jennifer exclaimed.

"Oh, she doesn't mean kill them, kill them. Just wait. You'll see," Thomas replied, placing a reassuring hand on Jennifer's arm, and, with a slight pull, prompting her to follow along.

As Jennifer followed in line behind Thomas, Gemma came to join him by his side. The rest of the group brought up the rear, their eyes still wide with wonder.

"Try to keep up people!" Theresa hollered out, causing those in the back of the line to scurry. "We've got a long way to go!"

The trail they were on twisted around a bend, and as it did, the group noticed a steady decline in the volume and frequency of birdsong. It wasn't soon until it faded completely away.

"Oh my goodness," Jennifer said, breathing deeply, "the birds are gone!"

"This is too much," Adrianna added, shaking her head gently with awe.

"Okay, Theresa, what's next?" Thomas asked.

Theresa giggled softly, enraptured by the feelings gathering within her.

"Far too many plants!" she announced, her gait beginning to bounce slightly. "My faith world wouldn't have this many plants."

The group continued on, and the path turned around another bend. As they approached and turned the corner, Theresa began to see random empty patches peeking out between the flowers and grass. The further they walked, the more empty patches there were, until Theresa was satisfied.

"That's better. But can you make them look less...alive?" she asked.

"What do you mean?" Thomas inquired.

"Do you remember the story I told you of the flower? The one that was halfway dying? The one I saw that day in the desert?"

"Yeah...I remember the story," he replied.

"Well, make them look like that. Endlessly dying."

"You're the boss," Thomas said, trying to suppress a laugh as he did.

"Okay, someone needs to explain what's going on," Terence said. "Cause, this is getting a little weird."

"Don't worry, Tee," Gemma said, placing her hand on his shoulder. "The three of us have been here before. Let me explain."

Gemma began to explain to the group what had happened when she and Thomas had entered *her* spiritual world, and how he had asked her to change the landscape until it represented a world where she felt more at home. As she talked, Theresa periodically interrupted, calling out more changes she wanted for *her* spiritual realm; which was the one they were in now.

Fewer hills. Make the landscape more barren. Change this. Vary that. Add an abandoned vehicle over here. Put up a crumbling freeway overpass on this side. And toss a few collapsing buildings over there.

"But what about those evil creatures back in the real world? Won't they notice we're gone?" Brendan asked at one point.

"Time doesn't move here like it does back there," Gemma informed him. "Even if they did notice, we'll be back before they have time to respond."

"I really don't get how this all works," Jeremiah said, "but it's really super cool."

"Yeah, plus, Theresa's world is starting to look kinda post-apocalyptic," Sam mentioned.

"You mean," Theresa said, turning to give him a smile and a wink, "like Fallout Four?"

"Yes!" Sam shouted out, his eyes glowing with recognition. "That's exactly what I mean!"

Theresa laughed, then whispered something in Thomas' ear. He nodded at her, smiling broadly. Satisfied that Thomas understood her request, Theresa reached back and took hold of Sam's hand.

"Come on, gamer-boy. Let me show you where I keep my faith!"

Giggling joyfully, Theresa raced ahead, dragging Sam willingly behind.

The path wound around yet another bend, and as the horizon changed, a small hill rose up from the otherwise relatively-flat terrain. As they drew closer to the hill, a dark spot became evident on its face, which, as they approached, revealed itself to be the entrance to a cave. Theresa stopped at the mouth of the cavern, still holding Sam's hand. Finally, the rest of the group caught up, and Theresa waved them inside.

"Welcome to my Vault-Tec vault!"

"This is way too cool!" Francis said, squinting a bit as his eyes adjusted to the dimmer light inside.

"It's just like in the game!" Jeremiah added, his eyes aglow with delight.

"Yeah, isn't it great?" Theresa asked.

"Great?" Sam said, breaking free of Theresa's grasp to run both of his hands over a metal plaque hanging just inside the cave. "It's literally perfect! I didn't know you were a gamer, Theresa!"

"Why, because I'm a girl?" she replied, giving him a bit of attitude.

Sam shook his head, "No, no. I game with girls all the time. It's just, well, you seem different from all the other gamer girls."

Theresa gave him a shocked look, then turned away in a huff.

"Dude," Terence whispered softly, unaware Theresa could still hear him, "you're kinda digging yourself into a hole. Trust me. Don't mention '*all* the other gamer girls'."

Sam gave Terence a look like he had just been speaking Greek, then suddenly his eyes lit up and he nodded in recognition.

"Oh...yeah. Um, Theresa, I didn't really mean *all* the others. It's not like I know *all* the girls who play video games. There's only like..." he paused, then held up eight fingers so Terence could see.

Terence shook his head and held up just two fingers in reply.

Nodding his thanks to Terence, Sam continued, "...only two."

Theresa kept her back to Sam, who looked at Terence and shrugged his shoulders. Terence just shook his head, giving Sam a look that said, '*you're on your own here*'. A moment later, Theresa spun around with a sigh.

"I was just kidding," she said, unconvincingly. "I don't care how many girls you know."

"Oh, cool! Cause I know quite a few," Sam said.

Theresa gave Sam a hard look, growled, and looked away again.

"Did I do something wrong?" Sam whispered to Terence, as Theresa stared him down.

Terence placed his arm around Sam's shoulders and leaned in close.

"Epic fail, bro. Epic fail," he said, as Theresa moved back into the shadows of the cavern.

After climbing a short, metal stairway to a raised platform, Theresa approached a small control panel that stood in the middle of the platform. She flipped a switch on the console, then watched as a rainbow of lights flickered to life. Various gauges revealed the current status of the system. On one side of the console, an entire bank of lights changed from red to green, and a series of clicks could be heard over the hum of servomotors. Looking up, Theresa began to count heads. She counted ten, including herself, meaning two people were missing.

"Who's not here?" she asked quietly.

"Jeremiah and Francis," Jennifer said with a grin as she pointed towards the rearmost wall. "I think they're in gamer heaven."

Several of the group snickered, or grinned, or simply nodded their head at the comment.

Theresa turned in the direction Jennifer had pointed, seeing the two missing members of the group standing as close as they could to a large, metal door. The structure was at least two stories tall, and was roughly spherical, with nine protrusions placed in equidistant segments. The door had the appearance of a giant sprocket or cog.

"Uh, Francis? Jeremiah? You guys might be a little too close," Theresa said as more servomotors hissed and sputtered, preparing to engage.

When the two had retreated to a safe distance, Theresa flipped a switch and then pushed a large, red button. Immediately lights began to flash, and a computerized, female voice blared from multiple speakers throughout the room.

"*Attention. Vault door cycling sequence initiated. Please stand back!*"

A loud hiss sounded as the hydraulics were flooded with air, causing pistons to extend, and the machine began to move. A large, box-shaped apparatus came to life, spun one-hundred-and-eighty degrees around, and then moved towards the giant, metal door. As the group continued to watch—a look of wonder in their eyes—a circular slot opened at the center of the cog-shaped door. On the front of the box-shaped apparatus was an extension made of shiny, stainless steel that appeared as if it would fit perfectly in the spherical slot. A moment later, this was confirmed as the 'key' slid soundlessly into the 'lock'. The rest of the process was not so soundless, and half of the group found themselves placing their hands over their ears. Metal scraped on metal, and dusty, rust-covered parts screeched as the door began to slide open.

The box-like contraption that held the 'key' moved backward again, though, this time, it pulled the door with it, accompanied by an even greater symphony of eardrum-splitting sounds. Finally, the door was out, and the box-like structure moved to the right side of the cavern; the cog-like door rolling obediently along. As the door rolled away, a metal walkway extended, allowing them to enter the next area without climbing over the section of wall where the door used to be.

Theresa turned to where Francis, Jeremiah, and now Sam were all standing, and watched as the three gave each other an excited 'high-five'.

"Come on. Let's go inside," Theresa sighed, rolling her eyes as she started to cross the metal walkway, not waiting for the others to follow.

The group crossed over the low bridge, then found themselves standing in a pristine, though featureless, antechamber. Theresa approached the back wall and placed her hand on a square panel to the side of what looked like the door of a freight elevator. The panel illuminated with a dim, blue glow. A moment later, a soft *thud* echoed through the large room, followed by a distant hum.

"Where does this elevator go?" Adriana inquired as the humming grew louder, and a slight tremor began to shake the room.

"Well, a typical Vault-Tec vault would have twenty-five levels, but I only use three. The main living quarters are on the bottom floor," Theresa responded.

"What's on the other two?" Jennifer asked.

"Level two is crafting rooms for weapons, outfits, armor; that sort of stuff. And the other level is a huge training room," Theresa stated, then turned to face Sam. "If I explain how the controls work, do you think you could program a few training scenarios for us? Something like what we might be up against when we return to the physical world again."

Sam nodded with enthusiasm.

"Oh, heck yeah. Just let me know the level of difficulty you want. Are we talking full on noob? Or more like Kobayashi Maru?"

"Somewhere in between would probably work out fine," Theresa stated, then turned to watch the metal door separate into four sections, each pulling away from the others in a different direction.

The sound of metal grinding on metal sent a shiver down her spine. When the doors had fully retracted, Theresa led the group inside.

"If there are only three floors, what are all the other buttons for?" Adrianna asked as she examined the elevator control panel.

"I might want to expand later," Theresa casually said as she pressed one of the middle level buttons.

The sound of metal on metal continued until the doors were completely sealed, and then the elevator began to descend.

"Brother Thomas," Theresa said, turning to face the young man.

"Yes, Theresa?" he asked.

"Why didn't the darkness follow us here; like it did in Gemma's world?"

Thomas shrugged his shoulders, his eyes scrunching together and his mouth twisting slightly as he considered her question.

"I don't know," he offered with an embarrassed look, as if he should have the answer. "Maybe because the darkness was already pursuing Gemma, or, maybe it was pursuing me until it could identify who it was that I would give the Armor of God to."

"So, you don't think it sees me as a threat?"

"Oh, I definitely think it sees each of us as a threat; otherwise none of this would have happened. We would have simply gone back to the mission site after dinner. None of this would have happened at all."

At that moment, the elevator shook slightly, indicating it had arrived at the destination. A loud *thud* echoed through the elevator shaft in both directions. This time, when the doors opened, they made barely a sound.

"Come on," Theresa said, stepping into the hallway and waving for the others to follow. "Let's get geared up."

CHAPTER TWENTY
DESIGNING HEROES

Thomas was following closely behind Theresa, his mind stuck on the question she had asked him while they were on the elevator. Why *wasn't* the darkness pursuing them here, in Theresa's spiritual realm? There were only two answers he could think of. First, the darkness had no reason to pursue them, because nothing the Guardians did while in Theresa's world would have any impact on the battle waiting for them back in the physical world. And second, nothing that the *darkness* would do in Theresa's realm would matter, either.

With no evidence to support either theory, he tabled the question, pushing it to the back of his mind where his subconscious could gnaw on it uninterrupted. Hopefully, while he was doing something completely unrelated to finding the answer, the answer would reveal itself. That was the way things always seemed to work; the harder he searched for an answer, the more difficult it was to find. Yet, if he took his attention away for a bit, the answer always mysteriously appeared.

Theresa had every right to be a target of the evil schemes that the Prince of Darkness might be crafting. In fact, every member of the Guardians should be a threat to the agents of Hell. On their own, Thomas knew that the strength of their individual faith would be enough to stop even the vilest demon. When combined, their faith would be unstoppable; but only if they didn't doubt what they were capable of.

Doubt was a curious thing, and something Thomas had dealt with for nearly his entire life. Even now, with everything he had experienced since he had first felt his powers come alive, he still had doubts. Inside his heart there was a battle constantly being waged as half of him wanted nothing more than to cast aside all doubt, while the other half was always insecure in his faith. Thomas had seen how lives could be impacted by carrying too much doubt. He had watched it tear apart some of those he loved the most. His own father had been torn apart by doubt and fear, and now his sister, Julianna, was fighting that same battle. The worst part was, Thomas felt as if there was nothing he could do. The choice to lay down whatever burdens Julianna was carrying lay in her hands and hers alone. All he could do for now was to pray that none of the other Guardians would fall.

The hallway they were traversing came to a split, and Theresa took the corridor to the right, which turned out to be a short passage, ending in at a doorway. On the side of the door, in large, bold letters, a single word was stenciled: Crafting. Thomas wondered what they would find on the other side of the door. He didn't have to wait for long, as Theresa placed her palm on another of the rectangular panels like the one she had used to call the elevator. The door slid open with barely a whisper, and Thomas and the others followed Theresa inside.

The room wasn't large, but it was spacious enough to not feel cramped. Three of the walls were lined from corner to corner, and from the floor nearly to the ceiling, with storage cabinets. Each cabinet held a label describing what was inside. Thomas quickly scanned a few of the labels closest to him: Fasteners, cloth fabric, water-resistant mesh, leather, rubber, metallic trim.

Across the main floor of the room there were two small workstations with hand tools in every shape and size. Hammers, awls, punches, pliers, screwdrivers. Everything the average hobbyist would want or need.

"Hey, Gemma," Theresa said, turning around with a sly smile. "Remember that ninja skinsuit I wore during the battle we had in your spiritual realm?"

"Oh, definitely. It was gorgeous. Is this where you came up with the idea?"

Theresa shook her head.

"No. More like the other way around. I envisioned that outfit on the spur of the moment, but it got me thinking; if I had a spiritual realm like you did, what would it look like? This is my first time visiting mine. Until we visited yours, I didn't even know something like this could exist; which is why I've only had time to design three floors," she said, grinning widely.

"Yeah, I hear you. I can't wait to get back into my world and make more adjustments," Gemma responded. "But, from what I've seen so far, your world is extremely creative and well thought out!"

"Thanks, Gemma! It's kinda been in the back of my mind this whole time. Now, let's get everyone dressed! I'll go first so you guys understand how this works," Theresa said as she sat down at a computer terminal. "First thing you need is an idea of what you want your outfit to look like. Here's a picture of mine."

She leaned to the side and turned the monitor so everyone could see. Pictured on the screen was a picture of a female ninja assassin.

"Wow, Theresa," Sam said, clearly impressed with the design she had chosen. "That looks like a combination of Rubi Malone and Silk Fox!"

Theresa turned bright red, an uncontrollably large smile dominating her face.

"Thanks, Sam! That's exactly the look I was going for!" she said, then bashfully turned back to the terminal and entered a few commands.

The click and buzz of a dot-matrix printer could be heard, and shortly after, an index card shot out of a slot on the side of the terminal. Theresa grabbed the card and pulled it out, looking over the information printed on the front for a moment.

"See this here on the left side?" she asked the huddled group before her as they leaned in closer to get a better look. "This is the list of items you will need. On the right is the locker and bin number for each item."

She held the card out in front of her.

"You'll find the corresponding numbers above the lockers," she said, pointing to a small plaque above one of the lockers. Then, she opened the locker doors and pointed to a smaller plaque on the corner of one of the bins. "The bin numbers are on each of the bins, right here. Does anyone have any questions?"

"Yeah," Francis hesitantly said, "I'm not that great at sewing. Once I have the materials I need, how do I get them assembled?"

"Oh, I can help you with that," Beth offered.

"Yeah, I can, too," Gemma added.

"Same," said Brendan, then when a few of the others gave him quizzical looks, he added, "What? My grandma taught me how to sew when I was little. She said it might come in handy one day."

"Smart grandma!" Francis said, smiling, then added, "Can I design my outfit next? I already have an idea what it is that I want."

"Well, there's more than one terminal," Theresa said, motioning with her hand to a group of terminals stationed on side of the room.

There was an instant buzz as the Guardians began to shuffle into position, each one wanting to be one of the first to use a terminal.

"Before we do anything else," Thomas interrupted, catching the group just before chaos broke out, "I think this would be a good time to share something I think you'll all want to incorporate on your gear."

He paused, ensuring he had everyone's attention.

"Theresa, I believe if you check on the table by the terminal you just used, you'll find a USB drive. There will be only one file on the drive, a jpeg image titled, *The Guardians Crest*. Can you pull that up for me?"

Theresa nodded, then turned and picked up the drive. She didn't ask Thomas where the drive had come from, she simply plugged it in. A window popped open on the terminal, and she clicked on the image of a folder, and then on the only file she found inside the folder. An image appeared. A few 'ooh' and 'ahh' sounds were heard as the Guardians looked over the image.

"I found this image during a trip I made deep into Gemma's spiritual world; a realm only available by visiting the first level, such as we are doing right now inside Theresa's heart. This is how I believe things work: the outer level is where you hold your 'public' faith; that's the faith that you let the world see. Since your faith is personal to you, you get to design the environment any way you want.

"The second level is your inner faith. This is where you keep the part of your faith that's just between you and God. For some, this is faith that you may not yet realize you have. The environment for this deeper level is designed for you by God. This inner level is always calling to you. It's that feeling you sometimes have that your life is of a greater purpose than what you've accomplished so far. Discovering the path into this inner level is the goal of every Christian, for within that realm lies the answers to all the questions you have about your life; questions like who you are, and why you were born. It is the part that allows your spiritual life to blossom and bear fruit."

"What did you see when you went inside mine?" Gemma inquired.

It was Father Dominic who answered.

"He can't share that, Gemma. We can help you find the path, but no one can tell you what's there. That part of your faith is something that you alone must find."

Thomas could see that Gemma was a bit disappointed that he had seen what was inside this inner world of hers, yet she had not.

"I'll promise you this, Gemma, let's finish this current mission, and then you and I will spend as much time together as we need for you to find your inner faith on your own. Agreed?"

Gemma nodded softly, turning to wipe a small tear from her eye.

"Now, back to the Crest. Since I found this image within Gemma's inner faith, I know it comes from truth, and I'd like for us to adopt it as the symbol for who we are, and what we stand for as a group."

"What does it mean?" Beth asked, stepping a bit closer to the screen. "What are all of the symbols?"

"I believe I can shed some light on that subject," Father Dominic offered.

CHAPTER TWENTY-ONE
THE GUARDIANS CREST

"Has anyone here, besides Brother Thomas, heard of the Guardians before?" Father Dominic inquired.

Ten pairs of eyes glanced from one face to the next. When no one responded, Father Dominic simply shook his head.

"Very well. Let's take this one step at a time. This symbol, known as the Guardians Crest, is the symbol that represents the Guardians of Zion. I'll bet you would never guess who it was that created the original design."

Again, he waited while the young adults before him looked at everything but him, as if they were praying that he would call on anyone but themselves.

"The symbol was designed by Hildegard of Bingen, a medieval mystic who was possessed with tremendous visions, including one in which she was given an image of the Holy Trinity itself! And not the simple, ordinary triangle shape that you probably learned in your first-year religious education class, but a symbol that was energetic, holistic and fluid. An image that shows how perfectly the Holy Trinity can move in our lives, even in the most difficult of times.

"Imagine for a moment how hard it would be to drive a car if the tires were triangular," he said, waving his hands as if to erase the image he had just described. "The car would bump and jerk worse than those damnable rollercoasters you young people are always trying to get me to ride."

Father Dominic shook his head and chuckled to himself, then continued on.

"Now, translate that to your own life. Does your life ever feel like that car, bumping and jerking from one day to the next? And what does the world tell you to do when you feel that way? Just keep going, don't give up, or choose happiness. But that's like putting a Band-Aid on a severed limb."

The priest took a deep breath.

"Following the ways of the world usually gets you into more trouble than the trouble you were trying to solve. Trust me on this. The ways of the world focus on treating the symptoms of our distress and disbelief; but they do nothing to change what's causing that distress. In fact, it's because of the diametrically opposing messages between the world view and the faith view that so many young people are choosing to walk away from the church. Just keep going. Bah!"

Father Dominic took another small pause, once more shaking his head softly.

"But a circular Trinity, one that casts aside anthropomorphism in its attempt to explain the unexplainable...now that is something that provides real value in our understanding of God. It addresses the *cause* of the distress we feel. It not only recognizes that our wheels aren't the right shape, but it allows us to replace them with wheels that do work. It gives us the tools to move forward as we are meant to, without the chaotic circus that leaves most of us emotionally numb."

"Uh...I'm sorry, Father. You lost me there," Terence admitted. "Anthropo-what?"

Father Dominic grinned and mumbled, "There's one in every class!"

Terence blushed, then, as he realized the priest was only teasing, he gave Father Dominic a wink.

"Anthropomorphism is just a really big word used to describe what happens when you try to assign human characteristics to something that is not human."

"Oh..." Terence said, grinning broadly, "Now that, I can understand."

"Good. Then, let's begin, shall we? What do you see at the very top center of the shield?"

Terence turned to look at the computer screen, then turned back towards Father Dominic.

"It looks like a star, but different somehow. Like, it has a tail or something?"

"In our faith, Terence, what star is the one we reference the most?" Father Dominic prodded, then, seeing Terence's blank expression, he continued, "I'll give you a hint. We talk about it at Christmas time."

"The Star of Bethlehem," Terence said, the statement sounding more like a question.

"Yes. The Star of Bethlehem, which represents the coming of Christ. Why would you think this symbol is centered at the top of the Crest?"

"Probably to remind us what our mission as Guardians should be," Jennifer answered.

"Very good, Jennifer. Keep that thought in mind. We will come back to it in a bit," Father Dominic stated with a warm smile. "Let's see...who is next. Ah, how about you, Francis?"

Francis' eyes popped open wide and he suddenly stood up straight.

"What do you see on each side of the star?"

Now, it was Francis' turn to look once more at the computer display.

"More stars, and some kind of branch, or plant?" he said, though not with much conviction.

"Yes. Twelve stars, in fact. One for each member of the Guardians. Each one of you here is represented by one of those twelve stars."

"Is that why you're here with us, Father? Are you the twelfth Guardian?" Theresa inquired, her words carrying just a hint of sadness.

Father Dominic walked over to Theresa and took her hands in his. He gazed into her eyes for a long moment, then softly, he said, "You know who the twelfth Guardian is, Theresa. It is not me. I am here only as your mentor, your guide. You know who the final Guardian is, the one who should be here with you now."

"Julianna," Theresa whispered, the tiniest glint of a tear in her eye.

"Yes. Julianna," Father Dominic said, his voice filled with compassion.

The air in the room grew heavy and thick, and no one wanted to be the one to ask the question they were all thinking. Finally, Thomas did.

"So, did we already fail in our quest? Did losing Julianna mean we lost the fight?" he asked tentatively, not wanting to hear what the answer might be.

Still holding one of Theresa's hands, Father Dominic turned to face Thomas.

"No, my son, you did not fail Julianna. You are not responsible for the Guardians. That job is mine to bear. I failed your sister, Thomas. And I'm sorry that I did. I thought she was stronger, and that she would make the right decision when the darkness challenged her, like it had challenged you. I am the one who is to blame for where she is right now."

"Where is she?" Thomas asked, his anxiety more than evident in his tone.

"Lost and alone right now," Father Dominic stated. "But, there is still hope. There is always hope. Never forget that, Thomas. When the world seems empty and desolate, when your heart is filled with anger and hate, never forget that there is always hope."

After a lingering moment, broken only by muffled sniffling and sighs, Thomas spoke again.

"Then, I have to go after her, Father Dominic. I *have* to go after her."

"Indeed, you will, my son. Indeed, you will. But first, know this," he cautioned. "The darkness has been planning for a thousand years for this moment. Most of you have had your powers for only a very short amount of time, and most of you have just learned that you are a Guardian of Zion, and what that even means. I know you want to get back out there and fight, that you want to track down your sister and bring her back to the group, but for now, you need to be here. There is much to learn, and much more to prepare for.

"Here, you have a powerful advantage. Theresa's faith cannot be breached, not like the darkness did with Gemma when you traveled into her spiritual realm. Theresa's faith is different. I cannot explain how or why that is right now; I just need you to trust me. Let me finish explaining the Crest and what we need to do to prepare. Then, I promise, when you are ready, which won't be that long from now, the first thing we'll do, is find Julianna."

Thomas could only nod. The burden he was carrying for his sister was so heavy, that even if his heart could find the right words to say, his lips would have refused to speak them.

Father Dominic could only do so much. The young men and women around him in the room needed time to grieve. In a very short span of time, they not only learned that they were a large part of an ongoing battle between good and evil, but they also believed they had already lost the first member of their group. He could tell that they all carried a small amount of hope that Julianna wasn't lost forever, but since this had been their first taste of the anger and hate that had driven their young friend away, it was hitting them hard. After several long moments, Beth broke the silence.

"I should have known. I've spent more time with Julianna before coming to Panama than anyone here. I should have sensed something."

"Trust me when I tell you, this is not something to be ashamed of, or to beat yourselves up over. How many of those here in this room have ever hidden behind a mask, sheltered their true feelings deep inside and pretended to be 'okay'?" Father Dominic asked.

Slowly, every hand in the room went up.

"We humans are amazingly well-gifted at hiding when we feel weak, and disguising our brokenness, too. If Julianna didn't want anyone to know, then that was her choice. Unfortunately, it was exactly what the Unholy Trinity wanted. She played right into their plans."

Thomas took a deep breath, letting the air slide out past partly pursed lips. The sound seemed to go on forever, and it became more wretched along the way. Finally, he breathed back in.

"I know my power is supposed to come from faith, which means I should probably start using it," he said, his head cast down as his eyes locked on the floor. Then, as his head came up and his eyes turned to Father Dominic, he added, "My faith might be all I have right now, but, hopefully, that's all that I need. Please, Father, continue with the Crest."

Father Dominic walked over to his protégé, placing a hand compassionately on Thomas' shoulder.

"Thomas, your trust in God is always the only thing you need. He will always provide. Always."

Thomas smiled at him, his eyes wet with tears, then turned and looked back at the image of the Crest.

"So, the stars, they represent the twelve Guardians. But what about those stalks of wheat?"

"Jesus used wheat many times in his parables," Father Dominic explained. "And seeds, and farming, too. The people he spoke to could understand these terms, being that a good number of them were farmers. Here, the wheat represents the parable of the farmer who sows good seed fields, and then, while he's asleep, his enemy comes and sows weeds in the same field. The grain sprouts first. It was good wheat, and strong. But then the weeds come up, too, and begin to choke the wheat.

"His workers ask if they should pull the weeds, but the farmer says to leave them. He says that they might unintentionally pull some of the wheat along with the weeds, and that they should let them grow together. He says that, at harvest, they could be separated out. This is the importance of the wheat on the Crest. It is a reminder that there will be times when you are among the weeds, and when those times come, to not be afraid. Simply lean towards the light, as these stalks here are reaching for the light of the stars above them. Do not fear the things that threaten you, sap your strength, or try to choke you out. When the time comes for the harvest, the wheat will be gathered in the barn, and the weeds will be burned."

The eleven faces that faced him were still placid and emotionless, their thoughts still on their lost friend. He waited in silence until, one by one, they began to turn their attention back to him. Finally, Brendan spoke.

"And the rest of the Crest's symbols, Father? What do they mean?"

"Ah, those. Those are my favorite parts of all."

"Yes, please go on," Gemma stated. "I've literally got goosebumps waiting to hear more."

Father Dominic gave Gemma a quick glance, wondering if she was teasing him, but found no malice in her face or tone of words.

"Ah, Gemma, you are the one who wears The Armor of God, yes?" he asked.

"I am!" Gemma admitted excitedly.

"Good, good. That is good," Father Dominic said, shaking his head gently. "Then you, of all those gathered here, should know and understand the symbolism of the shield and the rook."

At first, Gemma said nothing, believing the statement to be rhetorical. Thomas could see the look on her face change dramatically when she realized Father Dominic was actually waiting for her to respond, and his heart went out to her. He was familiar with the way in which Father Dominic worked to draw his students into sharing answers that, though they may be nervous to share at first, were actually correct. It was a strange talent Father Dominic had, this ability to know how much someone else knew and understood about even arbitrary or abstract concepts, especially when the person themselves had no idea the knowledge was already theirs. Just as Father Dominic was about to say something else, Gemma replied.

"The shield itself is the representation of our faith. Just like it is the device that the knights of the crusades used to defend themselves from the swords and arrows of their enemies, our faith shields us from the attacks of those that serve the evil one. And the rook, or stone keep, is not just a symbol of strength and stability, but also a symbol of trust."

Father Dominic gave Gemma a look of surprise and admiration.

"Someone has studied the philosophies of the game of chess!" he announced.

"I had an advanced placement philosophy class my junior year in high school. The teacher was a bit of a chess nut," Gemma announced, proud she remembered something that she had learned nearly four years ago.

"And do you still find it coincidental, in the light of the superpower you have, that you were placed in that class rather than the early childhood development course you had hoped for?"

Gemma gasped.

"How did you know?" she whispered.

Father Dominic simply shrugged and gave Gemma a conspiratorial wink.

"What you have just heard is true," he stated to the larger group. "The symbolism of the rook as it is used here is a representation not only of strength, but of patience and trust. Who here can tell me what it means to 'castle' your king?"

Jeremiah raised his hand and Father Dominic nodded to him.

"It means the king and the rook switch places."

Father Dominic nodded slightly, giving Jeremiah an approving look.

"That it does. But there is far more to this move than just two pieces trading places. Gemma," the priest said, turning his attention her way, "what is the underlying philosophy of the 'castle' maneuver?"

Gemma squinted her eyes a bit and looked up toward the ceiling, then back to Father Dominic.

"Though the two pieces change places, as Jeremiah said, there is a deeper meaning. The king actually *calls* the rook to him. Before this happens the rook is trapped. He is in a corner, with a pawn on one side, and a bishop on the other. Or, as it was explained to me, the pawn, which represents the world, and the bishop, which represents religion or faith, stand in the way of the rook making his first move. It is only through his response to the king that he takes his rightful place as protector and defender of the kingdom; but, this must happen as the rook's first move, or it can never take place."

"Well done!" Father Dominic said, smiling brightly. "That is exactly what the rook symbolizes. To become a Guardian of Zion, your first move must always be to protect the king! Otherwise, you will be trapped, torn between being *in* the world, and being *of* the world."

"Wow…" Adrianna sighed. "That's deep. Like, really, really deep."

"And yet, so simple, too," Brendan admitted, thoroughly engrossed in the conversation.

"Let's move on," Father Dominic stated, looking around the room. "Ah, there is a chair. Sam, would you mind bringing it to me?"

Sam, who was the closest to the chair Father Dominic had indicated, picked it up and brought it over, then set it down beside where the priest was currently standing. Father Dominic sat down.

"I do apologize. It was a very long hike," he said, smiling. "Now, who knows the two symbols that are emblazoned on the front of the rook?"

All eyes turned towards the computer display again. Jeremiah, who was an avid church history buff, was the first to speak.

"Those are the chi-rho and the trinity knot."

"Precisely! And what do you know about them?"

"I know the knot represents the Holy Trinity, but other than that I don't know much."

"And the chi-rho?"

"That was used before the time of Christ, mostly by the Greeks, since it is a symbol created by two letters; chi, which is the same shape as the letter 'x', and rho, which is the shape of the letter 'p'. Originally, it was formed to represent the Greek word, *chreston*, which meant 'good' or 'important', and was used as a marker to indicate parts of books that were more important than others, including passages within the Bible.

"Later, it was adopted to represent the word *christos*, since the first two letters are the same. But it really didn't catch on or become that popular until Emperor Constantine used it during the Battle of the Milvian Bridge, just outside Rome. The story goes that Constantine, who had not yet legalized Christianity as a religion, was shown the symbol in a dream as his men were preparing for battle. He then had their shields painted with the symbol, and, after they won the battle, it became his standard bearer."

"Ah, a believer who knows his history! Now, I know you said you didn't know much about the Trinity Knot, but can you share what is it that you do know?" Father Dominic prompted.

"Well, again, it was used as a symbol well before the birth of Christ, mostly within the pagan beliefs. To them, the three points represented earth, air, and water. Other groups have interpreted it to mean birth, death, and rebirth. Whatever the origins were, it was Christianity that added the circle to the middle of original design."

"Very good, Jeremiah. And, you are correct. Both symbols did start prior to Christianity, even before the birth of Christ. Now, while some would say that this invalidates their meaning, or that the church in those days acted like a strong-arm, taking whatever they wanted from the pagan faiths, and making it their own, Hildegard saw things differently. In her vision, these two symbols were included on the front of the rook as a way to show inclusiveness and respect. They are there to remind those who stand behind this crest that the battle between good and evil will never be won through division, but through inclusion. The Guardians of Zion do not fight to eradicate evil, nor do they fight with the goal of destroying whatever enemy they face. No, the Guardians of Zion fight only to defend what is good, what is right, and what is true. They fight to bring those who follow the darkness back to the light. Inclusion, never exclusion."

"Then I think it's time for us to do exactly that," Thomas said abruptly, rising to his feet. "One hour, team. That's it. After that, we need to start training."

Chapter Twenty-Two
Outnumbered and Alone

Father Dominic watched the young adults as they turned their attention to the task of designing and crafting the outfits they would wear whenever they travelled to one of the spiritual realms. Their excitement and energy was infectious, and he wanted to participate with them, but there was something even more pressing that demanded his attention. Slowly, so as not to draw attention, he began moving towards the door. When he reached it, he turned back around.

"Thomas?" he whispered softly, hoping no one else would hear. "Can I speak with you for a moment?"

"Certainly," his young friend responded.

Theresa suddenly looked over, most likely having heard Thomas' reply. Her eyes locked on Thomas as he moved to join him in the open doorway. Father Dominic could tell she knew what was about to happen, and he felt his shoulders tense just slightly as she walked over.

"Brother Thomas," Theresa said in a quiet voice, "what about your outfit? Don't you want one?"

Thomas paused. Father Dominic could tell that designing a hero costume was the last thing Thomas wanted to do, but the young man didn't want to hurt Theresa's feelings, either, and so he spoke quickly, before Thomas could say a word.

"I have an idea, Theresa!" he said, layering as much charm as he could. "You've already designed your own outfit, right?"

Theresa nodded, a slight twinkle in her eye, as if she could anticipate what was coming next.

"Then, I'm sure Brother Thomas would be more than happy if you would design his."

"Yeah," Thomas exclaimed, smiling at Theresa. "Would you do that for me, Theresa?"

"Oh, yeah, sure I could!" Theresa replied.

"Oh, good! Nothing too fancy though."

"Me? Do something fancy? Ha! No problem, Brother Thomas. I've got the perfect image in mind."

Thomas smiled at her, then turned and went out into the hall. Father Dominic followed behind, already aware of the things that were troubling Thomas' mind. They continued down the hall until the excited sounds from the young adults behind them began to fade, then Thomas turned and faced his mentor and friend. The two stood staring at each other for a few moments. Then, finally, Thomas spoke.

"I think you already know what I'm about to say."

"I do," Father Dominic replied.

"Then you also probably know that nothing you say can change my mind, right?" Thomas admitted.

"I do, indeed," he replied again, this time with a tinge of sadness in the words.

"I have to go, Father. I have to. She's my sister," Thomas said, starting to break down.

"Yes, she is, and she always will be. Regardless of what happens; regardless if you turn her back to the light or not, she will be your sister. Nothing changes that."

"Yeah, I know," Thomas admitted, sighing heavily. "And I know what you're about to say next is probably right, too. The Guardians need me now just as much as she does, and that it would be better to go after her as a team. But, you heard them laughing and joking with each other when we left. And you saw them when they wouldn't let Julianna hurt those men, even after all those men had done. They're already a team, Father."

"A team, yes; but one without a leader if you go," Father Dominic interjected.

Thomas sighed once more.

"You know what this is like, don't you?" Father Dominic inquired.

"No, I don't. What is this like?"

"Remember the day you wound up in the fight with the five kids who tried to steal your bike?"

Thomas frowned. He knew exactly the day that Father Dominic was referring to, and he gave his mentor a sideways glance.

"Yeah, I remember that day."

"Well, here you go again; about to face yet another enemy, alone and outnumbered."

"Alone, yes. But not outnumbered. I know the Guardians will be there when I need them."

"But, who's going to lead them, Thomas?"

"Terence can, or Gemma, or Beth. Or maybe all three. In fact, maybe that's another reason why the Trinity Knot is on the Crest."

"Oh?" Father Dominic asked with a curious look.

"Maybe we're supposed to do everything together. Think of it this way. When Gemma and I defeated the demon that Satan had sent to prevent her from becoming The Paladin, there were three of us. When we came back to the physical world and tracked down the rest of our group that had been kidnapped, three again. Maybe the reason our powers could combine during those times is that there was always three of us."

Father Dominic's face scrunched in thought.

"There may be something to that, Thomas, and it's worth testing your theory out. But, if what you are saying is true, then when you find Julianna, that still only makes two. Shouldn't you have a third? Shouldn't you have someone with you to help bring her back into the light? Doesn't it make sense, then, if everything else is established under a Trinitarian law, that you should take someone with you?"

Thomas thought about that for a moment. He realized that it did make sense. But who would he take? Who could he trust to stand beside him in this battle?

"Let's say you're right, Father, then the next question, is who? Which one of the Guardians is the right one for this moment? Jeremiah is a possibility. He already proved that he can stop Julianna's energy blasts. Or Brendan, perhaps. We might need his power to teleport into or out of a fight quickly," he said, then glanced down at the floor, shrugging his shoulder. "I just wish I knew what all of their powers are, and which of the Fruits of the Holy Spirit they come from."

"Well, we know that yours is based on Faith, and the opposite of Faith is Doubt. That is what the dark forces have been trying to flood your heart and mind with all these years: Doubt. Trust me when I say they won't stop, either. Not until the final battle is waged."

"What about Julianna? What are her powers supposed to be?"

"I believe Julianna was given the gift of Kindness, and the opposite of that is…?"

"Indifference," Thomas answered after a brief moment of thought. "It has to be. Julianna hates the world right now, but she's indifferent to what her actions are doing. That's what I'm up against, right? This isn't a fight between brother and sister, it's a battle between kindness and indifference. That's what I'm facing."

"Indeed."

"Then, which power, mixed with faith, would be strongest against indifference?" Thomas asked.

"Perhaps if we list what we know of the other's powers, you'll find the answer," Father Dominic offered.

"Okay, let's start with Terence. His entire body burns with a radiant light, and he can shoot beams of white energy from his hands, like he did when he helped rescue Theresa. Which Fruit of the Spirit would that power come from?"

"I believe that power comes from joy. There is no brighter light than the light which is born from joy."

"I don't see how that would help. I know when I'm not in a good mood, and someone tries to cheer me up by being overly joyful, it can have the opposite reaction. I can just imagine what Julianna's reaction might be."

"What about Gemma? Perhaps having The Paladin with you will be of some good."

"I thought of that, especially with her power to heal, but I've only seen her heal physical wounds, where Julianna's wounds seem to be emotional," Thomas said, shaking his head slightly. "By the way, what Fruit is Gemma's powers based on?"

"Chastity," Father Dominic said.

"Chastity? How does that even relate?"

Father Dominic chuckled, then motioned for Thomas to follow as he began to walk some more.

"Don't think of the powers as literal translations of the Fruits from which they are born. For example, Theresa's power of invisibility, and the way she can share her power to boost another Guardian's power, those all come from charity. Now, you might ask why charity would grant invisibility, and I would say that to believe otherwise tells me you don't understand what charity is. Charity, to be pure, must be completely transparent. Otherwise, call it a good deed, or call it a benevolent gesture, just not charity. If the party who is giving is also receiving anything in return—feeling good about themselves for a while, or feeling less guilty about their abundance—then it is a transaction, not charity. Which means..." Father Dominic began, waving his hand to indicate he wanted Thomas to complete the thought.

"For charity to be pure, it must be invisible," Thomas said. "I get that now. So, in the case of chastity, then, how does that relate to healing?"

"Those who are chaste are said to be pure, correct?" Father Dominic asked.

"Yeah," Thomas replied, deep in thought. "So anything that is not pure, needs to be healed! Is that it?"

"More or less, yes. That is the basic principle. For someone who was not living a chaste life before, and wants to do so now, the first thing they must do is heal themselves of any guilt they have for the lifestyle they had been living. Of course, they are forgiven the moment they ask for that healing, too."

"This is starting to make sense," Thomas said, as he suddenly stopped. "So, we've talked about faith, charity, joy, kindness, and chastity. That leaves self-control, modesty, gentleness, generosity, peace, patience, and goodness. Of all of those, there are two that seem to be the best defense against indifference."

"And which two would those be?"

"Self-control, and peace."

"Both of those are good choices, Thomas, but which one would be the best one to choose?"

Thomas thought about each of the Fruits of the Holy Spirit, and what the rest of their powers must be. He considered that the root-like tendrils he had seen growing from Sam's legs represented an ability to stand firm, and concluded that Sam had been granted the fruit of self-control. He also knew that goodness was born from an ability to be consistent with the purpose God intended for the order of things. This led him to believe that goodness was the power that Beth used when she created her shields, since those things that were not good, or were not consistent with God's will, were not able to pass through her golden dome. Jeremiah, he knew, must have been using the gift of patience, with his ability to freeze time. That left, Brendan, who had the power to teleport. Which of the Fruits that would translate into, Thomas had no clue. As for the rest of the group, he had yet to see what they could do.

Feeling a bit unsure of what to do, he suddenly remembered what Saint Thérèse had said to him during the dream she had visited him in. The first thing he recalled her saying was, *"Go into the desert, Thomas. Find the Guardians of Zion. God has faith in you."* And the second, was *"Never hesitate to fall back on love. Even if that seems to be the only thing you have left. Love never fails. Never."*

At first, he had thought Saint Thérèse meant an actual desert, like something he might find in Arizona, or Africa. But now, after the conversation he had had with Father Dominic, he realized that Saint Thérèse was most likely being metaphorical in her statement. Just like the powers that the Guardians had been given didn't directly relate to the Fruit of the Holy Spirit from which they had come, the desert that Saint Thérèse meant was more than likely not a real place either. If so, then he had to find which of the Guardians would have a spiritual realm that would be so devoid of life that it would resemble a desert if he traveled to it.

He thought about how Theresa and Gemma had designed their worlds, and how perfectly suited they were to their personalities. He considered each of the remaining Guardians, wondering if perhaps any of them would choose a desert as their landscape. None of them, he knew, would. They all had faith lives that were far too vibrant and alive. All except for one. Suddenly, it was clear what he was meant to do, and he turned to Father Dominic with a smile.

"I know now what I need to do, Father." Thomas said. "And I know who it is that I need to take."

"Good! And do I get to know this secret of yours?"

"In time, yes. But, for now, we need to go back to the group. There's something I need Theresa to do."

Father Dominic nodded at him.

"You go on ahead. I'm sure your legs will carry you at a much faster pace than I can keep up with. It always takes some time to fully recover when I go through a transformation like I did. To be honest, my calves have been killing me since we arrived here."

"Okay, Father. I'll see you soon."

Thomas turned and hurried off down the hallway, back the way they had come. Soon, he arrived at the door where he had left the rest of the Guardians, and he quietly stepped inside. The team was busy at work designing their outfits, or finding the materials they needed to craft them. The mood in the room was light and comfortable, a much different emotion than they had all held at the moment Beth's dome had collapsed. He was glad to see them working together so easily, as if they had been friends for a long, long time.

He spied Theresa standing over against one of the side walls. In one hand she held a basket, and in the other she held some of the materials she would need to craft the costume she was making for him. The basket held the rest of what she would need.

"Theresa," he said as he walked over.

"Oh! Brother Thomas! You startled me," she said, her face flushing with embarrassment.

"I'm sorry, Theresa," he replied.

"Did you want to see the outfit I've been working on for you? I almost have all of the materials in my basket. There are just a few items left to grab."

Thomas smiled at her youthful enthusiasm, realizing this was the first time he had seen her emotional signature looking comfortable and free.

"Of course I want to see it," he said, emulating the same level of excitement that she was showing, "but first, I have a question for you. Do you remember when you made that drawing that Sunday night after the retreat? You know, the night I showed up in your room?"

"Yeah, I think so. Why?"

"Well, I'm curious. Did you draw it like that because that was how you felt about yourself?"

Theresa shook her head, blushing slightly.

"No, actually. I didn't."

Thomas smiled. He had hoped that this would be the answer she would give.

"Then, who was it that inspired you to draw it like that; the dark forest on one side, and the crystal cathedral on the other?"

Theresa paused a moment, and their eyes met. Thomas could see hesitation behind her eyes, and wondered why she was afraid to admit whatever it was she was about to say.

"It's okay, Theresa. Honestly. You can trust me with whatever it is."

Theresa stared at him for a few moments longer, then quietly said, "You."

Thomas smiled at her warmly, and she blinked a few times and breathed in deeply.

"Can I ask why you chose to draw it that way? What is it that made you think I was divided like that?"

Again, Theresa hesitated, and again, Thomas tried to console her.

"Theresa, you're not going to be in trouble or anything, regardless of what you say. I just need to know, because I think you may have one more power that you have not yet discovered."

"Oh, really? What power is that?" she asked, her eyes lighting up.

"The power to see things as they really are. Like the way I see people's emotions and can tell when they are being genuine with their words or not. You can do the same, but you see it in other's actions."

Theresa's face relaxed, as if she had been afraid Thomas would have said anything but what he just had.

"Yeah, that's how it feels," she admitted. "Like, on the retreat, you were carrying yourself with such confidence, like you had everything all figured out. But, somehow, I knew that deep down inside, you were torn. That's the reason I came to talk to you on Saturday night, because I could tell that you were just like me, that you had a secret you didn't want anyone to know. I could tell that, even with the way you were acting and behaving, you still had some deep doubts about your faith. And, because of that, because you had those doubts but were still willing to stand up for what you believed in, I just knew I could tell you what my secret was, too."

Thomas smiled, then reached out and wrapped his arms around Theresa, pulling her close to his chest. He simply held her for a moment, as understanding and awareness of everything that had happened since the day he had first faced the darkness four years ago began to fall into place. Then, as he let go of the embrace and stepped back, he knew he was on the right track.

"First of all," he began, "I want to thank you for coming to me that night. A part of me knows now that, if you hadn't, we wouldn't be where we are. So I want to honor your courage for taking that leap. And, you're right. That night we met, I was divided. Although I believe my faith is one of my strengths, there are still so many doubts. I think that there may always be doubts, regardless of how strong my faith grows. But maybe that's the way it's supposed to be. Maybe there's no reason to have faith unless you also have doubts. Maybe it's in the way we overcome those doubts that gives us the faith we need to take on the next challenge."

Theresa just smiled.

"Anyway, I need you to do something for me."

"Sure. I'd love to help. What do you need?"

"Were you and Julianna friends at all before this trip? Did you two spend much time together?"

Theresa's face twisted a bit as she thought.

"Not really," she said. "I mean, we hung out at youth group sometimes, and we kinda knew each other from school. But, not really. Why?"

"Did you ever tell her the story about the endlessly dying flower?"

Theresa's eyes rolled up and to the left, and she placed her hand on her chin. Then, suddenly her entire face lit up.

"Yes!" she announced, loudly enough to startle a few of those in the room. "We did talk about it once!"

Thomas smiled.

"Then, this is what I need you to do."

Chapter Twenty-Three
The Desert Rose

Thomas waited in one corner of the room, looking over the design Theresa had come up with for his superhero outfit. He had to admit, her idea for his outfit was far better than anything he might have come up with on his own. She really had a way of seeing people for who, and what, they really were. The design was simple, too, which he was glad to see. He really didn't want anything flashy or colorful, and her design was anything but.

The main part of the costume was the most familiar, as it looked almost exactly like his Franciscan robes. It even had the simple corded rope belt and hood like his official garments did; though the robe she had designed was a bit more tailored. The sleeves weren't as long, and the bottom of the robe was made from overlapping flaps, allowing his legs to move more freely without fear of getting tangled in the fabric. The robe was mostly brown, but it had some blue highlights as well, including long strips of fabric that were meant to wrap around his forearms and hands. The wrappings reminded him of a picture he once saw of a boxer in the early days of that sport.

The colors Theresa chose were perfect, too. He knew there were biblical meanings behind each. For example, the color brown represented the poor, the downtrodden, and the outcast. In a lot of ways, these were the people whom Christianity was first given to, as Christ walked among the poorest and most alienated people of his time. And the blue she had used for his hand-wraps had several meanings in scripture. Authority, was one of those meanings, and the Word of God was another. He also knew that the Holy Spirit was represented in blue. Since his hands were the only weapon Thomas would ever use, to him, the color choice meant that he held in his hands the authority of the Holy Spirit, and the power of the Word of God.

Lost in thought, he didn't notice when Father Dominic had come back into the room, nor did he notice when Theresa approached and dropped a folded sheet of paper in front of him. It wasn't until she cleared her throat that he turned her way.

"Oh, Theresa. Sorry. I was thinking about this outfit you designed."

"Oh, yeah?" she said, sullenly, as if she feared his next words would be that he didn't like it, or that something needed to be changed.

"Yeah. And I have to say, I love it!" he answered, watching as her face brightened up at his words.

"Really? You do?" she asked.

"Yeah. I really, really do," he said, waving Father Dominic over. "What do you think, Father?"

Father Dominic took a moment to examine the drawing, then a bright smile washed over his face.

"I think it's perfect! Well done, Theresa!" he exclaimed with a smile.

Theresa turned away as her cheeks began to flush.

"When are you going to wear it?" Father Dominic asked, looking over the drawing.

"As soon as I have it in my hands," Thomas said.

Theresa glanced at him with a proud smile and a gleam in her eyes.

"I can have it done in three minutes!" she exclaimed, grabbing the basket of materials she had set aside. "Five minutes tops!"

Thomas and Father Dominic shared a smile.

"Oh the exuberance of youth!" Father Dominic said, then in a more serious tone added, "You know, Thomas, this is a great group of young people that are gathered here."

"I agree, Father. They definitely are."

"Can I ask what it is that you're holding there?" Father Dominic inquired, motioning to the paper Theresa had dropped on the desk.

"This," Thomas said, unfolding it so they both could see, "is everything I need to save Julianna."

Father Dominic looked at it, a bit puzzled.

"I don't think I understand. What will you do with that?" he asked.

"You'll see, Father. You'll see."

A few minutes later, now dressed in the apparel that Theresa had crafted for him, Thomas was feeling strangely confident, and completely comfortable. Once more he was standing looking over the drawing Theresa had done for him. Most of the page was covered with an illustration of a dried-up riverbed, and had been drawn using colored pencils in shades of tan and yellow and light brown. The ground looked hard and cracked, and the surface appeared to be peeling away in places. It was dirty, dusty, and bare, and the depth and dimension with which Theresa had drawn it made the images look and feel as if they were real.

In the middle of the barren landscape was a small, grayish-brown shape that looked very much like a melting lump of clay; with one small difference. On top of the lump, standing out like a beacon of life against the drab, empty desert within which it was planted, was a single desert rose. The main part of the blossoms, with five petals, was a deep, royal purple. The base of each petal, where they attached to the sepal, was highlighted in the most brilliant red, with small dots of white between each one. The very center was yellow, and was as bright as the sun.

Thomas laid the page on the floor, and sat down, preparing to meditate. Before he did, however, there were a few items he needed to take care of. Looking up, he gazed into the eyes of each of the Guardians as they stood, now dressed in their new outfits as well.

"Where I am going, none of you can follow. However, I am not able to make the journey on my own, and will need every ounce of strength and energy that all of you can provide," Thomas stated, his face serious.

"Where are you going?" Adrianna asked, a look of worry and concern dominating her expression.

"As you all know, we are currently in the depths of Theresa's spiritual realm. To get here, she had to open her heart and invite me in. The rest of you came along because we were joined together, and because your desire was to be of service. Before we came here, I thought I had only done this once before, when I had entered Gemma's world, as I explained earlier. But, as I just recently learned, there was one other time I made a journey like this.

"A few months ago, I saw a picture that Theresa had drawn. It was a picture of a landscape, with a dark, twisted forest on one side, and a crystal cathedral on the other. At the time I first saw that picture, I thought it was just that, a drawing. Well, it turns out that Theresa has another power. What she drew was *my* spiritual realm.

How she knew what it looked like without having been there, I have no idea, but it was perfect for me, and exactly the way I would have created my own spiritual realm.

"Now, I have a feeling that I was able to travel to my own spiritual realm without realizing that's what I was doing, because I didn't have to open my heart to myself," Thomas explained, pausing for a brief moment before continuing on. "But, what I'm about to do, I believe will be much harder. Much, much harder, in fact; which is why I'm going to need your help."

He paused again, taking a moment to look at each of his friends in the eye, ensuring they understood the gravity of the situation, then he continued.

"A little while ago, I asked Theresa to draw for me a picture of what she believes Julianna's spiritual realm might look like, and this," he said, waving a hand over the picture in front of him, "is what she came up with. I'll have to admit, if this is correct, then I'm going to face perhaps my greatest challenge. Julianna's spirituality is nearly dead. We all saw the way she was acting back in the physical realm, the way she looked like she wanted to kill those men.

"I'm not sure, but I think at some point in her life, she invited the enemy into her heart. Perhaps she was tricked into doing it, perhaps she didn't feel like she had a choice. I really don't know. What I do know is this: right now, time is on our side. The spiritual realm doesn't operate like the physical realm does. Time moves far faster here than it does there. When Gemma, Theresa and I were in Gemma's spiritual realm, we spent an entire day and night there before coming back. When we returned, hardly any time at all had passed, maybe a minute or two, but that's it.

"But, that also means, regardless how long we stay here, that army of demons that was about to crash in on us is still there. We haven't changed the real world, we've just delayed it. Something tells me that if we went back right now, we might win that fight, but we might not. And the reason I say that, is, we aren't yet the Guardians of Zion; not while one of us is missing.

"We need Julianna, and I'm going to go get her. I'm going into her spiritual realm, and I'm going to face whatever demons are driving her away from the light, then I'm going to bring her back here. Then, as a team, with the combined power of *all* of the Fruits of the Holy Spirit, I know we will win."

There was a moment of silence as the group digested what Thomas said, then Beth stepped forward.

"What do you need us to do, Brother Thomas?" she asked, standing tall and confident.

"Yeah, how can we help you?" Sam added.

"You know you're not in this on your own, right Brother Thomas?" Jennifer asked.

"We're with you, Thomas," Terence shared, giving his roommate a broad smile.

"Yeah, we're with you," Gemma agreed.

Thomas smiled. He could tell by the look on the faces of his friends that they were ready to do whatever it took to ensure that evil did not triumph. Had he been able to hand pick the other eleven people to make up the Guardians of Zion, he couldn't imagine having selected a better group than this.

"I don't know if you can help," Thomas admitted. "I don't know if I can take you with me for this."

"Why not? We'll open our hearts, or whatever we need to do," Francis offered.

"I don't think it's that easy, Francis," Thomas explained with a frown.

"Why not?" Jeremiah inquired. "Isn't this why we were all called to be Guardians?"

Thomas paused for a moment, searching his heart for the right words to say.

"A few months ago, back when all of this craziness was just getting started, I had a dream. In that dream, I was visited by Saint Thérèse, and she told me that this challenge was coming. She also told me that I needed to go into the desert, and that I needed to find the Guardians. This," he said, waving his hand over the picture Theresa had drawn, "is definitely the desert. But, Saint Thérèse didn't say to *bring* the Guardians. She said to *find* the Guardians. That's why I don't think I can bring you with me. I think you're all already there."

CHAPTER TWENTY-FOUR
FAMILY REUNION

Stars. Thousands of them. There were tiny, white sparks of single stars standing alone; and larger, brighter spots where two or three or four stars were clustered together. From one horizon to the next, there was nothing but a solid dome of stars. Across the center, the milky-white ribbon that had first granted the galaxy its name was visible. It was like being on the inside of a snow globe where every glittering flake had been suspended in time. It didn't matter which direction Thomas faced, the view was always the same.

Around him, the wind created ghost-like serpents that twisted and spun, dancing to music only they could hear, then disappearing back into the dusty ground. The wind carried more than just magic, dancing sand serpents. It carried a message, too.

"This is a dangerous land, earth-walker. Nothing lives out here but the wind. You should not be here. Turn around now, and go back. Return to the safety of your world," the wind sighed as it caressed the skin of his ears.

Thomas breathed in deep, smelling the clear, clean fragrance of this uninhabited land. He had experienced so many magical and exotic events recently that speaking to the wind did not seem strange, it was just another peculiar encounter in a life that became more miraculous every day. Grinning to himself, he rose to his feet.

"I will not turn back," he called out loudly, not sure which way he should face.

"You will not find what you seek, Follower of the Light," the wind moaned louder, growing in strength and scattering so much sand that Thomas had to shield his eyes. *"The wind will not let you find it. If you come close, the wind will rise and blow more fiercely than you have ever felt. The wind has the power to wipe out your tracks. The wind can spin you around until you have no idea where you were going, where you are, or where you have been. The wind will make it impossible for you to find your way."*

"Even so, I will not stop, for I have something that you do not," Thomas replied.

"You have nothing but impermanence. You are temporary, no more than dust. I am eternal. I have blown before this desert existed, and well before man first breathed me in."

"It is true that my body is temporary, and it is true that the wind was born at the beginning of time. And it is true that, given enough time, the wind can destroy even the strongest of stone. But that still will not stop me, and it means nothing compared to what I have."

The wind was silent for a moment, and the sand lay perfectly still. Then, once more it began to blow, though it blew gently now.

"Tell me what it is you have," the wind demanded.

"I will, on one condition only," Thomas replied.

"Mortal! You are in no position to barter with the wind!" the wind shouted at him with hurricane force.*"*

"Then, I will simply sit here, and wait," Thomas said, sitting back down and crossing his legs while the wind howled around him, the sand brushing past him so hard it scratched his skin.

Thomas pulled his hood until it covered his face, and then gathered the fabric of his robe around his arms and legs until nothing was outside the robe except for his hands, though they were covered as well. Thick strips of bright-blue cloth wrapped from his knuckles up his arm, stopping just below his elbows. Though he knew the Wind could eventually tear the fabric to shreds, it would still take some time; and time was one thing Thomas had on his side. And so he sat, and waited, while around him the wind continued to howl and moan.

At first his mind wandered from one thought to the next, but as he focused on his breathing, even his thoughts faded away. There was nothing but the gusts of wind, and his determination to endure. Thomas had no idea how long he waited, but, eventually, the wind died down, and Thomas shook the gathered sand off his robe.

"Okay, mortal. You win, this time. The wind can see that you are determined. And though the wind could blow forever, there is a limit to how much interest the wind has in doing just that. What is the condition you wish to appoint?"

Thomas let a smile stretch in his mind, but on the outside, his face remained still and emotionless.

"Only this. Once I explain what it is that I have, and that you do not, if you agree then you will reveal what it is that I seek. As I said, I am willing to search forever. However, there is a limit to how much interest I have in taking that long to find what I seek. Therefore, if you agree that what I have is something you do not, then you will not only leave me alone, but assist me in whatever way you can. Agreed?"

A moment of silent, barely salient breezes whispered past Thomas. Then, all was still.

"The wind accepts your challenge. However, if the Wind does not agree with your reply, then every moment you linger in this land, the wind will grow stronger. The wind will rip the flesh from your body, and turn your very bones to dust."

Thomas thought for a moment, extending a silent prayer that the idea he held in his mind was correct, then he stood and nodded his head.

"I agree," Thomas said confidently.

"*Then, come, speak!*" The wind demanded. "*What is it you have that the wind does not?*"

Thomas took a moment to steady his nerves, focusing on and releasing any tension he felt, then he spoke just one word.

"Hope."

He could feel the wind begin to gather, preparing once more to blow.

"*Hope? What need does the wind have for hope? You have lost, mortal! Prepare to spend your last days wishing you had not upset the wind!*"

The gentle breeze grew quickly to a gale, but Thomas stood still, his face determined and resolute.

"Not so fast!" he shouted. "I have not lost!"

The gale blew harder than he had felt yet, nearly knocking Thomas off his feet.

"I did not say I had something that you need. I said I had something you do not!" he screamed, his throat burning from the force of his words. "Now…be still!"

The billowing sand that had been scratching and burning his exposed skin suddenly stopped, and the tiny grains fell harmlessly to the ground. Thomas waited patiently for the wind to admit defeat, but no sound came. All was still. Then, just off to his right, in a place where the sands had piled higher than the rest, Thomas saw a tiny dust devil begin to form. The small cyclone grew until it was double its original size, but it did not travel. It was as if the small end of the twisting cloud was fixed on that one, single point.

Faster and faster the cyclone spun, and as it did, it began to lift the sand from under where it spun, and as the sand began to lift and blow away, Thomas could see there was something buried underneath. At first, there was just a small glimmer of deep, royal purple, but as more sand shifted, Thomas could see it for what it was. It was the desert rose that Theresa had drawn. It had been right at his side the entire time.

The cyclone continued spinning, though he could tell it was getting smaller now. Then, when the last grain of sand had been lifted away, and the rose was fully exposed, the small tornado itself lifted away, and the air was once more still. Thomas approached the fragile plant, knowing full well it was not just a random desert bloom that he set his eyes upon. No, what he looked at now, was Julianna's faith. It was the last lingering bit in the vast desert that had become her spiritual realm, but it would have to be enough.

Thomas reached down, placing one hand on each side of the tiny blossom, as if to shield it from the desolate landscape that could easily swallow it whole. Then, as he leaned in close, letting his nose savor the flower's heavenly scent, a small tear broke free, dropping from his cheek and landing at the base of the plant where it quickly disappeared in the dry, colorless sand. A moment later, the plant began to grow. Rather than just one blossom, suddenly there were two, then four, and then a dozen. From the point where the branch of the plant attached to the trunk, a new branch came forth, extending outward and giving birth to a host of blossoms of its own. As he watched, the evolution continued; the trunk growing in size, extending branches, and the branches sprouting limbs, all of which held flowers.

When the plant was nearly as tall as Thomas, the base split, forming two separate trunks, and near the top, two limbs grew longer than the rest. As these longer branches continued to stretch, they remained without flowers, nor did they sprout any additional branches. Then, when they were about three feet long, the ends formed into small round balls, and five tiny branches stuck out. Thomas watched as these ten small branches formed into fingers, and the balls became hands. A moment later, he realized what the plant was forming. And then, a noise behind him made him spin around, and he came face to face with a demon so evil, so twisted and dark, Thomas could feel his face go pale. This was the source of the dark energy he had felt when he had connected with the shadow-sprite in the jungle.

The demon, which stood on two long, powerful, lion-like legs, was covered in a ghostly gray skin that looked like it had been pulled far too thin, especially across its dog-shaped face. In one hand the creature carried a long spear, and in the other, a poisonous snake. On its back, the monster sprouted two dark, blood-red leathery wings. Every cell of Thomas' body wanted to run, but his legs wouldn't respond. The demon leaned in closer, and then closer still, until Thomas nearly wretched from the stench of its breath. Just as Thomas felt as if he was about to pass out, he heard a familiar voice.

"Astaroth, is that any way to greet our guest?"

Thomas turned slowly, not wanting to, and yet knowing he had no choice. He had to face the woman who was now standing behind him, the one who had been formed from the desert rose. As he turned, he felt his eyes start to water and burn. He blinked several times to clear the gathered moisture, then looked to see at the young woman standing there. She was dressed in a midnight-black and royal purple gown, with sleeves made from spider-web lace. Around her shoulders hung a black cloak, fastened about her neck with a bird-skull clasp.

At first, Thomas didn't recognize her; he had never seen her wearing makeup like this before, and she had added crimson highlights in her hair that matched the color of her long, pointed nails. Still, with everything that had changed, there was one thing that hadn't. She was still his sister.

"Julianna…" Thomas sighed.

"Hello, Thomas. We've been waiting for you," she said with a sneer.

With that, she spun on her heels and walked away.

"Astaroth!" she called out over her shoulder, "be so kind as to bring my brother along, will you please? We've got an awfully long way to go."

Thomas heard the beast give out a low, menacing growl, and wondered for a moment which of the two was the master, and which, the slave. But the thought disappeared as he felt the fangs of Astaroth's serpent bite deep into his neck. The burning sensation of poison spread throughout his body, and he felt his mind go numb. Then, with fear in his heart, Thomas crumbled to the ground. The world around him faded to black.

The story will conclude in
Book Four – Apocalypsis

Michael Chrobak has been involved in working with Youth and Youth Ministry programs since he was a teen himself; a long, long time ago. He has held the position of Director of Religious Education and Youth Minister for St. Bonaventure's Parish in Concord, CA, and also as Youth Minister for St. Michael's Parish in Livermore, CA. He has survived raising four children of his own and now lives in Oakley, CA where he continues to stay involved in Youth Ministry through his blogs and books.

How to Connect:

Facebook: https://www.facebook.com/michaelchrobakauthor
Twitter: https://twitter.com/MChrobakAuthor
Instagram: https://www.instagram.com/mchrobakauthor
Website: https://michaelchrobakauthor.com